“Wounds heal.”

Risk straightened, the silver chain he wore at his neck shifting to fall over his collarbone, right where the wound he’d had yesterday should have been. But the skin was as tanned and unmarred as the rest of his bare chest.

He turned the knife, watching the light glint off its length. “Some wounds.”

Kara rubbed her damp palms on the legs of her jeans. “And, the other night, you…saved me?”

“I guess you could say that.”

Kara shifted her weight from one hip to the other. “And last night…? You disappeared.”

“Not my choice.”

Before she could pull back, his hand captured hers, his fingers warm and strong. He rubbed his thumb across the bones of her hand, emotion warring behind his eyes.

They stood there frozen.

Available in September 2009 from Mills & Boon® Intrigue

The Sheriff's Amnesiac Bride
by Linda Conrad
&
Soldier's Secret Child
by Caridad Piñeiro

Her Best Friend's Husband
by Justine Davis
&
The Beast Within
by Lisa Renee Jones

Questioning the Heiress
by Delores Fossen
&
Daredevil's Run
by Kathleen Creighton

The Mystery Man of Whitehorse
by BJ Daniels

Unbound
by Lori Devoti

Private S.W.A.T Takeover
by Julie Miller

UNBOUND

BY
LORI DEVOTI

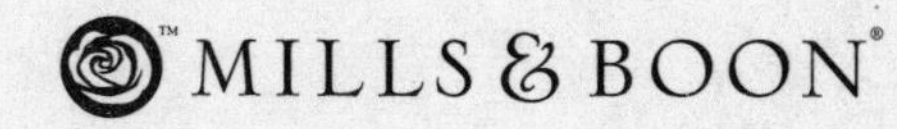

First published in Great Britain 2009
Harlequin Mills & Boon Limited,
Eton House, 18-24 Paradise Road, Richmond, Surrey TW9 1SR

ISBN: 978 0 263 87324 5

46-0909

Harlequin Mills & Boon policy is to use papers that are natural, renewable and recyclable products and made from wood grown in sustainable forests. The logging and manufacturing processes conform to the legal environmental regulations of the country of origin.

Printed and bound in Spain
by Litografia Rosés S.A., Barcelona

Lori Devoti grew up in southern Missouri and attended college at the University of Missouri-Columbia where she earned a bachelor of journalism. However, she made it clear to anyone who asked, she was not a writer; she worked for the dark side – advertising. Now, twenty years later, she's proud to declare herself a writer and visit her dark side by writing paranormals for the Intrigue Nocturne line.

Lori lives in Wisconsin with her husband, daughter, son, an extremely patient shepherd-mix dog and the world's pushiest Siberian husky. To learn more about what Lori is working on now, visit her website at www.loridevoti.com.

To Holly Root and Jenny Bent for "hounding"
me to embrace my dark side.

To Tara Gavin for inviting me to be part of this line,
and for being such a dream to work with.

To Eve Silver for believing in me and this book even
in its earliest stages. Your input kept me sane.

And to the rest of Romance Unleashed –
I love you, each and every one.

Chapter 1

It was the fear he smelled first, a pheromone-laden scent almost irresistible to the hellhound within him. She was here—somewhere.

Risk Leidolf spun on one worn boot heel, searching the dim interior of the bar for his latest assignment. He didn't have much information: young and pretty, Lusse had said. She hadn't bothered to tell him anything more. It didn't matter. Whatever Lusse's latest target brought to the fight—talents or temptations—she would be no match for him. They never were.

The room was a kaleidoscope of sounds, smells and emotions—an onslaught that would be overwhelming to a less experienced hunter, but sadly for his prey, it would barely slow Risk down. He inhaled, dissecting the surrounding scents. Stale beer and human sweat. He shoved them aside.

Emotion was what he sought. What he craved.

A tinge of desperation wafted toward him. He ignored it, too. Despair and what followed, guilt and sorrow, held no appeal for Risk. No, much as he wished it different, adrenaline was what lured him—fear, anger. They called to him, making him a slave to urges he wished he could forget.

Clearing his senses, he concentrated, listening to the low murmur of voices around him. It was quiet for a bar, but an undercurrent ran through the place, a vibration of danger humming around him like a tuning fork held to his ear.

The bar held secrets, but Risk was unconcerned. He had one job tonight—to retrieve the female for Lusse, and save himself from another period of service in the kennels. Torture he could handle, but being forced to live with the other hounds, fighting daily just to survive, perhaps even losing the small piece of territory he had secured for himself in this world, that would surely drive him mad.

He laughed, a dry hollow sound. Like a hellhound could ever be called anything but mad, soulless, according to his owner.

Thoughts of Lusse caused his jaw to tense, brought him back to his purpose. *Enough. Get on with it.*

Adjusting his dark glasses down his nose until he could peer over their tops, he studied the room. Grizzled men and timeworn women filled battered tables around him. Not sparing them more than a glance, his gaze shifted to the back, where the shadows grew deeper. Instinctively, he knew that was where he would find her.

She might think the gloom would disguise her, but it offered no protection from hell's hunters. With a sigh, he continued his scrutiny.

The booths were empty—save one. Huddled in the cubby farthest from the door was a small lone figure. His prey. Even with Lusse's vague description he couldn't miss her. Young, pretty and fresh. She stood out in the place like an angel dropped into a pit filled with vipers.

Leaning against the rough paneling on the wall behind him, he took a moment to study her. Petite, probably only 110 pounds, and with dark hair that fell past her shoulders, she seemed lost in thought. Her hand hovered over a shot glass of amber liquid and a crumpled paper was smoothed out on the table in front of her.

Now that he had her located, he focused on her fully. *Fear.* The strength of it caught him off guard. Placing his hand on the unfinished wood, he inhaled, nostrils flaring. How did one so small contain so much emotion? Willing himself to stay controlled, he turned to her again. Yes, fear, but there was sorrow, too, and… She plucked the shot glass off the table with her finger and thumb, and tossed the liquid to the back of her throat… Determination.

She might be afraid, but it wasn't for herself.

This one was a fighter.

A sliver of respect sliced into him. With a shake of his head, he tamped it down.

Let her fight.

A lot of good it would do.

The cynical thought should have urged him to action, but he waited still. She would be easy to capture—why rush?

The female slid the empty glass across the table and signaled the waitress for another. As she waited, she ran a pale hand over the crumpled paper in front of her, caressing it, as if trying to gain reassurance or knowledge from its length.

The waitress returned and his prey looked up to thank her, but her gaze wandered to Risk instead. Startled, he stepped sideways, farther into the gloom. Could she see him? He had guarded himself carefully tonight. Perhaps Lusse was right. Perhaps his human half was growing too strong, weakening the hellhound, weakening his hunting powers. And, as Lusse was fond of pointing out, weakness equaled only one thing—death.

He peered back at his prey. Did she see him?

Her gaze passed over him, and he relaxed. Just coincidence, but still…he hesitated. There was something different about this female, something that made him reluctant to deliver her to Lusse, the witch who kept him chained in her service.

He shook his head. This was insane—he should just be done with it, lure the female to the parking lot, change and carry her to Lusse.

The female downed her second drink, picked up the paper and stood to leave. This was Risk's chance. One husky whisper in her ear, and it would be over. Another soul, another power, in payment toward his eternal debt.

The female strode past him, close enough he could smell the undertones of spice in her perfume, and he let her pass.

He pushed his glasses back into place, hiding eyes that almost surely glimmered red by this time. What was wrong? Why was he reluctant? Why did a piece of him almost wish she had seen him—proven he was more human than beast? Why did the thought of destroying one more life seem a much bigger price than the torture and loss he faced if he didn't?

Cursing, he concentrated on that loss. This female was nothing to him, but he, he had an eternity to suffer.

Damn Lusse, and her quest for souls.

He forced his hand to the silver chain around his neck,

letting the ancient metal links dig into his palm. This was who he was—property, nothing more. Pulling his coat more closely around him, he turned to follow.

A cold blast of air hit Kara Shane as soon as she left the bar. The two whiskeys she'd drunk did little to warm her now, and they'd done nothing to lessen the pain of losing Kelly.

Her sister had been missing a full week today. The police seemed to have given up hope, but not Kara. Kelly was out there somewhere—she had to be; Kara couldn't accept anything else.

She gathered her coat more closely around her and walked into the wind. Maybe the frigid air would do what the whiskey hadn't—knock loose some idea that would lead her to Kelly. Something different than the dead end that had brought her here tonight. A discarded matchbook, how cliché. Was she really so pathetic she'd jump at any straw?

She'd known she was out of her element as soon as she'd stepped into the bar. Part-time employees of cute little tea shops did not stride into a place like the Guardian's Keep and leave with the name of their sister's abductor in hand. No, part-time employees of cute little tea shops were lucky they left…at all.

She'd thought she could brazen it out. Even borrowed Kelly's floor-length leather coat—very *Matrix*—but it couldn't make her strong, confident, something she wasn't. The bartender hadn't bothered to look at the "missing" flyer she'd edged under his nose. The waitress was worse, coarsely suggesting she take her size-four ass back to the mall while she still had a chance, and the patrons…well, Kara didn't even have the courage to approach them.

She was failing, and Kelly was somewhere, suffering because of it.

Lost in her thoughts, it took a few seconds for her to realize something wasn't right, that she was being followed. There was no sound, just a sensation. An eerie knowledge that something was behind her and getting closer. With an uncharacteristic calmness, perhaps brought on by the whiskey or the numbness from losing Kelly, she slipped a hand inside her coat and removed the can of Mace her sister always kept tucked in the inside pocket.

Kelly with her "I can take on the world" outlook wouldn't be afraid—neither would Kara. She slipped her thumb under the safety cap.

Despite her resolve, the combination of alcohol, pain and adrenaline made her almost giddy. Why didn't the bastard just jump her and get it over with?

She didn't have to wait much longer. Within seconds, the heat of his breath crawled over the back of her neck. She spun, the can hissing as it released a steady stream of Mace.

Instantly, she realized her error. Too soon. Her would-be attacker was still fifteen feet away, and…she took a steadying breath…wasn't human.

A shaggy-looking dog stared back at her.

"Go home, puppy," she called, suppressing the sudden surge of panic that threatened to drive her to her knees. Dogs; she hated dogs. Had since… Refusing to let her mind slip back in time, she gripped the Mace can, the feel of the cool metal against her palm reassuring.

Stay calm, she recited mentally. That was what the trainer she'd talked with afterward had told her. *Don't panic. Don't run. It is very rare that a dog attacks for no reason. Don't give him one.* Filling her lungs with air, she forced herself to stand still. "No food on me," she murmured.

The ginger-colored dog tilted his head as if studying her, then lifting his nose, took a long whiff of the frigid air.

Nothing to be afraid of. Just a lost dog, a stray. She wasn't in his yard, his territory. Nothing about her was threatening. It would wander off now. She willed the thought to be true.

Kara waited, her breath puffing white in front of her.

The dog lowered its head then lifted it one more time to study her.

Kara froze. "Go home, puppy," she whispered.

The dog glanced over its shoulder, then turned to face her. Taking two steps forward, it glanced up.

Kara's next breath caught in her chest.

Its eyes…were red.

Kara blinked, unable to believe what she was seeing. The dog moved forward a step, then two. His head held low, his tail stiff behind him, he glanced at her, an almost human intelligence in his eyes. The cold determination she saw there sent a shiver dancing up her spine.

This was no ordinary dog.

No, she corrected herself. It was. It had to be. Her mind was just playing tricks on her—too many sleepless nights worrying about Kelly causing old phobias to come back and haunt her.

Now firmly in the circle of light, the dog stood facing Kara, its jaws gaping, drool streaming from its mouth, red eyes flickering like windows in a burning building.

Ordinary? Not quite. What was wrong with the thing?

Her hand tense around the Mace, Kara kept her gaze steady. When you looked away, that was when they attacked. Or at least that was what had happened with Jessie.

The dog had been there one second, staring her and her friend down, then Kara had looked away, just to search for an escape, and the dog had sprung. Not on Kara, no, on Jessie. Just on Jessie. Kara didn't remember much after that, except the screams—always the screams. She still didn't know if they were hers or her friend's.

Tears threatened to spill from her eyes. This wasn't helping. Forget the past.

Blinking hard, she edged backward, making what she hoped were soothing sounds. "Nice dog. Nothing to eat here." *Be strong. Think like Kelly.* Kelly who had saved her that day, and had kept her sane every day since.

Cell phone. She had her cell phone. Tugging it from the pocket in her backpack with her free hand, she continued talking. "How would you like to meet some new friends?"

Friends with shock collars and nice strong steel cages.

The dog raised his lip in a snarl, revealing three-inch-long canines.

Maybe a friend with a nice .38 would be better. Kara used her thumb to flip open the phone, and began punching. She would survive this.

She had to survive this.

The squeal of a wrong number answered her. Damn. She glanced down to redial…and instantly realized her mistake.

The dog backed up, bracing itself on its hind legs as it prepared to leap. With nowhere to run, Kara pointed the can in the creature's direction and steeled herself for the impending attack.

For the second time that night, the can hissed, but the dog didn't waver. With a chilling growl, it shot off the ground soaring directly toward Kara.

The world slowed around her. She should run now. She

knew it, but somehow she couldn't. All she could do was wait, knowing there was no way she would survive this attack.

As the parking lot swirled around her, the dog close enough she could smell the stench of his breath, a blur of silver shot forward from the shadows, knocking her assailant to the asphalt.

Elation swept over her. A second dog, a silver one, stood poised above the first. Kara used a shaking hand to brush hair from her face. He'd saved her.

The new arrival glanced up. Red eyes glowed back at her.

Her own rounded in horror.

The second dog barely had time to give her a snarl before the first began thrashing beneath him. Dropping his head, he attempted to grip the first dog's neck in his jaws. The ginger-haired dog bucked beneath him, placing its hind feet on the larger dog's stomach for leverage. The two grappled for control, ginger hair mixing with silver until they looked like one throbbing mass.

Her palms damp with sweat, Kara took advantage of their distraction by quickly pressing 9-1-1 on her phone and then Talk.

The dogs rolled across the ground toward her, their teeth flashing as each tried to lay claim to the other's throat. The ginger dog twisted to the side, latching onto the larger dog's neck. His teeth embedded in fur and flesh, he grappled for a stronger hold. Blood seeped through silver fur, staining both animals.

Kara stood frozen, waiting for the scream of pain, the crunch of breaking bones, the smell of the blood. How could she be going through this again?

His eyes burning, the silver dog fell onto his back, pulling the ginger dog with him.

This was it. The first dog would kill the second then come for Kara. In her mind she saw Jessie lying on the ground beneath the mutt they'd stumbled on while exploring. They hadn't realized anything was in the yard when they'd crawled under the fence. Hadn't even seen the dog until it had been too late. Until it had jumped on Jessie, and thrown her on the ground like a discarded rag doll. Then, not satisfied with simply disabling her friend, the beast had scissored its massive jaws against her throat, crushing tissue and bone all in one vicious bite. And Kara had done nothing. Nothing.

She'd just stood there staring as the dog had lifted its head, its eyes darting wildly around the yard, its feet immersed in her dead friend's blood. When it had finally focused on her, she'd known it was her turn. Soon she'd be lying on the ground just like Jessie, blood mixing with the dry dirt beneath her. Then there had been screaming—it had to have been her—and Kelly had come charging from nowhere, a metal pole in her hand. Kara had tried to yell out, to tell Kelly to go back, but her voice had failed her. Pole in front of her, Kelly had grabbed Kara and stepped between her and the dog. That was all Kara remembered; they'd told her later she'd passed out. Kelly had scared off the dog and dragged Kara back under the fence.

No one knew what had happened to the dog or why it had run from Kelly rather than just adding her to its list of victims. But Kara knew one thing. Her sister had saved her while Kara had been too frozen by fear to even warn Kelly away.

Without Kelly, she would never have survived.

A chilling growl snapped her back to the present. The silver dog sprang to his feet, the ginger dog still attached to his neck, but not for long. The silver dog surged to the side, yanking himself free. The two animals stood facing each other, breath escaping their mouths in rasping pants, clumps of silver hair dangling from the ginger dog's mouth. In unison, they lowered their heads and charged forward. Their bodies collided in another swirl of fur and teeth, the pair pushing closer and closer to Kara as the silver animal overpowered the ginger one.

Scrambling to get out of their way, Kara slipped on the damp pavement, from snow or blood she couldn't tell, sending her cell phone dancing across the lot. She watched it, her stomach clenching at the sight. No Kelly to save her and now no hope of calling anyone else.

The silver dog shoved the ginger one against the outside of the bar building, inches from Kara. With one last snarl, he pinned the smaller animal to the ground, grabbed it by the neck—then rotating his massive body, tossed the ginger dog across the parking lot.

The animal landed in a crumpled heap in the darkest part of the lot. The silver dog waited on stiff legs, his body tense, then apparently content his competition was beaten, turned his glowing eyes on Kara. Blood mingled with saliva, falling from his open jaws in a steady drip.

Kara's gaze dashed around the lot searching for an escape. The silver dog stood between her and the street where her ancient Honda sat. She was trapped between him, two brick buildings, and a six-foot-tall chain-link fence. Her phone was six feet away. She had completed the dial. A 9-1-1 operator wouldn't just hang up, would they? Could whoever was on the other end of the line hear her?

"We are at the Guardian's Keep. Did you know that, doggy?" Kara spoke as loud as she could, her voice rough with fear. "It's a bar, near the lake. Not a good neighborhood at all."

Sweat trickled down Kara's back, her heart pounding so loudly she was sure the beast in front of her could hear it, too.

The dog's pants slowed until they were barely a whisper in the still night. Nothing else broke the quiet—no bar patrons stumbling out to their cars, no sirens answering her call, no Kelly rushing in from nowhere to rescue her. It was just Kara all alone with no one to save her but herself.

Kara stared at the massive animal in front of her. Damn it. She wouldn't die now. She'd survived too much, and she still had to find Kelly. If she could survive this, anything was possible. Maybe there was still hope. There had to be.

The dog tilted his head as if thinking.

"Not a place a woman should come by herself—the Guardian's Keep," she repeated, her voice stronger. "But who knew rabid dogs were running loose? Is that your problem, doggy? Don't feel well?"

The dog wrinkled his nose. She could have sworn it was in a snort. Crazy. She was going crazy.

She shook off the instant of weakness. No time for doubts. She had to do something, so she edged an inch closer to the phone. At the movement, the dog moved closer, too.

Kara froze. She still had the Mace. Would it stop over two hundred pounds of rabid dog? She doubted it, but she would try.

The dog took another step. Kara positioned her finger over the spray can, her hand trembling so badly she almost dropped it. She wrapped her other hand around the metal cylinder, then concentrated on the dog and her last chance at life. Not close enough yet. One shot. She would get one shot. Spray and run. That was it.

Something moved behind the silver animal—the ginger dog teetering to his feet.

Kara bit her lip. If they got into another fight, farther away, she could use that time to escape. "Looks like your friend's awake, buddy." She nodded toward the ginger dog. It shook its head as if trying to reorient itself.

To her surprise the silver dog seemed to understand her, he glanced over his shoulder at the other animal. Kara rose onto the balls of her feet in a crouch—ready to run.

The ginger dog glared at them both. Kara held her breath, hope flickering in her chest. Then in a shimmer—like heat rising off hot asphalt on a summer day—the animal disappeared.

Kara gave a quick intake of breath. She *was* crazy. Lock-her-up, throw-away-the-key crazy.

Would anyone be surprised?

The silver dog turned back to Kara, and she could have sworn he was smiling. Glimmering eyes focused on her, he padded closer.

Hatred poured into Kara. A dog had killed her friend, would she let one kill her, too? Crazy or not, Kara wouldn't make it easy. Not this time.

She waited until he was a couple arms' lengths away then pressed the spray nozzle. The dog barely blinked.

Tossing the empty can away, Kara lunged to the side. The dog cut her off, knocking her to the ground and standing over her just as he had the ginger dog.

If Kara believed in God, this would have been a good time to pray. Instead she stared up at the animal, trying to ignore the unsettling eyes that seemed to burn into her. Where were the police?

In her delirium, she heard a reply in her head. "No one's

coming. Not in time. Relax. Fighting will only make it worse."

How funny, the giant dog was telling her to relax. A hysterical giggle formed in her throat. A throat about to be crushed and torn until no sound could escape. The giggle bubbled upward, sounding foreign and unreal to her ears.

God, how embarrassing. Faced with death, and she giggled. Kelly never giggled.

The dog leaned down, pressed his nose to her mouth and exhaled. She twisted her head to the side, but there was nowhere to go. Hot breath filled her lungs.

Oh, Kelly, I'm sorry.

Everything faded to black.

Chapter 2

Lusse stood in front of the floor-to-ceiling windows of her mountain home. But even the cold starkness of the scenery couldn't soothe her today.

Risk should have returned by now.

His mission had been simple—the girl didn't even realize her own power. It would be like crushing a still-blind puppy—easy, but also rewarding.

Except Lusse didn't need the girl crushed, not yet. Not until Lusse'd drained her of any power she held. But Lusse did need Risk to obey her.

He had potential to be great. The most powerful alpha her pack of hellhounds had ever answered to, but an annoying thread of humanity weakened him. Lusse had been patient, waiting almost five hundred years for him to lose the tendency on his own, but with the exception of one slight slip over a score of years ago, he'd stubbornly refused to embrace his demon nature. If anything, that slip had actually strengthened his resolve. Finally, she'd faced reality. He needed a few pointed prods to help find his way.

She sighed. Hellhounds. Her domination of them was one of her greatest strengths and also one of her greatest trials. Praise Yggdrasil, there were some paybacks. A shiver of pleasure danced up her spine as her finger reached out to flick the silver manacles that hung from her gilded ceiling.

After six months of confinement in the kennels with the others, daily training...her lips curved in a wistful smile...and the threat of taking the inconsequential piece of territory he thought of as his in the human world, she'd believed she had him under control.

But now she was beginning to wonder.

"Bader." She spoke in a normal tone. Even though her servant was elsewhere in the mansion, he would hear her.

Within minutes the old servant shuffled into the room.

"Have you heard from Risk?" she asked in the most casual tone she could muster.

Before he could reply, she stopped him. "Don't answer. Of course, you haven't. If you had, you would have told me. Correct?" She raised one elegant brow.

He nodded.

No Risk and no innocent. Luckily she'd planned for such a problem.

"Did you do as I asked?"

Bader's round eyes blinked back at her.

"Venge, did you send him?"

Another nod.

Lusse relaxed into the velvet comfort of her favorite chair, her ankles crossed delicately on the matching ottoman. Another plan perfectly executed.

* * *

Kara stretched out one leg, pointing her toe, then flexing her foot. Fur tickled her inner thigh. Rolling onto her stomach, she buried her face into the soft pelt beneath her.

Fur? Pelt?

She flipped back over and jerked to a sitting position. The white fur covering her dropped to her waist, revealing naked breasts—*her naked breasts.* She stared stupidly at the white flesh before coming to her senses and yanking the pelt back up to her chin.

Where was she? The room was dark, the only light coming from an oversize rock fireplace. The crackle of the blaze and the smell of wood smoke was ominous rather than reassuring. She spun on her knees, the fur still gathered around her. Peeled-log chairs and a couch sat beside her; behind them she could make out a rock breakfast bar and what appeared to be a kitchen.

No dogs, and no people.

For now.

Dogs… The memory of red eyes, and dripping canines, sent a tremor of unease through her. Real or a slip from sanity, she didn't know, and at the moment she didn't care.

Her breath ragged, she stared down at the fur she held pressed to her breast. She was naked in a strange house.

Who had brought her here? What had happened last night? The thoughts pinged around in her brain. Her fingers curled into the fur.

She pulled the cover more tightly around her and closed her eyes. *Slow breaths. In. Out. Listen to the fire. In. Out.* Finally, her exhalation barely audible over the crackle coming from the hearth, she opened her eyes.

Calmer, she was able to think. She had to get out of

here. Get home where she could go quietly insane in her own space.

A quick glance around the room didn't reveal her clothing. There was a closed door behind the couch, but Kara wouldn't risk opening it and alerting whoever or whatever had brought her here.

At the thought of what might lie behind the door, her heart sped up. She pressed her palms onto the cold wood floor beside her and ordered her mind to focus.

Calm. She had to stay calm. Eyes closed, she practiced her breathing again, visualizing her heart rate slowing, her body relaxing just the way that last counselor had taught her. Steady, she opened her eyes and glanced down at her hands. No shaking. She inhaled. No problem breathing.

She was improving. Maybe next time the panic wouldn't even appear. The thought pushed her spine a little straighter. She could do this. Filled with a strange confidence, she glanced around the room again.

Her situation wasn't any better; still no sign of her clothes, and the door was still closed hiding God knew what, but…she'd be damned if she'd sit here waiting.

Naked or not, she was leaving.

Jamming the pelt under her arms for a better grip, she sprinted to the front door. Made of rough-hewn lumber, it had only an old-fashioned wrought-iron latch as a lock. She flipped up the metal strip and yanked on the handle.

Her barrier to freedom didn't budge. A hot flush crept up her body. *No. She wouldn't panic. Try again.*

She jerked harder. Nothing.

Cursing, she dropped the fur, grabbed the handle with both hands, and used every ounce of her 110-pound frame to dislodge the recalcitrant door.

"Aren't you cold?" a composed male voice asked from behind her.

Kara froze, the sharp edge of the door's handle cutting into her fingers. Biting her lip, she waited. Who was he? Would he rape her? Kill her? Let her leave?

"Here, this might help." Her shirt and jeans landed in a heap beside her.

She glanced at her clothing. That was good, wasn't it? Would a rapist toss her her jeans? Unless he wanted her off guard, wanted to trick her into trusting him. She gave the door one more subtle tug.

"That's not the way out." The voice sounded amused.

Kara paused. Of course not, why would she think that? Obviously, she should be scrambling up the chimney or searching for a mouse hole. The hysteria from the night before returned.

Her bare foot brushed against the rough material of her shirt. Glancing down, she saw the folded edge of Kelly's "missing" flyer poking out of the pocket.

Kelly. Kara had let her down for a week. Doing nothing to find her—trusting in the police. Now, one day after she'd found a clue, as worthless as it had proven to be, this.

Her fear began to bubble and change inside her until it had evaporated, leaving pure cleansing anger in its place. Reaching down, she jerked up her clothes and began tugging them on. Fully dressed, she spun to face her captor.

He was huge, at least six-six, silvery blond hair and dark eyes—she couldn't make out the color. A heavy silver chain hung from his neck, bisecting a huge gash at the base of his throat. She skipped over the wound. His size alone made him intimidating; thinking about what he'd battled to get such an injury would send her back into a panic.

Swallowing hard, she forced her gaze to move on. His chest was bare. She paused again, this time fixated on the smooth muscle, mesmerized by the up-and-down movement of his breath.

He crossed his arms over his chest, a sound close to a growl rumbling from his lips.

Her mouth suddenly dry, Kara remembered the danger she was most likely in. Snapping her gaze back to his face, she said, "I'd like to leave."

"Would you?" He sauntered forward, his eyes burning into hers.

She folded her fingers into her palms, forcing herself to stay focused and calm. "Who are you?"

He stopped just short of touching her. His gaze flitted from her face to her neck, and then continued the descent to her still bare feet.

The wood floor seemed to warm beneath her.

Flight of imagination. Ignore it.

"How did I get here?" she asked, her voice coming out stronger than she felt.

He paused, then glanced back at her face.

Kara's blood pulsed through her veins. She felt bare, as if he could see inside her, but she resisted the urge to shrink back against the door.

"Who are you?" she repeated, forcing an edge to her voice.

He took another step forward, and with a slow deliberate motion, twisted a lock of her auburn hair around one finger. "You first. Who are you, and why does Lusse want you?"

Risk stared down at the tiny woman in front of him. The air was thick with her emotions, which were just as mercurial this morning as they had been last night. Fear to anger, with no stop in between.

He fought the urge to step even closer, to gorge himself on the heady scents.

"Why does Lusse want you?" he repeated, asking himself as much as her.

She blinked up at him, confusion clouding her eyes.

Risk twisted his finger farther into her hair. Using the physical contact to strengthen his senses, he focused on her, searching for something that would draw Lusse.

A fist to his gut broke his concentration. Huge eyes dark with anger glared up at him. The self-imposed leash he kept on his instincts slipped in response. Anger. So hard to resist. The blood surged a little quicker in his veins, but he kept his face blank, undisturbed.

"Who are *you*?" she demanded.

She was verging on full rage. His pulse quickening, Risk leaned lower and burrowed his nose into the waves of her hair. Annoyance, rage, fear; they all were there, and…he placed his palms flat against the door behind her, trapping her into place…something else, something barely tapped. Ignoring the blood pooling in his groin, he pulled his head back and stared into her eyes. They flickered with one of the few colors he could truly identify—the violet of unsullied power.

The intensity of her emotions engulfed him, making him reluctant to leave her side. "What *are* you?" he whispered.

Her lower lip disappeared between her teeth as she stared up at him. Another gleam of violet.

Whatever she was hiding, it was growing stronger. Like most power, it must be tied to her emotions—and with the strength of hers, whatever she was, unfettered she would be formidable.

He should stop now, take the female to Lusse. Let the witch wring whatever she desired out of her. But…the female's eyes flashed again…she wasn't like his normal Lusse-directed prey. This female's power was…he hesitated…pure. An inaudible laugh escaped him. Pure power. It was impossible, a myth. Power corrupted. It was true, cliché though it was.

No being could grow to adulthood with power over others and not use it to help themselves, harming those around them in the process. Then, once the power was realized, they turned to it again and again, until *all* that mattered was power. He jerked his hand from behind her head and grabbed on to the chain around his neck. This was proof of that. Lusse's quest for power had held him for five hundred years. Five hundred hell-filled years.

Spinning away from the female, he fisted his hands at his side. Power, another witch perhaps. Lusse had a particular love of destroying her own kind. He had taken no small amount of joy in it, too. Each one represented Lusse in his mind.

He should kill her himself. Why wait? Why give Lusse the chance to bleed her of her strength?

Kill her before she turned. It would be easy.

A low growl forming in his throat, he spun slowly back toward the door, and his prey.

Lusse whirled from the window, her blond hair snapping as she turned. "Where is he?"

Bader shuffled forward, his gaze glued to the white pile rug beneath their feet. "Venge is in the foyer. He was bloody. I didn't think you would want him dripping on the carpet," he mumbled.

"Not the whelp. I have no need for him. Risk. Where is Risk?"

Bader's eyes darted toward the white double doors that opened to the hall.

"Where is he?" she repeated.

"Missing." Bader hunched his shoulders, waiting for a deserved blow.

Like she had time to mess with him.

"I thought you said he fought the boy. Didn't he return with him?"

Bader gave a slight shake of his squat head.

Pausing in front of a gilt mirror, Lusse ran her forefinger over her brows. "And the girl?"

Another shake.

"Words, use words." She glared at Bader's reflection. "Did she survive their fight?"

"I'm not sure, but there were no signs of her blood on Venge, or much of…Risk's…" he finished.

Not a surprise. Lusse didn't expect Venge to get the best of Risk. In fact, she'd hoped Risk would be angered enough by the whelp's appearance, in what she knew Risk thought of as his territory, that he would allow his hellhound nature to take over completely. She'd hoped to have little more than a ginger-colored hide left of the whelp as a result of his dedicated service.

She turned her back on the mirror, pressing her spine against the marble top of the server that set beneath it. Risk had potential to be unstoppable, but his annoying edge of humanity kept getting in his way—her way.

She pressed her palms and fingers together in front of her face.

"Should I call him?" A carved horn hung from a leather strap in Bader's hand.

Lusse glanced from the horn to Bader's flat face. "Not yet. Let's talk to Venge first. I need to know what's keeping Risk before I summon him."

With a short nod, Bader shuffled from the room.

Lusse spun back around to study her reflection. This had not gone at all as she had planned. She plucked a tube of lipstick from the tray in front of her and smeared a line of red across her lips. Risk should be here now, fresh from the capture of the girl—a total innocent.

Lusse'd laid out a test for him and he'd failed.

The boy was just insurance, but even that part of her plan had fallen short.

Not only had Risk not returned with the young witch, he'd allowed another hellhound to step into his territory and survive. It was unthinkable.

She threw the lipstick down. The open cosmetic rolled across the marble before thunking onto the white carpet below.

Risk should be here, finally embracing his darkest side. Finally ready to lead Lusse's hounds in more than name only. With Risk as pack leader, willingly following her, she would be unstoppable.

Lusse gripped the sides of the server and stared into the mirror at her reflection. The months she'd spent training him, molding him. It couldn't have been wasted. She had been sure he was ready. No, something was keeping him, and when she found out what it was, she would destroy it and any bit of humanity left in her favorite.

The smell of blood drew her attention back to the room.

The boy stumbled in, barely moving faster than Bader who followed behind, his gaze on the floor.

"I see what you mean." She smiled, admiring Risk's work. The neck of the young man in front of her was thick with dried blood. "No real damage?" She stepped forward, running a finger along one particularly deep cut.

Bader's head gave a slight shake. "You know hellhounds—"

"Near impossible to kill. Yes, I know." She folded her arms over her chest, and studied the other man's face. So handsome, with his blue eyes and ginger hair. And his physique showed promise, too. Broad shoulders, long muscular legs. But, all in all, he was still nothing compared to Risk.

"What happened?" she asked.

Eyes, void of emotion, stared back at her. "He won."

She tapped a finger against her arm. Hellhounds were such a pain to break. Although there was a certain amount of joy in the act. She motioned for Bader to retrieve her favorite toy.

Eyes darting, Bader scurried to the silver-strapped chest she kept stuffed with items guaranteed to brighten an otherwise dull day. He flipped the lid up, then hovered above the open chest as if lost.

"The whip," she ordered, then looking back at Venge, added, "…the special one."

A tremor shook Bader's back.

"Now," she demanded, narrowing her eyes at her servant. Really, he was becoming tiresome, but lucky for him, she had bigger concerns today.

Nodding and mumbling to himself, he crept forward, the cat-o'-nine-tails balanced over his upturned palms.

Finally. She snatched the leather toy from his hands.

"Now, Venge, what did you say happened?" She let the black tails of the whip trail through her fingers.

His gaze didn't waver. "He won," he repeated.

Damn hellhound pride. They never learned. She snapped the whip, the tails sparking yellow as they struck together.

Venge's eyes widened just enough.

He knew what was coming.

Tingles of pleasure danced through Lusse's center. "There's no shame in giving in. Your father has often enough."

It was a lie, of course.

She slid closer, the whip whispering to her, begging for the feel of flesh against its tips.

"Are you protecting him?" she murmured, her lips brushing against the young man's ear, her tongue darting inside. "He wouldn't do the same for you, would he?"

Venge's eyes flashed in response, but his lips stayed firmly closed.

"Ah, why must it always come to this?" With a smile she raised her arm, adrenaline surging through her. Pain. Sweet, sweet pain. Without it life would be so dull.

Sated, Lusse fell against the fur cushion of her chaise longue. Her arm and shoulder were tired, but in oh, such a satisfying way. Smiling, she allowed one of her female servants to knead oils into her overtaxed muscles with smooth steady strokes.

Venge had exhibited the same tenacity as his father. Rewarding, but also a problem. She was no closer to learning what had happened to her favorite.

Hours had passed. Something had to have gone wrong. With Risk or the plan? A line formed between her brows.

Lusse had been sure he was ready and she so hated to be wrong, but she couldn't think of anyone with the exception of a very select group of gods, and herself, of course, who could touch Risk.

"Bader," she yelled.

He looked up from where he knelt, a bloodstained cloth clutched to his chest.

"Leave that." She waved her hand in the air. "Let one of the others tend to it." Why the old servant was so fixated on cleaning up every little drop of blood as soon as it was spilled was beyond her. She rather enjoyed the scent herself.

"Bring the horn. I think it's time we called Risk home."

His eyes darting from side to side, Bader gave a slight bow and scurried from the room.

Her hands fisted at her sides, Kara watched as her captor spun away. His fingers, just seconds before wrapped into her hair, now gripped the silver chain at his neck. The firm muscles of his back tensed as if engaged in some kind of internal disagreement.

Now would be a good time to escape, but how? Keeping her body immobile, her breath soft and steady, she let her gaze flit around the room. There was a small window over the kitchen sink, but unless she quickly developed the ability to fly, there was no way she could reach it before the man in front of her realized her plan.

Her cell phone—where was it? Not in her clothes, that was for sure. She would have felt the weight of it when she'd dressed. Probably still lying on the cold asphalt outside the Guardian's Keep. She tilted her head back, letting it bang softly against the wood.

What good was conquering your fears if it didn't help save you from reality?

A sudden wave of heat swept over her. She leveled her gaze to see her captor had settled whatever battle he had been waging and again stood facing her.

Every muscle in his body was tense, like an animal ready to spring. A vein in his neck pulsed a steady primitive beat. Even his wound seemed darker, angry. His eyes focused on her as if looking for any sign of movement.

No place to run. No way to defend herself. What was left? Words. It wasn't much, but it was all she had. All she had ever been very good at wielding.

Biting her lip, she looked up.

His eyes flickered back at her.

Chapter 3

Kara pressed her palms flat against the door behind her, unable to remove her eyes from those of the man in front of her. Unblinking, he stood there, his pupils barely visible in the surrounding glow, like a pebble tossed into a pool of molten lava. Instinctively she knew when that pebble sank all hope of saving herself would be lost.

Drugs? Some virus? Whatever was causing this strange condition didn't matter. She had to bring him back from whatever hell he was descending into.

Feeling unreal, as if she were watching the scene from within someone else's body, she asked, "You feeling all right? You want me to call someone?"

Muscles still tensed, the man took a deliberate step toward her. "Who are you?" The question fell from firm lips that barely seemed to move.

Kara swallowed. A name. He wanted a name. That was

simple, normal. She could supply that. She clung to the feel of the hard wood door behind her to keep her centered. "Kara. Kara Shane."

He held out his hand, brushing the backs of his fingers against her cheek. "What are you?" he asked.

At the simple gesture, a tingle of awareness rippled through Kara. Refusing to acknowledge it, she concentrated on his question.

What was she? Fair enough. Hadn't she been asking herself the same thing for as long as she could remember? Her throat closed in, making it hard to answer. "Poet, baker, candlestick maker. That's me." She pressed a hand to her neck willing the muscles to relax.

The man in front of her seemed to vibrate with a raw sexual energy, and her own body, ignoring the screams of her rational brain, pulsed in response. Everything was unreal, surreal. Her hand stole out toward him, wanting to touch his chest, check to see if his skin was warm or hot like the simmering in his eyes.

He made a small movement as if to move closer and she stopped, her hand frozen in midair. This was unreal. It had to be.

Grasping at the moment of reason before it slipped away, she closed her eyes and willed the nightmare she was captured in to dissolve, focused on waking as she had so many times before, alone and terrified, but safe in her bed.

"Poet?"

The soft questioning word caused her eyelids to fly open. He was still there. Still tense, and still emitting a strange energy that made her heart quicken and her breath turn to small shallow puffs in her chest. "Yes, poet." Her voice seemed loud in the quiet room. Suddenly annoyed with his response, she dropped her hand to her side and continued. "There's nothing wrong with poetry, you know. We can't all rape, plunder and pillage for a hobby."

Her captor froze, the carmine-tint of his eyes deepening to a dark burgundy. "I do not rape."

"Oh, sorry. Just the pillaging then? My mistake." She crossed her arms over her chest and glowered back at him, all the fear inside her draining away, leaving just an exhausted shell of resentment. How dare he bring her here, strip her naked, and then question her, as if she were the guilty party?

He looked back at her, a furrow of doubt, perhaps even sadness, etched between his eyes.

And despite all rational thought, she felt it again—the tug toward him, but this time it was less sexual and more kindred, a recognition of pain and a desire to alleviate it. Suddenly calm, she blinked. His eyes, now a swirl of green, gray and brown, not a single dash of red, seemed to hold as much confusion as she felt.

Swallowing hard, she forged on. "Who are you?" she asked.

"Risk." The name came out in a low growl.

Strangely, Kara didn't feel intimidated, though, more…intrigued.

"Strange name. You're what? A rock star?" Her tone was dry, the question brazen, the type of thing Kelly would have asked.

Kelly. Her gaze dropped to the paper at her feet.

"What's that?" Bending his knees, the man slid down to retrieve the flyer, his body brushing hers as he did.

Kara reached out to snatch it away.

"Patience, please." A frown settled on his face as he studied the paper, his body now close enough Kara could smell his warm masculine scent. She shifted her stance, long-neglected muscles at the apex of her thighs tightening.

Keeping her gaze steady, she ignored the quickening of her heart and the dampness forming in her too-tight jeans.

"I thought you said your name was Kara?" He held out the flyer; a picture of Kelly dressed for kickboxing stared back at them.

"I did." She reached for the paper again, but he simply slid closer, his arm extended over her head, less than an inch separating them now.

"Then this is…?"

He was too close. His chest brushed her breasts, and his breath moved her hair as he lowered his face back toward her neck.

"Then this is…?" he whispered against her ear.

A shiver darted up her spine. "My sister," she replied, the words coming out rough and sharp.

He pulled back far enough to look her in the eyes, his own gaze intense. "You're a twin? An *identical* twin?"

Kara pressed her sweat-dampened palms against her jeans, and tried to ignore the rapid beat of her heart. Afraid or excited? She'd lost track of her own emotions. Did it matter? However he affected her, she had to escape. She had to act strong. "That's right. Wouldn't want to break up a pair, would you?" Another very Kelly-ish question.

He stepped back until there were a few feet separating them. "A pair," he murmured. "Is it possible?" He stared at her again, his gaze wandering from her still bare feet to the top of her head. Kara felt another ripple of awareness, but when his gaze snapped back to her face, his eyes held nothing but cool analysis.

He turned again, striding toward the door at the back of the room.

Kara frowned at his dismissal. "What about me?"

He paused, placing his hand on the door frame in front of him, then slowly pushed himself back around to face her. "Yes, what about you?"

His gaze pierced her, pinning her to the door. Regretting the impulsive question that drew his attention back to her, Kara clamped her teeth onto her lower lip.

"She's lost?" He held the flyer toward her.

Kara nodded, her reply barely more than a whisper. "For a week."

"Not dead?"

The word sounded harsh, callous. Kara's chin jerked upward and she shook her head with a short definite motion. No, Kelly wasn't dead. She didn't know where she was, but she was alive—Kara could feel her.

"Can you find her?" he asked.

Kara blinked back the dampness that threatened to form in her eyes. "I…haven't."

"Maybe…" he folded the flyer up and shoved it into the front pocket of his jeans "…you haven't been looking in the right places."

Kara took a step forward, a seed of hope fluttering to life in her chest. "You mean, you'll help? You'll help me try to find Kelly?"

"No." Not bothering to give her another glance, he disappeared behind the door.

The blood drained from Kara's face, and her knees bent beneath her. Retreating before she sagged to the floor, she rested her head against the wood door. What was she thinking? Why would he help her, and why would she want him to? She didn't even know him.

Her tormentor emerged from the back room, a flannel shirt in his hand. He shoved his arms into the sleeves and began sliding buttons into place. Even disheartened by his refusal, her traitorous gaze zeroed in on the disappearing muscles of his chest.

He rolled up his sleeves, leaving his toned forearms bare. "I won't try."

Kara rolled her eyes to the ceiling, counting the log beams to keep from screaming her frustration. She was pathetic, leaping at the first hint someone might help her, and now what? He was going to lord her idiocy over her?

"I *will* find her."

Kara's gaze dropped to see him spin on one bare heel and stride into the kitchen.

Risk finished placing the last platter on the table and nodded for Kara to join him. She hesitated, hands gripping the top of her chair, anxiety wafting off her like mist off the sea.

"You eat like this all the time?" Her gaze darted over the plates of meat arranged on the table's top.

"Not all the time." When he was on a hunt he didn't eat at all. He could go days, even weeks without eating, but when he was preparing for a hunt, like now, he ate and he ate well.

And that was what he intended to do right now. Let the female fend for herself. Giving her one last impatient glance, he pulled out a chair and sat down.

"You have anything less…red?" she asked, a crack in her voice.

He frowned. “It’s cooked.”

“Barely,” she mumbled. Then, gesturing toward the refrigerator, she continued, “No, I mean like something green or yellow. You know, fruits, vegetables?”

Picking up a fork, he speared a slice of venison. “Prey eats plants.”

The mist of emotion around her thickened to a cloud. Cursing silently, he lay down his fork, the venison still on it. “Eat,” he commanded.

Something flickered in her eyes—not her power—fear; the scent hit him squarely in the face. Damn. Gripping the edge of the table, he fought the need to press her against the wall; to bury his nose in her hair; to control, dominate and conquer.

Why was the urge so strong? Fear and anger always pulled at him, but he had learned to manage his reaction. But with this bit of a witch, the tug on him was more intense than any he had ever experienced. Heat glowed to life behind his eyes and his nostrils flared. He dropped his gaze to the tabletop. He had to get her calmed down.

Taking a deep breath, he willed his body to relax then looked up, his teeth bared in what he hoped was a nonintimidating manner. “There might be bread and peanut butter.” He pointed to a drawer near the sink.

Chewing on her lower lip, she nodded.

With her facing the refrigerator, he studied her. She was attractive enough for a witch—small, rounded buttocks, legs long for her height, and hair with just enough curl to tempt his fingers to weave deep into its depths. His cock twitched at the thought. Disturbed by his body’s betrayal, he adjusted on the hard chair.

He had to focus on the hunt. If the tales of twin witches

were true, Kara and her sister could be invaluable to him. Perhaps even powerful enough to free him from Lusse forever. But if he hoped to find her sister and use their magic to break Lusse's hold, he couldn't be getting sidetracked every few minutes by the alluring scent of her overactive emotions or the equally alluring sight of her rounded buttocks.

He had to get her calm and himself focused. Concentrate on the need to find the missing sister not the desire to take this one.

He avoided looking at her again until she had returned, a loaf of sourdough bread in her hand. "You want some?" she asked.

Risk stared at the white slice in front of him. He mainly kept bread to lure animals to his traps. He glanced up at her heart-shaped face. The scent of fear had faded again, but anxiety still clung to her.

She watched him, eyes huge, the hand holding the bread quavering ever so slightly.

Have to keep her calm. Brows lowered, he took the bread.

A breath he hadn't realized she was holding escaped her lips in a huff. Then pulling out the chair across from him, she collapsed on the seat.

"So, you're really going to help me find my sister?" she murmured, the slice of bread pressed to her lips.

His gaze on his plate, he nodded.

She stuck a knife into the jar and spread a slow zigzag of peanut butter onto the bread. "How..." Her lower lip disappeared in her mouth again. "How do I know I can trust you?"

"You don't." He picked up the carving knife, whacked the leg off a roasted duck and felt her pull back.

Damn, this nonintimidating thing was hard.

* * *

Kara jumped at the sound of the knife chopping through bone and sinew.

Not exactly a man of culture, her host. Eyeing him nervously, she folded the bread in half, making a little sandwich, and nibbled at the corner. This whole situation was just weird—the dogs last night, his eyes today, being here at all for that matter. For a bit she'd truly thought he was going to rip her throat out—wasn't completely sure still that he wouldn't. But…she stole a glance in Risk's direction…he hadn't done anything *obviously* aggressive since he'd started layering the table with plates. A little disturbing perhaps, what with the knife, talk of prey and such, but he hadn't actually threatened her and she hadn't seen any sign of glowing eyes.

Both good things.

Her common sense told her to take advantage of his slight mellowing by beating a fast exit out the door, but he had promised to find Kelly, and despite her fear of him, or perhaps because of it, Kara believed he could.

"Where do we start?" she asked, forcing the bite of sandwich down her dry throat.

"You tell me. How did she disappear?"

Trying to ignore the fact that he still held the gleaming knife in one hand, Kara willed herself to relax, to remember. "Kelly is…different." By most people's standards this was an understatement, but he didn't need all the details, surely. "She's always believed things other people don't." She edged a glance at him to see how he was reacting. He drove the knife into a turkey carcass then gestured for her to continue.

Suppressing a shiver, she said, "About six months ago,

she started taking classes online, hanging out on bulletin boards, stuff like that. And she was going out, a lot, at night."

"She have a mate?" he asked.

Kara paused for a second, thrown by his strange choice of words, then gave her head a slight shake. "No, Kelly isn't much for dating—neither of us are."

He raised an eyebrow, but didn't interrupt.

"I got the feeling she was…" Kara squeezed the bread in her hand until peanut butter squished out the sides. A brown glob dropped onto her lap.

What to tell him? Swallowing, she made the decision. Might as well be the truth. He might even believe her. "Hunting. I think she was hunting something."

"And maybe she got caught instead?" He ran a finger along his lower lip. Kara's eyes followed its path. "Your sister, you said she was different. How exactly?"

Dropping her gaze before he could notice her interest, Kara used her finger to swipe the peanut butter off her leg. She had chosen her path, might as well stick with it now. "She's, you know…new age-y. Incense. Little statues. Dead animal parts." Grabbing a napkin, she wiped her finger clean, then glanced up. No expression, not even a glimmer of interest showed on his face. "Did she practice?" he asked.

Kara frowned. "Practice what?"

His only answer was a deep breath, as if calming himself.

Afraid he was about to slip back into berserker mode, Kara hurried to continue. "Well, I guess you could say she practiced. Kelly is what you might call determined."

He arched one brow.

"Like a terrier. Give her a challenge and she'll put 120 percent into conquering it. She's physical, too, you know? Hands-on? She's a big believer in being able to take care of yourself. Studied some self-defense stuff—the same thing used by the Israeli Army. She took classes five days a week for a while. They were closed the other two." And she'd tried talking Kara into taking the classes with her, over and over. Based on the last twenty-four hours, Kara was beginning to wish she had agreed.

"A hunting warrior female. Your sister sounds interesting." His hand wandered to the silver chain at his throat. "How about you? Do you practice?"

Kara dropped the sandwich onto the wooden tabletop. "No." The last came out a bit abruptly. Kara had always accepted that Kelly was the dedicated one—the one everyone admired. It had never bothered her before, but hearing the edge of respect in Risk's voice when he spoke of her sister brought the truth home more clearly than ever before. She could never measure up—apparently, even a complete stranger who had never met Kelly could sense that.

Uncomfortable with the topic, she changed it. "What about you?" she asked.

"What about me?" He turned back to the plate in front of him.

Kara hesitated again. Did she dare push her luck by questioning him, and what to ask first? His eyes, had they been her imagination? Too personal. Why would he help her? Didn't want to put the idea not to in his head. Finally, she settled on a question. "How did I get here?"

He barely glanced up. "I brought you."

His abruptness set her back for a second, but when he continued eating, she relaxed—a bit. "But how, and where are we?"

"I carried you, and about eighty miles from the city. If you want to measure like that."

Eighty miles? All hope of an easy exit died. Then the other part of his answer registered. "How else would I measure, and how do you carry someone eighty miles?"

He smiled, a sad somewhat self-mocking slant to his lips. "Oh, I've carried…"

Kara waited for him to finish, but Risk's attention appeared to have shifted. He froze, his eyes suddenly alert, and tilted his head slightly to the side.

"What is it?" she asked.

Clapping his hands over his ears, he stumbled away from the table and began to crumple slowly toward the floor.

Kara jumped up and ran around the table to kneel beside him. His hands gripped the chain at his neck with such force his knuckles turned white and Kara thought the metal might imbed itself into the back of his neck.

A seizure, it had to be. Kara reached out to pry his fingers loose. He was going to hurt himself.

He let go of the chain to push her hand away. "Jeep, in back. Take it…"

What the hell was he talking about? She couldn't leave him like this.

"Is there a phone? I'll call someone. Or medication, do you need something?"

She placed her hand on his shoulder; he began to shimmer beneath her, just like the ginger dog the night before. She could feel her own hand begin to shimmer, too, an unsettling sensation as if her hand had fallen asleep and now was in the painful process of waking up.

"No." He pulled back his leg and, using one bare foot, shoved her across the oak floor away from him.

Her head knocked against the cabinet with such force, she couldn't be sure what she saw next actually happened.

Just like with the dog, the air around him turned into waves, and with a growl, he disappeared.

Kara stared blankly at the space where Risk had been. He was gone. Impossible. Rubbing the back of her head, she scrambled along the floor until she reached the spot where he had disappeared. She ran a trembling hand along the length of the wood. The floor radiated heat, like a stove burner that was just turned off seconds before.

What would cause that?

Curling her fingers into her palms, Kara willed herself to stay rational. Grown men did not just disappear. There had to be an explanation. She pressed her palm against the boards. They were still warm, though already cooler to touch. In a few more seconds even this sign of Risk's disappearance would be gone.

It wouldn't change things, though. He was there, then he was gone. This couldn't be explained away. She looked around. She was still in a cabin—a strange cabin—and Risk had been real. He *had* been there.

The dog, now Risk. It was too much for her to comprehend. Kara slid onto the spot, letting the last fragments of heat seep into her.

Strange things had happened around Kara all her life, but none so blatant as this. None that couldn't be explained away somehow.

But a full-grown man disappearing in front of her eyes, there were only two possible explanations for that. Either Kara truly *was* insane, or there was something else going on here. Something that didn't play by the rules of the world she knew.

She wasn't completely sure which she hoped was true.

Chapter 4

Risk shimmered to solidity on Lusse's plush carpet. Once he had pushed Kara away, he had given in to Lusse's call. Ignoring her would only have made things worse. She or one of her minions might even have come looking for him, might have violated the only personal space allowed him, and worse, found Kara.

The thought startled him. He gripped the wool pile with curled fingers.

He couldn't care about the little witch.

Even with the streak of humanity Lusse claimed he had, Risk didn't care about anyone—not even himself. Yes, he wanted to be free of Lusse, but only to cause Lusse pain. To loll in the knowledge that she had lost what she valued most—power. Even if it was just the power to torment and torture him, it would gnaw at Lusse, and Risk would savor every gratifying moment.

No, he didn't care about the witch, he told himself, relaxing his fingers. He was only concerned Lusse would find her before Risk tracked down her twin and convinced them to assist him. Until then, he had to protect her, that was all.

The hollow sound of Lusse's horn landing on marble broke through his thoughts; then the pointed toe of Lusse's diamond-encrusted shoe slid into view. "Ah, my favorite pet has arrived."

Eyes focused on the white rug, Risk gritted his teeth at the term. As a child, he had made the mistake of letting Lusse know when something she said or did angered him. Not anymore. Better to endure in silence, pretend pleasure even, than give the sadistic witch the joy of seeing him suffer.

"What is that you're wearing?" Her hand hovered over the flannel shirt on his back, the energy crackling from her hand signaling her displeasure. "Remove it."

Steeling his mind to hide his annoyance, he leaned back on his heels and reached for the buttons. "A shirt," he replied, forcing his lips into a false smile.

"I detest it. Remove it. Immediately." She spun, the skirt of her silk dress slapping against her legs as she strode to her chair. Once seated, she waited, her fingers caressing the velvet armrests.

His chest now bare, the icy air of Lusse's home assaulted Risk's skin, causing a shiver he barely contained.

"Cold?" she asked, one brow arched.

"Never around you, Lusse," he answered with indifference. Risk knew she would prefer a term more suiting her proprietary position, but it was a deference Risk had never afforded her. He didn't intend to start now.

"So, pet, where have you been?" The question was casual, her tone almost a purr, but Risk knew better than to answer lightly.

"Serving you, as always." He kept his gaze steady to hide his lie.

"Really? Have you?" She stood, pausing to pluck one of her toys, a gem-covered glove, from a table, then wandered past him to stand under the silver manacles that dangled from her ceiling.

"I must admit I wondered. Just a tad, you understand." She brushed her foot along the marble tiles that covered the floor under the shackles, then shook her head. "My, Bader is slipping. He seems to have missed a spot." Her shoe darted out to point at the bright red gleam of fresh blood on the white marble.

Risk cocked one brow in feigned interest.

"It took you so long, and with no word. I found myself bored." With a whoosh of her arm, she appeared beside him. Grasping his chin until her long nails dug into his skin, she pulled his face up so he had no choice but to look at her. "You know what I do when I'm bored, don't you?"

Risk stared evenly into her stormy-sea-colored eyes, not having to pretend the disinterest he felt. "Yes, Lusse, I do."

"What, no contrition? No apology? No 'I'll do better, Lusse'?" Her thumb slipped over his lower lip, the pressure as slight as a butterfly landing on a petal. "I worry about you so, and you have nothing for me?" she whispered, tugging on one glove. "And, worst of all…" She pulled back her hand, stared at him for a second, her eyes gleaming, then in a streak of sparkling jewels, struck him across the face. "No witch."

The diamonds sliced into Risk's face; the pain of a thousand icicles piercing his skin soon followed.

How nice, Lusse had added a little extra treat to this particular toy of hers. Was this how she cured her boredom while he was gone, or were there more surprises in store?

Still on his knees, Risk maintained his pose, ignoring the numbness creeping across his face, and the blood swelling from the cuts.

"Have you failed me, alpha? Was all my attention and care over the past years for nothing?" She turned again, striding across the room. Her dress billowed in a cloud of purple silk as she lowered her body into her chair.

"Where is my witch?" she asked.

Risk stared ahead. Kara would do him little good if he were dead, but five hundred years of torture told him Lusse wouldn't go that far, and if he was wrong…well, so be it.

"I don't have her," he replied.

"You *did* fail?" Her tone revealed disbelief.

"There were issues…" Blood from his wounds trickled into his mouth as he spoke. He swallowed the salty liquid.

"Hellhounds don't have *issues*. Hellhounds do as they are told. Isn't that right, Risk?"

"Of course." Paralysis overtook the corner of his mouth, a blessing since it made it impossible to fulfill the urge to bare his teeth in a snarl.

"Do you know where you got your name, Risk?" she asked, her gloved fingers tapping the padded armrest.

"From you, Lusse," he answered.

"Yes, that's right, but do you know why I gave you such a name?"

"No, Lusse," he mumbled, half his face now immobilized by her blow.

"When I bought you…your parents were quite happy

to be rid of you, you know, one less mouth to feed and all that, plus the honor of being chosen by me, I barely paid them half your worth..." she chuckled as if exchanging warm childhood memories "...I picked you from your brothers and sisters because even as a boy you stood out. The others wanted to please, as much as any of your sort does anyway, but not you. No toy could tempt you and no threat could break you. I was intrigued, and I knew you had the potential to be unstoppable, if I could train you. It was a risk, but one I thought I could manage. And if I couldn't, well, I'd be out a few gold coins and some time."

The numbness in Risk's face shifted and changed into a shooting coldness, like a frigid sword boring down the length of his spine. Tightening his shoulders, he withstood the torment.

"So, tell me. Did I name you well? Were you worth the risk?" Lusse clenched and unclenched her fist, watching as the light caught the gems on her glove and split into a million tiny rainbows.

"Of course, Lusse." Risk's words came out so garbled, even he couldn't decipher them.

"So..." She looked up from the glove. "Where is she? Where is my witch?"

Whatever the magic in Lusse's blow, it continued to grow, gathering speed as time progressed. Pain shot from Risk's back to his thighs to his stomach, like an icy comet bouncing around inside him. Gritting his teeth, Risk blocked out the pain.

What to tell Lusse—too little and she would know he was lying. Too much and she might realize his plans.

"Safe," he mumbled.

"Safe?" A flicker of interest lit Lusse's eyes. "From what?"

"There was a—" Pain sliced through Risk's head, cutting off his speech.

"There was a what?" Lusse demanded.

"A…" Risk sucked in air through his teeth, forcing his brain to overcome the glove's magical poison and form the sentence. "Problem."

"Yes, yes, a problem. What else?" Lusse lowered both brows. "Talk."

Risk opened his mouth again, but this time only a guttural noise came out. Frosty wires wound around his lungs, slowly cutting off his oxygen. He locked his body into an upright position and waited for Lusse's spell to weave its final net.

"Yggdrasil! Obstinate alpha." Lusse jerked the glove from her hand. Then, pulling a small vial from the folds of her skirt, strode toward him.

If her spell hadn't frozen him in place, he would have jerked backward, evaded her cure—just for the sheer pleasure of thwarting her. How it would have irked her to have killed him herself and without learning about the witch she'd sent him to retrieve. The thought made him smile inwardly, but unable to move, all he could manage was a slight sway sideways before warm liquid splashed onto his face.

Within seconds his wounds changed from icy numbness to blazing fire then simmered to a dull, throbbing ache.

As the potion followed the course of the poison, the pressure on Risk's lungs lessened, making it easier to breathe, but refusing the need to gulp air, he kept his posture steady and his breaths controlled. With silent effort he stamped down the last remnants of pain.

Lusse stood a few feet away, eyes assessing, her toe tapping, and the empty vial dangling from two fingers. "Bader," she snapped. "Bring in the whelp."

So, Lusse was ready to end her game. What treat did she have planned for him now? Whatever her ploy, Risk was grateful for the delay; it gave him a few more seconds to compose his answer regarding Kara.

"Bader," Lusse repeated, her voice cutting through the room like an arctic wind.

The double doors leading to the hall crept open on silent hinges, followed by Lusse's ancient servant, Bader, his polished dress shoes barely leaving the floor as he inched along. In his hand was a silver box; following close behind was a young redheaded hellhound in human form. The youth, the hound who'd invaded Risk's territory, Risk guessed, walked steadily behind the servant. A strand of energy crackled from Bader's tiny box tugging the younger male forward as it connected with the chain around his neck. Despite that insult and the numerous wounds that decorated his body, the youth kept his posture stiff, his eyes focused forward.

"See, it's as I told you." Lusse directed her question to the boy, her outstretched arm gesturing to Risk. "Your father knows his proper place." Raising her hand, she signaled Bader to bring the other male forward.

Risk stared blankly at the scene in front of him, one word echoing through his brain. *Father?*

As Bader twisted a dial on the box, pulling the chain around the younger hound's neck taut, Lusse turned a blinding smile on Risk. "Oh, I forgot. You haven't been introduced, have you? Risk, this—" she gestured to the youth "—is your son. Venge, this is the father I've told you so much about."

The younger male, his eyes focused on a spot somewhere behind Lusse, didn't acknowledge Risk or the old servant Bader, who rose on his tiptoes in an effort to control the surging energy and bring the youth to his knees.

Seeing her servant's ungraceful position, Lusse's eyes flashed, a spark of cream in her naturally dark color. Briefly, Risk wondered what the true color of her power was to someone not hampered by the colorblindness of a hound. Not the pure violet of Kara's eyes. That was certain.

"Bader," Lusse bit out the name, then with an impatient toss of her head, held her closed fist, palm up, toward him and the other male.

"No." Risk's order broke through the tense scene like a hammer through glass.

Lusse paused, tilting her head toward him. A slow lethal smile transformed her. "What, Risk? You object to a little discipline?" She wandered toward him, her uncurled hand trailing over tabletops and chair backs as she came. Circling him, nails rasping over the bare skin of his shoulders and chest, she continued, "A show of fatherly love, perhaps?" Reaching his back, she stopped and leaned forward until her cold breath puffed against his neck.

Realizing his mistake, Risk stared ahead. Lusse said the other male was his son, but she'd offered no proof, and even if what she said was true, what did it matter to Risk? It didn't change his reality, his goal—to defeat Lusse.

"What? Cat got your tongue?" Lusse giggled, a sound as different from Kara's feminine laugh as the hiss of a cobra from the coo of a dove.

"He is yours, you know. Same strong shoulders…" Lusse's hands cupped Risk's. "Same solid chest…" Her hands slipped lower, her palms rubbing his chest, her breasts pressed against his back. "Same delectable taste." Her tongue flicked out, lapping at his neck.

Risk contained the urge to toss her across the room, to hear her spine snap as her body collided with a wall.

"Same stubborn disposition…" In one fluid movement, she held out her fist and uncurled her fingers. Power arched from her outstretched hand, hitting the chain on the younger male's neck. The surging power raced around the silver links encircling the youth's neck before merging with the line of energy pulsing from the metal box still clasped in Bader's fist.

Bader watched, eyes rounding as the combined force raced toward him. As it hit, his body thrashed like a sheet caught in the wind. Lusse smiled, her free hand still stroking Risk's back.

The younger male grabbed at his throat, attempting to yank the chain from his neck, his eyes squeezed shut in an obvious effort to ignore the pain arching through him. One knee buckled, and he threw out his arm, grabbing the wall beside him for support. His body jerked, the power popping and snapping as it continued to flow from Lusse to the collar and into him. Still vibrating against the surging energy, he raised his eyelids and glowered at Lusse and Risk.

With a bored sigh, Lusse muttered against Risk's ear, "See, obstinate." Standing, she yelled, "Enough." Then, holding out both arms, let loose another stream of magic.

The thick scent of the youth's fury clouded the air.

Risk tensed, the desire to turn on Lusse even stronger than before. How long could the boy survive such force? Risk had survived worse, but this hound was young, not possessed of his full strength yet. Would Lusse kill him to make a point?

The beast inside Risk growled, eager to break out and turn Lusse's torture into a real fight—one, bound as he was by her magic, Risk was sure to lose. But, a growing voice inside him murmured, if the reward was just a few drops of Lusse's blood it would be well worth any price.

As the fire in his soul began to grow, his fingers curved into his palms. *Change. Change. Change,* the hound within him chanted.

The younger male pitched forward, both knees giving out at once, only the stream of energy flowing from Lusse stopping him from landing on the floor.

"At last," Lusse muttered. Flicking her wrists, she sent one more surge of magic into the chain, then apparently satisfied her message had been sent, dropped her arms.

Both Bader and the youth fell to the floor with a disturbing thump.

Risk took a deep breath, attempting to calm the unsatisfied animal inside him. *Keep with the plan.* Saving the girl was the only way to hurt Lusse.

Except… His gaze wandered to the near-comatose youth.

"So, Daddy, what do you think of your son? Is he everything you hoped for?" Lusse strolled to the younger male, picking up her long skirt to step over an unconscious Bader on the way.

"I don't have a son," Risk replied, turning a now cool gaze on Lusse.

"Oh, but you do." Lusse placed the sole of her shoe on the boy's back. "Big, beautiful and brazen—he's definitely yours. Don't tell me you don't even remember? How sad."

The youth raised his eyelids, his gaze simmering with impotent fury.

At Risk or Lusse?

"Poor Venge. His daddy won't claim him." Lusse knelt beside the youth, then reached out to draw circles on his sweat-dampened back.

Snapping her gaze back to Risk, she continued, "Such a special night. So full of promise. Don't you remember? The battles, the bloodlust? The weeks of training to get you to the point where you would lose control, to give yourself over to the power of the Hunt. It cost me six strong hounds, but it was worth it just to witness the completeness of your Change." She hugged herself, her fingers dancing up her arms in a shiver of joy.

The completeness of his Change, Risk's mind repeated. Yes, he remembered.

"But…" he began.

"Oh, that's right. How could I forget?" Lusse brushed a lock of hair out of the pup's face. "He thinks he killed your mother. He almost did. Tore her throat so thoroughly, she barely lasted long enough to deliver." She glanced back at Risk. "But, you see, she made it—for a while anyway. Long enough for what I needed from her." Lusse's hand brushed the length of the younger male's back. "Look closely, smell him. You'll recognize the truth."

Risk's mind traveled back—to the time he most wished he could forget. Lusse had starved him for weeks; used every toy she could devise to break him; locked him in with a pack of rogue males all intent on winning the spot of leader, and not caring if there was any pack left to lead. Then she had chained him to a wall in her torture chambers and pumped every drop of anger and fear she could extract from her victims into his face. There was no escaping it. By the time she had unloosed him and tossed the bitch in heat into his cell, he was lost. There was nothing human left—nothing but animal.

He'd torn into the female, mounting her even as his teeth had sunk into her neck, ripping through fur and skin. The metallic tang of her blood only adding to his pleasure, he'd forgotten everything except the heady sensations of sex, blood and finally death. Or so he had thought. After, when he had calmed and was back in his human form, Bader had come in to drag the bitch's lifeless form from the room.

Lusse had rewarded him by announcing his new position as pack alpha, but Lusse's ploy, instead of committing Risk to his demon half, had done the opposite. Memories of that night filled him with self-loathing, feeding his need to contain his true nature.

He had refused Lusse's position, instead accepting the torture that came with defying her. She had tried many times since to force him back to that place, but had never managed to push him that far.

And now Lusse was telling him the male in front of him was the product of that gruesome night.

"Still don't believe me? Risk, your lack of trust is so disturbing. Come closer." Lusse gestured with one hand.

But Risk didn't need to move closer, didn't trust himself nearer the witch. Instead, he closed his eyes and put faith in his senses. At first he smelled nothing more than hound—male hound, too close. *Kill. Kill*, his instincts yelled. In his hound form, Risk's hackles would have raised and his lips would have twisted into a snarl, but as a human, he was able to tamp these reactions down, his nostrils flaring the only visible response to the scent of a potential challenger so close.

Kill. Risk sat still, his hands fisted at his sides, waiting for the impulse to lunge toward the other male to subside. When he was confident of his control, he inhaled again, delving deeper into the scent.

Anger. And pain, but not just physical… Risk frowned. Emotional pain was a human tendency, not something natural to a hellhound. A human weakness, Lusse would say. The type of weakness she accused Risk of having…

Damn. Could it be true? Then hidden under layers of anger, hurt and testosterone, he found it, his scent—Risk's scent. Not exact, of course, but close—too close to deny.

The boy was his.

At the realization, his eyes opened.

"Ah, you see it now, don't you?" Lusse grinned, her hands clasped in front of her like a schoolgirl being presented with an unexpected gift.

Yes, he saw it. He had done the one thing he had sworn he would never do—condemned another hound to a life of hell serving Lusse. He could imagine Lusse bent over the boy's crib—if she'd allowed him that luxury—while she clipped the silver collar of her control around his neck. His mother dead, his father already trapped in bondage to the witch, leaving no one to stop her.

"So, are you proud of your little boy, Risk? He shows a lot of promise, you know. Not as strong as his father, but I suppose with the right training…" she pulled the gem-covered glove she'd used on Risk earlier from her pocket "… he might earn his keep. Or perhaps father more hounds, eventually I'd have to get at least one whelp without those annoying human sensibilities." She knelt down, resting her gloved hand lightly on the younger male's back.

"So, what did you say happened with the witch I sent you to retrieve?"

Chapter 5

Kara sat back on her heels, staring at just a few of the strange objects her sister had tucked inside an innocuous-looking rubber tub: a small statue of a woman draped in some kind of winged cloak, a silk bag filled with polished stones, and most disturbing, a very sharp, polished dagger with a bone handle.

Setting the knife carefully onto the ground beside her, Kara sighed. What had Kelly gotten herself involved in? She reached into the tub again, this time pulling out a rough cloth. A nub of white chalk fell from its folded length and plinked onto the cement floor of their shared basement. Kara's gaze followed as it rolled to a stop.

Well, that probably explained this, anyway. Kara stood up to retrieve the chalk then wandered to a space to the right of the stairs where the faint outline of a circle showed on the dusty floor.

Plopping down onto the cold concrete, Kara absently traced over the circle while her mind flitted back over the past few days.

After Risk had disappeared, Kara escaped the cabin—through the window. The door wouldn't budge even though she'd seen no sign of a lock, and there were no other exits. Made her wonder how she had got into the cabin in the first place, but with everything else swirling through her head, she hadn't wasted much time worrying over the trivial. She'd squirmed out the opening, and scurried to a small lean-to she'd found behind the house. Inside she'd found a Jeep with the keys conveniently in the ignition. Even though the vehicle had to be almost twenty years old, it had started without so much as a hiccup.

Not pausing to analyze her sudden change in luck, Kara had sped away, taking the only road she could—the one that dead-ended at the cabin. After an hour of bumping down the rutted dirt road, she'd finally hit pavement and a choice—left or right. Still having no clue where she was, she'd picked using pure instinct. As it turned out, her gut had served her well. Twenty minutes later she'd been back in familiar territory. Which, if she was allowing herself to analyze any of this too carefully, would be disturbing, since she had visited the gas station she found herself at many times last summer when she and Kelly had gone hiking, but she couldn't remember ever seeing the road that led to Risk's cabin.

Just an example of how little attention she paid to what was going on around her. A habit she was beginning to think she needed to break.

She paused for a moment, dusting the white chalk on her hand onto the leg of her jeans.

She'd escaped Risk's cabin, but not the questions that had continued to pile up around her. Who was Risk? How had she wound up with him and what had happened to him last night? In under twenty-four hours she had seen, or thought she had seen, two very large living beings disappear right in front of her eyes.

The dog was one thing. She'd been near hysteria at the time. She could easily have imagined that—but Risk?

She dropped the chalk and stared blindly at the white line she had traced. Shouldn't she be calling the police or something? He *was* missing.

She pressed a damp palm to her forehead. She could imagine the conversation. "This is Kara Shane, the woman who has been harassing you about her missing sister. I'd like to report a missing man now. No, don't know his full name. No, don't know his address, but I have his Jeep. Oh, and how do I know he's missing? He kind of just evaporated in front of me."

Yeah, that would work. She picked the chalk up and dotted it against the ground, leaving little white specks on the floor.

But he was missing, and for some reason, Kara felt responsible. She had to look for him, didn't she? She glanced down at the nub of chalk in her hand, then at the almost complete circle.

Finish what you start, Kara. First, she'd find Kelly. Then she'd look for Risk.

With new determination, she dropped the chalk and strode back to the rubber bin. As disturbing as her sister's belongings were, they were also the only hope Kara had of learning what might have happened to her. Even if the next thing she pulled out was a shriveled head, she was going to sift through every single strange object.

As her hand dropped back into the bin, her gaze drifted over to the almost-closed circle. *Finish what you start.* Nothing like a little symbolic gesture to put her on the right track. With a determined nod of her head, she strode back to the discarded chalk, and prepared to finish at least one thing today.

Risk stared at the sparkling gems on Lusse's glove. Would the sadistic witch use it on the boy? Boy. Risk shifted his gaze to the semiconscious male lying at Lusse's side. Risk's son, and no boy. No, he was a man—almost twenty years old if Risk's memory was right.

Old enough to be starting life as an adult. Moving away from his family and starting one of his own. Or training in one of the few career choices open to free hellhounds…or, something Risk had often dreamed of, mingling with humans and carving out a life for himself there.

Old enough for any of that, but far too young to be lying here on Lusse's fine wool rug, bleeding and beaten.

"So, Risk, where is my witch?" Lusse twisted her hand so the light caught a ruby-tinted jewel releasing a crimson blaze.

Tell her you lost her. Stick with the plan. Forget the boy—son or not, he's nothing to you.

Lusse stared back at him, one gem-covered finger tapping against the boy's back.

"I told you. There were…complications." Risk kept his gaze focused on Lusse's eyes and away from his son.

"Complications?" Lusse pushed one finger into Venge's back. The glove sizzled to life. The muscles of Venge's back twitched, and the line of his jaw tightened.

Damn Lusse. What would she do to the youth if Risk didn't deliver Kara?

"Yes, complications..." Risk began.

Lusse let a second finger drop, the pressure light, but her intention clear.

"But..." Risk continued. "Nothing I can't deal with."

"Of course. I have complete faith in you." Lusse curled her fingers toward her palm, breaking all contact with Venge's back. "I would, just out of curiosity you understand, like to know what exactly constitutes a complication."

Risk paused. Sunlight caught on the gemmed glove, sending a sprinkling of rainbows dancing across the room. A cold thread of dread uncoiled in Risk's stomach. If he didn't give up Kara or a believable reason why he wasn't, his son would suffer for it. Risk had already doomed the boy to a childhood of suffering. How could Risk, by his actions, sentence Venge to more?

"She has a twin." Risk let the words lie there, knowing Lusse would realize the importance of what this meant.

"A twin?" She stood up, peeling the glove from her hand as she stepped around the prone Venge. "That is wonderful news. Was there a problem? Did they learn of your coming?"

"No, not that. It's more complicated. The sister. She's missing." As the words fell from his lips, Risk's mind whirled ahead. All wasn't lost. Maybe he could still work the situation. Buy time.

"Missing? She ran off?" Lusse frowned.

"No, I don't think so. I think she's been taken."

"Dead?" Lusse twisted her lips to the side.

"Not according to Ka— the witch you sent me to retrieve."

A flicker of suspicion passed over Lusse's face at his slip, but Risk hardened his gaze and continued. "I knew you would want both, but to find the sister I need the help and trust of the first. That's what I was working on when you called."

"Building trust?" Lusse cocked her head. "And how, my alpha, do you go about doing that?"

Risk stared at her, his gaze cool, knowing.

She laughed. A sensual smile tipping her lips, she stepped closer. "A little mortal witch. How could she resist all this?"

While Risk held his breath, disguising his distaste, Lusse ran her bare palm up his stomach, over his ribs and onto his chest. "No chance at all."

As soon as Risk felt confident he'd reestablished at least a modicum of trust with Lusse, he prepared to leave. The boy, Venge, had sat up, his gaze distant, but Risk could feel the emotion pulsing beneath his son's carefully crafted facade. Venge was angry, seething. Given the chance, he would most likely rip out the throats of both Lusse and Risk. Risk accepted that. His son had been dealt an ugly hand. Rage was to be expected. But Venge would do what all hellhounds did, embrace his anger and use it to grow stronger.

Risk turned his thoughts to Kara, what he had promised Lusse and how he could possibly twist the situation to get everything he needed while accomplishing his goal. Lusse now knew about the sister, but thanks to her ego, also believed Risk was in the process of hunting the twin to deliver to Lusse. Of course, somehow, Risk had to avoid that—string Lusse along enough to keep his freedom to move about the human world, without actually delivering his part of the bargain.

And Kara, she expected him to help *her* find her sister. Which he would. He'd just need a little repayment from the pair before he released them. But, one step at a time. First he had to return to Kara.

Now that Risk knew the distinct scent of not only Kara's

human musk, but also her emotions, it would take him only moments to locate her. Inhaling deeply, he trusted his senses to lead him to his target and shimmered away from Lusse's mansion.

Even before he solidified completely, he began scanning the room. It was dim, cool, and smelled of damp. A disquieting energy thickened the air. The hairs on his forearms unfurled and his muscles tensed. Eyes scanning the space, Risk waited for his body to catch up with his senses. Solid, he stepped forward, toward a line of light leaking from under a nearby door.

Odd, if Kara was there—which his senses said she was—then why hadn't he shimmered closer, at least into the same room?

His instincts screamed at him. Something wasn't right. Immediately switching into hunting mode, he concentrated and pulled on his ability to blend, confuse the eye. He wasn't invisible, but unless a person expected to see him and had some magical ability of their own, Risk would blend into the background, going unnoticed until it was too late.

Unsure what awaited him, Risk padded closer, his muscles tensed and ready to spring. Keeping his body to the right of the closed door, he pushed the thin barrier open with one palm.

The space was illuminated from above by a bare bulb dangling from a single wire. Beneath it—her hand flung to the side, her body twisted like an abused doll—lay Kara.

An unfamiliar emotion snaked through Risk's gut. Pale, broken, the image of Kara lying on the cold cement floor seared into him, freezing him in place. Dead.

She couldn't be.

The thought snapped him into action. He jumped forward. A prayer that Kara was alive forming in his brain, he collided with a wall of pure power. He had no time to think or react—just flew backward, knocking into a plastic tub and sending its contents skittering across the floor.

Stunned, he sat for a moment, the aftershock of his collision reverberating like the roar of a souped-up engine in his ears. Kara lay as she had when he'd first seen her, not even a hair moved though the floor was now littered with small stones, statues and shards of broken pottery. Balling his fists, Risk reached out with his senses again—this time checking for anything or anyone that might have laid this trap. Nothing. Not even the faint remnants of an old emotion. No one besides Kara had been in the space for at least a week, maybe longer.

Satisfied there was no hidden danger, he concentrated again on Kara and what repelled him so thoroughly. He pushed himself to a stand and took a guarded step forward, ready to lash out if attacked. His bare foot landed on something small and hard, but before he could pull back, it flattened to white dust.

Chalk. Witches used chalk. For circles. Traps.

He glanced back at Kara, and for the first time noticed a thin white line traced in a perfect circle around her.

Yggdrasil. The witch was laying a trap and got caught somehow herself. What was she hunting? Him?

Heat simmered in his chest. Did she think him such easy prey she could act the innocent, blind him to her ways, and then catch him in a trap capable of deceiving only the simplest of beings?

All witches were the same. He'd known that. Any wavering he'd felt in his goal to use her and her sister to secure his freedom evaporated.

Now to get her out of her damned circle so he could find her sister, secure his freedom, and remove himself from anything even hinting of witch.

A roar ripped through the air, jolting Kara to awareness. Her eyes darted around as she tried to assess her situation. The ground beneath her was hard and cold, and a dull ache drilled through her hip, telling her she'd been lying in one position far too long. Above her the stark gleam of the uncovered lightbulb reminded her she was in the basement sorting through Kelly's things. No, she corrected herself, sketching a circle on the floor when suddenly electricity had seemed to shoot upward, startling her. She must have fallen and hit her head.

Still groggy, she lifted her body to lean on one elbow, and glanced around. Risk, dressed only in the worn jeans she'd last seen him in, stood inches away, his hands held close to his face, his fingers curled away from him, while he struggled with some invisible force as if fighting to separate two recalcitrant elevator doors.

Except there was nothing between his fingers but air. Her eyes rounding, she stared up at him. Was she hallucinating now?

"Erase the chalk," he gritted out through clenched teeth.

Kara moistened her lips. He was real. Angry and real.

"Erase the chalk," he repeated. A vein in his neck began to pulse, and a rivulet of sweat crept down his bare chest.

Kara inched backward, her heart jumping in her throat. What was he doing?

"Erase—" His tone shifted from labored to boiling.

Kara stared at him, knowing her eyes were wide and full of fear. She hated being afraid. Was so tired of it.

"Kara," he began.

Her gaze dropped to the chalk. What did it matter? It was chalk, on concrete. She frowned. She could do what he asked—erase the chalk…see if that calmed him down, or she could run, but he stood between her and the door.

Sparing him one last cautious glance, Kara licked her finger and rubbed the white line beside her. Gray cement quickly showed through. With a muttered curse, Risk relaxed, his arms dropping to his sides.

"What were you doing?" His words were low, controlled, but Kara could almost feel his rage, as if the air around them had thickened to the consistency of pudding.

Unsure if she could trust him, she raised to her knees, and forced her voice into a calm somewhat flip tone. "I'm fine. Thank you for asking."

Watching him from the corner of her eyes, she pressed her fingers into her hair and stood. No bump. Too bad. She could use an excuse right now for all the insanity she had been experiencing—and, her gaze shifted to the glaring Risk, was about to experience.

Every muscle in his body seemed to be on alert, and his eyes, she refused to look at them, sure she'd see that eerie glimmer she'd imagined before. Or hoped she'd imagined. If she didn't see it again, she could convince herself it was just a figment of her overly stressed imagination.

Her own muscles ached, and a pounding had started in the back of her head. Whatever had happened to her here in the basement had drained her of every bit of energy she had—even the energy to be afraid.

"I've done nothing wrong," she murmured.

"Really?" He motioned to the severed circle under his feet. "What game are you playing?"

"Game?" She frowned. "You really are..." She paused, her gaze drifting over him. His body tensed, and he returned her perusal with a look so intense, she felt the need to step backward—away from him.

"You were busy while I was gone," he murmured. He stepped forward, eating up the distance she had put between them. The heat of his body enveloped her. "Your trap was well drawn."

Trap? Kara pressed her fingers against her forehead and closed her eyes. She couldn't think right now. The pounding in her head was getting stronger, enough so, she could barely hear his words as he continued to speak. He was accusing her of something, but what?

She opened her mouth to tell him his threats were lost on her for the moment, and felt her body sway, her legs sagging beneath her.

Damnation, she was falling. All anger drained from Risk as he reached out to catch the tiny witch and pull her to his chest.

Her eyelids fluttered closed, leaving only a thin ribbon of blue visible. He pressed his cheek against the pale skin of her forehead. Cool. She was too cool.

He shifted her in his embrace, letting her head tilt backward over the arm that held her while he tucked his free arm under her legs. Cradling her, he looked for a place to lay her down.

She moved, a sigh escaping her lips. The knot he hadn't even realized was twisting in his stomach loosened. She was all right, just exhausted. The spell, the energy to complete the circle that had repelled him, it must have drained her. Lusse had said she would be weak without her sister, and she was. Weak. Fragile. And alone.

Risk pulled her closer to his chest. Her long hair pillowed around her face. Without thinking, he nuzzled in its depths. Female. Flowers. And Kara. The scents tugged at him. He trailed the tip of his nose down her face, briefly touching her nose with his own. Then after hovering briefly over her parted lips, he closed his eyes and dropped his lips to hers.

Chapter 6

Warmth filled Kara, rolling through her like whiskey on a December night. Strong, masculine fingers wove through her hair, pressing her face toward lips firm and soft at the same time. Kissing. She was kissing someone. Risk, her befuddled mind realized.

She should be concerned, a tiny muted voice in the back of her head warned. Afraid even. He was big, dangerous and basically unknown to her. She couldn't trust him.

His lips trailed from her mouth down her neck, leaving a line of heat that surged right to her core. His tongue circled her ear, moist, hot and compelling.

She straightened her legs, twisting her body in his embrace until she was pressed against him. One arm around his neck, her breasts flattened against his deliciously naked chest, she ran her palm down over sculpted muscles. His skin was hot, almost fevered. She pushed herself closer, letting his warmth seep into her. Her thin T-shirt suddenly felt confining, the material separating the heat of his skin from her own, sadistic.

He exhaled, murmured something in a language she didn't understand, then pulled her closer till her face was pressed into his neck, and her pelvis rubbed against his erection—long, hard and enticing.

Pull back, the voice said. *This could be your last chance.*

Risk shifted again, pressing her more firmly against the steely hardness. Muscles deep inside Kara tightened, moisture forming in invitation. Her mind was afraid, but her body elated.

Kara lifted her right leg, wrapped it around Risk's waist and kicked the little voice deep into a crevice she hoped it never escaped.

As Kara's right leg wrapped around his waist, Risk paused. She was irresistible. He couldn't get close enough to her, the musk of her sex, the silky feel of her skin, and the sirenlike moan falling from her lips, filled his senses.

He raised and lowered her, letting her mound skim over the length of him. The need to push her against a wall and plunge the full length of his throbbing shaft into her moist heat almost overwhelmed him.

Need. His mind shot back to the son he'd left beaten on Lusse's floor. He'd lost control before, given into his need of the moment.

His instincts were screaming, heat rolled inside him, demanding he forget everything except his craving—to meld with Kara, to plunge over and over into the soft pleasure of her body.

She was tiny, delicate, not as strong as Venge's mother,

and she tempted him more than any female he had ever encountered. Could she even survive the full force of his passion? Lost in his lust, could he control the beast that lived within him?

Kara's free leg inched up his thigh, over his hip until she clung to him, her body pressing tightly against his chest, stomach and groin. She moaned again, then lowered her mouth to nibble the rough line of his jaw.

A tremor rocked through Risk. He closed his eyes, fighting the building lust. She seized his earlobe between her teeth and suckled the trapped flesh.

He turned his head, capturing her eager lips with his own. As he did, her eyes rounded, then flashed an intense, almost fluorescent violet. She was losing control, too.

Risk groaned, his tongue delving into her mouth, even as his brain told him he had to stop. He knew the cost of losing control. She didn't. Didn't know the power she held.

She didn't know. He repeated the thought in his head. He believed that. She might have drawn the circle, but it wasn't with intent. Somehow she'd stumbled across the magic and got caught by it herself. She was innocent—unlike him.

Unable to resist, he stroked the inside of her mouth with his tongue. She responded by running her fingers down his sides, her fingernails blazing a trail to the tops of his low-riding jeans.

He was hard under the denim, ready. Beyond ready. Almost spilling just at the thought of melding with his little witch.

His little witch. What kind of spell had she cast on him?

With a muttered curse, he grasped her arms and pulled his mouth free. Her chest heaving with short, hard breaths, her eyes radiating violet, Kara looked up at him, confusion and hurt coloring her face.

Kara stared at Risk, her mind clouded with passion. Excitement she'd never known before. Rubbing against Risk, daring herself to lose control and have sex with him here on the cold concrete floor, had filled her with a sense of power she hadn't known she possessed.

Why had he stopped?

He pulled her close, resting his cheek on the top of her head. His chest moved up and down with his breath, and his heart pounded loudly in her ear. Then, abruptly, he pushed her aside and strode to the other side of the room. He stood for a moment, his back to her, his palm pressed against the wall.

"What is all this?" His voice rough, almost harsh, he gestured to the plastic tub that had held Kelly's things. Now it lay on one side, its contents scattered across the floor.

Kara blinked. Her heart was still racing, and her lips still swollen from his kisses. What had just happened?

"Uh, those are Kelly's…" The words came out weak, unsure, and she hated it, wanted to feel strong, as she had when lost in Risk's arms. She took a slight step toward him.

His face angled away from her, he knelt, picking up the statue Kara had noticed earlier and holding it in his hands.

"Freya," he said, his thumbs rubbing the stone in smooth hard circles.

"What?" Kara stared at the statue, her brows lowering.

"Nothing." He shoved the statue into the box. "Did you learn anything here?"

That was it? She'd appeared mysteriously in his home, then he'd disappeared in front of her eyes, and finally, they'd almost devoured each other in a passion she hadn't known she possessed, and he could only ask what she had learned?

"Why don't you tell *me* something?" she replied.

At the edge in her voice, he looked up, surprise in his eyes. To be honest, Kara was surprised, too. Best not to analyze her sudden courage.

"Who are you?" she asked.

He straightened, the silver chain he wore at his neck shifting to fall over his collarbone, right where the wound he'd had yesterday should have been. But it wasn't. The skin was as tan and unmarred as the rest of his bare chest.

"What happened to your wound?" The words spilled out.

Risk paused, a dagger in his hand. One brow curved, he replied, "Risk Leidolf and wounds heal." He turned the knife, watching the light glint off its length. "Some wounds."

"But…" It had been less than twenty-four hours ago when his injury had looked red and ragged. No one healed that quickly.

A wave of exhaustion swept over Kara. She pressed two fingers against the bridge of her nose. There was too much happening that she didn't understand. She wasn't sure how to deal with it—analyze it and maybe lose whatever was left of her mind in the process, or just go with whatever happened and hope in the end everything turned out all right?

"Risk Leidolf?" she asked. "That's what? Swedish?"

"Norwegian," he replied, not looking up as he dropped the knife into the box with the statue.

"Oh." She licked her lips, then paused, not sure what to say or do next. "And, the other night, you…saved me?"

He glanced up for a second, then back down, reaching for a handful of spilled stones. "I guess you could say that."

"The dog." Kara rubbed her damp palms on the legs of her jeans. "Did you see it, them? Were they real?"

"I saw him."

Kara sighed. At least part of this nightmare/dream, she hadn't decided which yet, was real. "And you took me back to your cabin…because…?"

He looked back up, his eyes unwavering. "I did."

Well, that answered that—kind of. Kara shifted her weight from one hip to the other. "And last night…?"

"Last night?" He arched a brow.

"You, uh, disappeared…"

He picked up a wooden bowl, flipped it over, then tossed it into the bin. "Yes, sorry. Not my choice."

A flare of anger lit inside Kara. "Not your choice? You *disappeared*."

He ran his hand along the floor, scooping up a handful of polished stones, then let them fall from his fingers one by one into the rubber bin.

Kara frowned. What to say now? He acted as if he'd just popped out the door when she hadn't been looking. Rude, but not occasion to call the paranormal press. The pounding she'd felt earlier returned. Damn. She couldn't deal with this. Maybe the pretending-all-was-normal route was the wiser, at least until she was alone and able to think.

Glancing around, her gaze lit on a small black object almost hidden under a toppled stack of old school books. She sighed, happy to have a reason to change the course of conversation.

"I did find this." She walked across the room, her gait a bit unsteady, to the small black notebook she'd found in Kelly's box earlier.

She flipped open the cover and scanned the first page for the fiftieth time. "It looks like a list of names."

"Really?" Risk shifted on the balls of his feet until he faced her. "What kind of names?"

Kara walked toward him, the notebook held out in front of her. "I don't know. Names." Her gaze flicked from his bare feet to his equally bare chest. Where were his clothes?

He glanced from the page to her face, his gaze intense, simmering. Kara licked her lips again. A vein at the base of Risk's neck began to pulse, and Kara suddenly didn't care about his strange answers or lack of shirt and shoes, she just longed to press her lips against the thrumming vein, to taste the saltiness of his skin.

"Do you want to see?" she asked.

He held out his hand. Kara started to slip her own into his grip, before remembering the notebook. "Oh." A small nervous sound in the quiet room. "Here."

The vein at his neck throbbing harder, he shifted his gaze to the paper. "Humans?"

"Uh, yes?" There he went again, making her think she should be running from the room instead of standing mesmerized by the lines of muscle that formed his back, or the way his worn jeans pulled across his thighs. Kara swallowed.

"Hmm." He balanced the book on his leg, and looked up at her. Silence filled the room.

Kara reached out to take the book back, and her fingers brushed over taut denim. Risk's eyes flashed, and Kara's breath caught in her throat. Tension pulsed between them. Before she could pull back, his hand captured hers, his fingers warm, strong and masculine.

They stood there frozen. Kara unsure whether to run or

to finish what they'd started earlier—to fling her legs on each side of his waist and trap his body with her own.

Risk rubbed his thumb across the bones of her hand. Emotion warring behind his eyes.

Kara opened her mouth, not sure what she was about to say, and the phone rang, breaking the spell.

Risk drew in a deep breath and followed Kara as she scampered out of the room. The dusty steps creaked under his weight as he climbed the stairs leading to the main house, leaving the dark basement behind him.

"This is Kara." Kara stood in a small kitchen, a cordless phone wedged under her chin.

Polished wood floors and a white-painted table made the room cozy and feminine. An intriguing mix of cinnamon, coffee and Kara perfumed the air.

"No, I haven't heard from her." Kara glanced up, nodded for Risk to sit at the table.

Risk pulled out a spindle-legged chair and stared uneasily at the lemon-yellow cushion balanced on its seat.

"No, I understand." Kara turned to face the wall, pressed her free hand to the back of her neck. "I…I can come now."

With a click she hung up the phone. "I have to go." Without looking at Risk, she strode to a cabinet and jerked out the drawer. "Where—? Damn it." She looked up at Risk, her eyes snapping with anger.

Leaning against a line of cabinets, he wrapped his fingers around the cheerful yellow countertop, and fought to ignore the onslaught of emotion rolling out of her. "Is there a problem?"

"Yes. No." Kara shook her head. "I don't know. My car. Where is it?"

"Car?" He stared back at her. If she had a car, he didn't know it. Most of his prey had bigger issues to worry about than lost transportation.

"Damn. It must still be at the bar—or towed." She mumbled something under her breath. Then snapped her head up. "Your car. I'll have to borrow it." She disappeared through a doorway into a hallway. There were sounds of shuffling objects then the tinkle of keys.

Risk raised a brow. Silly female. He'd loaned her his Jeep once—to escape Lusse. But did she really think he would let her waltz away in it again? Without him? Sighing, he strode through the door after her.

Kara stared through the small windshield of Risk's Jeep, refusing to look at the man himself. He had insisted on driving her to the morgue—despite the fact he was half-clothed. He'd just plucked the keys from her fingers and strode past her to the car. As distraught as she was, not knowing what awaited her, she'd followed, like a sheep.

When the detective had called, she'd lost her grip for a bit—her only thought to get to the morgue and prove the body they'd found wasn't Kelly—couldn't be Kelly. Even now, ten minutes later, her pulse pounded and she couldn't seem to sit still on the leather seat. She had wanted the police to call, but not like this—not to tell her they'd found a body matching the description of her sister.

A body. A body. Her mind chanted over and over.

Sun beat down on her, and despite the cold air outside, sweat beaded on Kara's neck and dribbled between her breasts. She stared out the window watching children with sleds whiz down a snow-covered hill as the Jeep zipped past.

Not Kelly. Not Kelly. Couldn't be Kelly.

Sloshing through half-melted snow, the Jeep spun into the circle drive in front of the county building and jostled to a stop.

Risk turned in his seat to look at her.

Kara closed her eyes and unclicked her seat belt. Time to prove them wrong.

Risk had dropped Kara at the door, then driven off to find a parking spot. When he joined her inside the building, he was wearing a flannel shirt and boots. Kara didn't bother to ask where they came from. She was beyond such details.

Detective Poulson was waiting for them at his desk. Kara had met him earlier, two days after she first reported Kelly missing. He was attractive in a slim marathon-runner kind of way. When he saw Kara, he smiled, flicked a chunk of too-long hair out of his eyes, then held out his hand. Before she could return the gesture, Risk stepped forward. The welcome in the detective's eyes changed to a question.

"You have something to show us?" Risk asked, ignoring the other man's hand.

Detective Poulson met Risk's gaze, then lowered his hand. "Are you here for the ID, too?"

"We are," Risk replied.

Poulson gave Risk a curious stare, but shrugged it off, switched his gaze back to Kara. "You ready for this? It isn't going to be easy. This woman…she didn't die an easy death."

Kara inhaled through her nose, held the breath for a second. "I'm ready." Ready or not. Right? There were just some things you'd never be ready for. Meeting the detective's gaze, she gave her head a firm nod. "I'm ready."

The detective looked as if he might say something else, then shook his head. "Follow me then. Might as well get this going."

They took an elevator to the lower level. Kara stared blindly at the silver doors. When the bell dinged, she didn't move. The detective cleared his throat, and Risk pressed a warm reassuring hand to the small of her back. Huffing out a breath, she stepped out of the elevator.

They stood in a short hall. Black scuff marks marred otherwise white walls. The air was cool; Kara wrapped her arms around herself, wishing Risk would replace his hand on her back or drape his arm around her shoulders. Wished someone would tell her this was all a mistake and motion them back into the elevator. Instead, Detective Poulson ushered them toward an older man in a white lab coat standing a few feet to their left.

"Dan is one of our forensic technicians. He'll take us in."

In the tech's hand were three surgical masks. "For the smell," he said with an apologetic note.

Risk waved the mask off, but Kara took one, her hands shaking as she tied it around her face. With one last concerned nod, the technician pulled open a nearby door and motioned them inside.

Even through the mask, the smell hit Kara hard—an unpleasant mix of sulfur and ammonia. Her lungs burned, and her eyes watered. Blinking back the wetness, she glanced around, praying she would see nothing that reminded her of Kelly.

The room was small, cold, and sterile. There were three tables in the back, only one occupied by a sheet-covered body. Their companion motioned them ahead, then walked toward the corpse. Kara took a shuddering breath and forced her feet to move one in front of the other, her hand tightening around Risk's arm with each step.

His eyes filled with sympathy, the technician placed his hand on the sheet. "Are you ready?" The question was directed at the detective, but the tech kept his gaze on Kara. Then before pulling back the sheet, he flicked a warning look to Risk.

Risk stepped closer, his large body seeming ready to shelter Kara from whatever lay underneath the white cloth.

Her gaze on the body in front of her, Kara nodded. Now or never. She had to know. Was it Kelly?

The tech flipped off the sheet then stepped back, his eyes focusing on something on the floor a few feet away. Kara ignored him. Ignored everything but the body on the table. She stifled a gasp as her gaze first lit on what she prayed wasn't her sister. Closing her eyes against the sight, she counted to ten, leaned her back against Risk's warmth then opened them again. She had to do this. Had to know.

It was a woman, her height. In other words, Kelly's height, but past that it was impossible to say how the woman had looked in life. The police detective was right, this had not been a pleasant death.

The body was black, but not in skin tone, burned, charred. From the neck down, Kara could make out clothing, but barely. It was as if whatever the woman had been wearing melted into her skin before being burned even further, almost beyond possible recognition as clothing. What hair was left was sparse and frizzled. There was no way to identify the color.

And the smell. It was horrid beyond imagination.

Kara's eyes filled again—the smell was stronger here, but it was more than that. She was trying to imagine the blackened thing lying in front of her filled with life, dancing at a club or kicking ass during fight training. She couldn't. The charred corpse could never have been as alive as her sister, could it?

"What...killed her?" The words spilled out of Kara.

The detective stepped forward, his gaze on the still sheet-covered part of the corpse. "We don't know. We suspect some kind of electric shock, maybe lightning, but there's no entrance point. There are some broken bones, but the coroner says that could just be from the body being flung into something like a wall when it got the jolt.

"...Had a case where a boy got flung twenty feet—"

Risk took a step forward, cutting the detective's monologue off short. Poulson tightened his jaw, then continued, "I know it's probably impossible to tell, but we have to ask. Is this your sister?"

Kara stared at the body for another minute before replying. "Can, can I touch her?"

The detective's eyebrows shot up, his surprise darting through his eyes.

Kara didn't know why she needed to touch the body, but somehow she knew it was the only way she'd know for sure. Was that...Kelly?

With a nod, Poulson gave his permission.

Kara curled her fingernails into her palm, bit her lip under the mask, then inched forward away from Risk and toward the body.

Risk placed a hand on each side of her waist, stopping her. "There are other ways. You don't have to do this."

He was right. Even as incinerated as the body was, it still had to offer DNA evidence. Kara was no forensics expert, and she knew that had to be a possibility, but she would have to wait for that. She knew she would never accept the truth, not unless she found out for herself, now.

One hand pressed to her mouth to help block the smell the mask couldn't disguise, she stepped away from Risk and placed her other hand on the dead woman's blackened forehead.

Nothing. Then memories flooded her. She was in someone's head—the woman's? She was sitting at a computer, worried, scared, and Kelly was there taking notes in the notebook Kara had found in the basement. Someone was missing—they would find them—the woman trusted Kelly. Had no one else to trust. Then she was alone—calm, laying out a statue, bowl and stones—all similar to the items Kara had found in Kelly's plastic tub—then she was somewhere new. It was smoky and dark. A knife pressed against her throat, and someone whispered roughly in her ear. Terror sliced into her, cutting off her voice, leaving her defenseless.

Kara scrambled to pull herself from the vision, to save what she had learned. The woman knew Kelly—had been somewhere Kara had been before. Kara clung to the thought, where?

Just as she felt the answer was within her grasp, she sank back in—smells, sights and sensations warring for her notice. A dank stench surrounded her; pain burned and twisted inside her and light exploded from behind her eyes. Then finally, when she knew she could stand no more, a scream ripped through her.

Chapter 7

Breath heaving, Kara realized someone had yanked her backward, breaking her contact with the charred body that used to be a person—a person someone loved surely, but not Kelly.

Thank God. It wasn't Kelly.

Kara glanced down at her fingers then clasped them in her other hand and pressed them tightly against her chest.

"What happened?" Risk grasped her shoulders so tightly his fingers dug into her flesh. Startled, she looked up at him.

He held her at arm's length, staring into her eyes, his simmering with an emotion she couldn't quite peg—anger, concern, what?

Poulson stepped toward them with brows lowered. A low growl rumbled from Risk's chest and he pulled her to his side, his arm draped around her. To Kara's surprise, she realized she was shaking.

"Are you all right?" the detective asked, bending to peer at her, crushed as she was against Risk.

Kara closed her eyes, grateful she hadn't passed out. That was becoming an annoying habit lately. She had to be strong—Kelly was still out there. Kara had to find her.

She opened her eyes and placed a hand on Risk's chest to push herself away. Once she was standing under her own power again, she looked at all three men. "Fine. I'm fine." She squeezed the words out of her constricted throat.

Three pairs of eyes stared back at her.

Another rumble started in Risk's throat and he reached for her again.

"No, really. I'm fine." She held out one hand, palm out. "Just a bit overwrought. That's all." She glanced at the technician, shoving her shaking hands into her jean pockets. "That's normal, right?"

"Sure it is. I'd be worried if this—" He glanced behind him and, seeming startled to find the body still there, tugged the white sheet over it, covering the corpse from their view. "I'd be worried if something like this didn't upset you. You're doing fine."

Kara smiled, grateful for the support, although she knew what she had just experienced wasn't normal—not in any way.

"What happened?" Risk asked as soon as they were both belted into his Jeep.

"Nothing. Just like I said, I was overwrought." Kara ran her fingers up and down the seat strap.

"It wasn't your sister?"

Kara sucked her lower lip into her mouth, held it there

between her teeth. Her eyes huge, she shook her head. “No. Not Kelly.”

Risk stared at her for a second. She was lying. Something had happened when she’d touched that body. Something that scared her, but if she said it wasn’t her sister, he believed her. She wouldn’t be able to hide the emotion that revelation would have brought with it.

He put the car into reverse and pulled out of the parking lot. He was getting closer. He could feel it. And Kara’s sister was still out there. He still had a chance to find her, for himself and…he glanced at Kara’s petite form…Kara.

The thought sneaked up on him. But him first, he corrected. He had to stick with his plan. He would save Kara’s sister, but for himself. If it saved Kara from a loss as well, that didn’t really matter.

He glanced at her again. Her hands lay limply on her lap.

Risk stared at her pale hands, at the fine bones and delicate fingers. She was tiny—how would she defend herself against Lusse once he’d secured his freedom and left?

She’d have her sister, he reminded himself. If the two of them could free him, they could surely defend themselves, right?

“What happened to her?” she asked, her voice shaking.

Risk glanced up at her wide eyes, startled by her question.

“That woman.” She jerked her head over her shoulder, toward the building they had just left. “What happened?”

“I don’t know,” he replied, and he didn’t. He’d never seen a corpse like the one lying under that sheet. A witch, he guessed. He couldn’t be sure, not with her life force missing, but there were hints. A lingering scent of power separate from whatever had killed her.

"Detective Poulson…he said, lightning. Do you think…?" She glanced up, her blue eyes filled with hope.

Risk balled his fists. Would lying to her help? No. It was time his little witch learned the truth—or most of it.

"Let's get back to your house. I think we need to talk."

Kara studied Risk's profile as a passing car's headlight illuminated the inside of his Jeep.

He wanted to talk. Kelly once told her someone wanting to talk could never be good—but a man? That was downright dangerous.

They pulled up in front of the small house Kara shared with her sister. Flat stones formed the walkway to the porch. Kara slid from the Jeep and stepped from one rock to the other. The thyme she'd planted last summer was still fragrant when she kicked off the light covering of snow and scuffed the herb with her shoe.

It was cold tonight, but not unbearably, not like the night she'd met Risk, seen the dogs. She took her time, stopping to pick up a dry maple leaf, the edges curled toward each other.

Once she opened the front door and stepped inside, heard whatever it was Risk wanted to tell her, she had a feeling her life was going to change forever.

By the time Risk stepped inside the house, Kara had already started a fire in the brick fireplace and was walking into the living room, a bottle of whiskey in one hand and two glasses in the other. Her feet were bare and her hips swayed back and forth as she padded toward him. He paused, tension curling like a fist inside him.

"Whiskey?" She held out a glass.

He shook his head.

With a shrug, she set the glasses down on an old chest that served as a coffee table, and filled one with the amber liquid. "No reason to be stingy, right? Might make what you're going to tell me easier to swallow." She held the glass up to the fire, watched the flame flicker through it for a second, then tilted it to her lips. After a long swallow, she set the half-empty glass back down. "Okay, let's talk."

She was acting brave, but the room was heavy with her anxiety. Risk stalked toward her, her emotion pulling at him. As he neared the table where the bottle of liquor sat, he stopped. He had to keep a clear head. Concentrate on convincing her to help him in trade for finding her sister.

He reached for the bottle and sloshed whiskey into the second glass. Then waited.

She shot him a curious look, then wandered to the couch and sat down, her legs crossed in front of her, the whiskey glass balanced on one knee.

"So, am I crazy?" she asked.

He sniffed his glass; the sharp scent of pine mixed with almonds assaulted him. He sat the glass down, turned to face her. "Crazy?"

"Yeah. Crazy." She took another sip of her drink. "You know that first night. The dogs? You only said you saw them, too. Never explained how I got to your house, escaped the giant hell-eyed canines. That alone is crazy, right? Why am I even here with you—a stranger. You said you'd help and I jumped on it. A week after my sister disappears, I trust a complete stranger. That alone's crazy, right?" She tossed the remaining liquid down her throat.

"Then that woman tonight? I touched her. I did. And I

saw things—saw her life, felt her joy, her peace, and finally her terror. I think…I think I saw her die."

Her eyes rounded; anxiety wafted off her. She glanced at Risk then down toward his untouched glass. Without a word, he picked it up and handed it to her.

She took the whiskey, an almost imperceptible shake in her fingers.

"Kara…" he began.

She lifted the glass again, looked at him for a second over the half-circle of the rim, then closed her eyes and swallowed.

"Kara. You're not crazy."

"Really. Well, that's a relief, I guess." She laughed, a rough sound like snow crunching underfoot. "You know I hate dogs. I was almost killed by one when I was a kid. My best friend was killed that night. At first I just blamed that for everything weird I was seeing. Posttraumatic stress or something like that. It would make me see things, don't you think?"

She hated dogs. Watched her friend be killed by one. Risk pulled back at the revelation. How had she survived being attacked by not one but two hellhounds?

"Risk?" Her voice startled him out of his thoughts. "You going to tell me what's going on? You know, don't you?"

Risk glanced around, part of him wishing for an escape. He wasn't used to talking to anyone longer than it took to let them know he held their life in his hands. But that wasn't the conversation he wanted to have with Kara—ever. When he found her sister he'd have to face that conversation, too, but first he had to tell her something that would turn her world upside down, then get her to trust him—so he could use her in a task she might not survive.

A shudder rippled through his body. Shaking his head, he flung the beginnings of guilt from his mind. She would have her sister, a chance at life—more than she would have had if he'd just taken her to Lusse; all in all, a more than fair exchange.

He inhaled deeply. He had to do this. Even if he told her everything, she'd still choose to find her sister—no matter the cost. Why worry over details that really didn't matter?

Clinging to that thought, he shoved the whiskey bottle aside and lowered himself onto the coffee table. Elbows resting on his knees, he faced her. "Your sister. You said she wasn't normal. And all those things in the basement—the statue, the athame, the rocks… You know what those are for?"

She held her glass in front of her, leaving only her eyes fully visible.

"Your sister, and that woman at the morgue. They have something in common. At least I think they do."

She lowered the glass slightly, moisture forming in her eyes. "You think Kelly is dead? Charred and dumped somewhere, like that woman?"

"No. No. I mean. I think they were…are witches."

Kara stared at the man in front of her. A witch. Her sister? That woman in the morgue? She held her glass up to her nose and inhaled the soothing aroma of whiskey. Warm and familiar, just the scent calmed her. It was a constant in a world that suddenly seemed to shift with every step. She took a tiny sip, let it sit on her tongue.

Kelly a witch. Was it possible?

The dagger, statues and other strange objects her sister

kept stored in the basement, plus the strange Web sites Kara had found bookmarked on Kelly's PC—they all added up to something, something strange.

Time to face facts.

Taking in a shuddering breath, she replied, "I told you Kelly was…different. I guess I knew all along she believed in some strange stuff. So, she thought she was a witch—what's the harm? Could be worse. She could think she was a vampire—or a werewolf. That would have been a nightmare, right?" She laughed. What a pair. A French poodle could send Kara into fits of terror and her sister, the sane one, had been practicing witchcraft in the basement.

Risk blinked, a shadow of unease passing behind his eyes. God. He thought she was crazy, too.

"I mean, so she burned some candles, chanted a little voodoo. That can't have anything to do with her disappearing—or that other woman…" She let the words drop off, not sure how to even voice what had happened to the body she'd touched.

"Kara." Risk placed a hand on her knee. "Listen to me. I'm not saying your sister *thinks* she's a witch. I'm saying she *is* a witch. And so are you."

Kara stared at the square masculine hand clasping her knee. Noticed the tiny blond hairs that dotted the top. She wasn't sure which was more startling—the zing of awareness that shot through her at his innocent touch, or his words. He thought her sister and she were witches.

"Kara." He squeezed her knee lightly, gave it a tiny shake, then using his free hand, tipped her chin up until her eyes met his. "You're not crazy and neither am I. You and your sister are both witches. That other woman in the morgue, she was too. And whoever/whatever killed her most likely has your sister now. We have to find her—fast."

Kara stared at him, absorbing the intensity in his eyes, the lines of his chiseled face. God. He was right. She'd been lying to herself. She'd known the truth as soon as she'd touched that woman's hand.

She was a witch. She sat for a moment, her eyes closed, her fingers digging into her thighs. The thought was boggling. Her body swayed slightly to the side; Risk's hand on her chin was all that kept her from toppling over.

She was a witch—what did that mean? Had her parents been witches, led a life she'd never suspected? How long had Kelly known? Had she been hiding it from Kara? So many questions and no time to sort them out now.

She pressed her lips together, opened her eyes and stared into Risk's. His gaze held hers, steady but filled with silent urgency.

He was right—she had to find Kelly. There was no time to wallow in what any of this meant to her future or how it colored her past. She had to live in the now. Deal with the moment. Determination surged over her. With Risk's help, she could do this.

Locking onto the thought, she placed her hand on his. "I think I know who she was—the woman."

Afraid if she hesitated, then the reality of what she was accepting as truth would hit her, Kara hopped up and hurried to the basement where she'd left the notebook earlier. After grabbing it, she raced back up the stairs. Risk sat where she'd left him.

"Here. The list of names. I think she's one of them." Trying to appear more sure than she was, she held out the pad. "I didn't say anything, but when I touched her, I saw things. Things from her life. Kelly was there with her. She was working on a computer and Kelly was taking notes—in this notebook.

"Look at the last name. It's written in red ink. All the rest are in blue. That name was added last. I think Kelly and that woman were looking for all the others and then…she disappeared, too."

Or was taken. Kara thought back to the last thing she'd seen after touching the woman—before the pain had sliced into her, breaking the connection.

She glanced at him, hope making her smile. They were getting closer. "Do you think someone took these people—" she pointed at the list he held in his hand "—because they are witches? Would someone do that?"

A short laugh escaped Risk's lips. "Yes, I most certainly do."

They talked for the next hour, Risk explaining to Kara that she had somehow closed a circle the night before when she'd knocked herself out. That while she didn't realize it, she actually had power—and that combined, she and Kelly might have a greater power capacity than any normal witch.

It was a lot for Kara to take in, to accept. She had never been more than average at anything, her fear always stopping her from trying all the things Kelly seemed to excel at naturally.

"And the dogs, they were real—I mean the eyes, the disappearing? Do you think they were sent by whoever took Kelly?"

Risk picked up an empty whiskey glass and twirled it around on his leg. Staring at a droplet that stubbornly clung to the glass wall, he replied, "No, I don't."

Kara frowned. "You mean they weren't real? Or they weren't part of Kelly's disappearance?"

His eyes flicked upward. "They were real, but they had nothing to do with Kelly."

"How can you be so sure? They were certainly threatening. Who's to say whoever took these witches didn't switch tactics and decide to use dogs instead?" She'd told him about the knife, and her belief that whoever wielded it had abducted the dead witch they'd seen at the morgue.

"I'm sure." He set the glass down on the chest beside him with a bang. "This is getting us nowhere. We need to concentrate on who did take those witches. Where's the last place you saw Kelly?"

Kara watched him, her brows lowered. There were still a lot of things she didn't understand. "Here at the house. She was going out. She was wearing all black. At the time I didn't think anything of it, even though she normally wears *some* color. Now, I think maybe it was because she was spying on someone…"

"Or hunting them," Risk finished.

"Yeah. That." Kara's mind flicked back to the bottles she'd seen Kelly tuck into her fanny pack. "I think she might have been armed—in a way."

Risk nodded, tension seeming to leak out of him as he considered her comments. "Anything else?"

"Well…" Kara twisted her mouth to the side. "There were the matches—but that was silly."

"What matches?"

She huffed out a breath, embarrassed. "It's nothing. I found some matches in Kelly's stuff. They had the name of a bar on them—the Guardian's Keep. That's why I went there—the night of the dogs. But I realize now, they were just matches. Kelly needed something to light those candles—for whatever." Kara still wasn't comfortable with the image of her sister going around lighting candles, chanting and who knew what else. "She'd probably had them for ages."

"No, she didn't."

Kara frowned at him. How could he possibly know how long Kelly had had a packet of matches?

"She's a witch," he continued.

Kara let her face go blank.

He sighed. "Witches store power. That's what they do. They collect it from around them and then channel it and release it when they need it. Even the weakest witch can light a candle without bothering with a match."

"I can store power? And release it—you mean like balls of fire?"

His lips thinned. "Depends on the witch. How the energy comes out's different from one to the other."

"But I've never—"

"I don't know how witches work. I don't *want* to know." He stood up, the chest he'd been sitting on creaking from the sudden loss of his weight.

Something shifted in the air around them, making the tiny hairs on the back of Kara's neck rise. She ignored it. "Could I be pulling energy from this room right now and not know it? And…" She held her closed hands out toward Risk, then flicked them open.

He moved to the side, so quickly it seemed almost instinctive. His eyes flashed, a spark there for a second then gone.

"Risk?" Suddenly wary, she edged sideways, placing her feet solidly on the floor. "You…you've never told me what you are. How you found me and how you know so much about witches. Are you…?"

Risk turned on his heel, strode to the front window and pulled back the drape, his hand clenched around the navy twill. "I…work for a witch. I was at the bar because she sent me to retrieve something for her. I walked out into the parking lot and found you. That's all there is to it."

Kara sat straighter. "You work for a witch? Can I meet her? Can she help us?"

He dropped the material, the floor-length drape catching on itself, wrinkled from his tight grip. "No."

Kara watched him, unsure where to go from here. "But surely, she could tell us something. Even if it was to just help me learn how to do things myself—maybe she'd have a book, or something."

"No." The terseness of his voice pushed Kara back against the sofa cushion. Her eyes widened.

He spun back toward the window and slapped his hand against the glass. He stood there, the muscles of his back flaring out with his breaths. A few seconds later, he turned back.

"Witches don't work together. They're like cats, territorial and possessive. You do not want to meet Lusse."

"But…" He made witches sound evil. Kelly wasn't territorial or possessive, and if Kara's vision was accurate, Kelly was actually working with a witch to find other witches. He had to be mistaken. "I don't think—"

He strode across the room until he towered over her. "You will not search out Lusse."

Kara stared up at him, something inside of her snapping in response. She jumped to her feet. "You make witches sound evil. Kelly is not evil. I'm not evil. Maybe you're wrong about Lusse, too."

The vein at the base of his throat began to pulse, and he fisted and unfisted one hand. Inhaling deeply, he stepped closer, wove his fingers deep into her hair.

Using her hair to hold her, he tilted her face up to his. "No, temptation. I am not wrong about Lusse. Just like I pray I am not wrong about you." Then he leaned forward and pressed his lips to hers in a kiss so fiery, heat surged through her, burning away every inhibition her sane side tried to push forward.

Chapter 8

Kara's scent engulfed him. Anger, fear—his usual downfalls, swirled around them. He fought to maintain the beast that roared to be set free. His tongue shoved past her parted lips. His hands gripped her head, his fingers tense with the struggle to stay under control; passion rolled through him, attacking his resolve.

Control. He had to maintain control. Couldn't risk a repeat of what had happened before, with Venge's mother.

With an effort so strenuous his body shook in objection, he slowed his kiss and concentrated on the woman trapped by his hands, returning his embrace. Something shifted inside him, moving further from the beast and closer to the man.

Soft hair wove around his fingers. He ran his thumbs over the angle of her cheekbones; her skin was smooth, cool to his touch. And her scent, he inhaled deeply taking in not only her emotions, which had morphed from anger to excitement, but also the spice that was Kara. A rumble formed deep in his throat.

He should pull away. He knew it, but her scent was addictive. It made him react in ways he'd never reacted before. Made him fear—for her. The thought of her finding Lusse had sent him into a rage, but one laced with panic. His hellhound blood running cold at the image of what Lusse would do to his little witch.

Fear. It was an emotion Risk drew from others, not one he emitted himself. It was a weakness, he knew that. And he could afford no weakness, not now. He should separate himself from the source—leave Kara behind and search for her sister alone. Nothing good could come of this liaison. If he leaned on his hellhound nature, he'd endanger her; if he let himself slip to his human side, she'd endanger him.

His traitorous lungs expanded again, taking in another wave of Kara. His hands softened, his fingers stroking her scalp. Addictive. She was addictive, and he wasn't strong enough to walk away.

Accepting his weakness and the threat to himself, he pushed all thoughts of the consequences of what he was doing from his mind, and instead concentrated on the undeniable pleasure of her lips moving against his. He let his human side take over.

As he relaxed, her tongue darting shyly then more boldly into his mouth. Her hands, once passive at her side, now traveling up the length of his body, tugging at his shirt. Her fingers found his bare stomach, glided over the muscles there.

He growled, freed one of his hands from her hair to shove her cotton shirt up until his palm touched the skimpy lace of the undergarment covering her breasts.

A puff of breath escaped her lips, blowing cool across his neck. He groaned and ran his thumb under the tight band of her bra, pushing the material up until her full breast fell into his hand. He palmed her flesh, rolling her nipple between his thumb and index finger. Twisting and pulling until it hardened in response.

"The shirt," she murmured, one hand leaving his side to pull at the T-shirt lodged under her arms.

He quickly skimmed his hands up her body, catching her shirt and bra and pulling them over her head. She stood before him, her breasts full and tempting, her nipples hard, her areolas rose-tinted and puckered. He longed to cover them with his lips, suck, taste and tease until she begged him to plunge deep inside her.

His erection pressed against his jeans. The urge to fulfill the thought was almost irresistible. Not yet. Too much to see, to taste, to devour.

As if sharing his battle, she reached for him, grabbed the top of his jeans in both hands, her fingers slipping the first metal button through its hole. Her nail jabbing the tender skin behind it in the process.

He ran a finger along her face, slipped her hair behind her ear, then whispered, "Wait."

She glanced up at him, her eyes clouded with passion and confusion. "Wait?" she repeated.

A slow smile tilting his lips, he nodded and lowered his mouth to her breast. Slowly, tantalizingly, he swirled his tongue around one tight bud. Then pulling it into his mouth, he nipped and suckled until she arched against him, her hair falling down her back, her hand pushing her other breast toward him.

His nostrils flared. He pushed both breasts upward, held

them in the V of his hands. He swung his head back and forth, his lips teasing first one then the other, dropping his nose for a second into the cleavage formed by the mounded flesh.

Blood pounded hot in his veins. The pungent perfume of the wetness pooling between her legs called to him; making him want to nuzzle her there, to taste her.

The scent almost sent him over the edge.

Her fingers clutched at his side, her fingernails digging into his skin. Then without warning, she shoved her hand down the front of his jeans and held his pulsing erection. Her fingers wrapped around him, squeezing. The tightness making him wonder how small she would be. How her body would feel contracting around him as he slid in and out, over and over, until she screamed for release.

Heat built to a roar inside Risk. With one hand he flipped the remaining buttons on his fly, releasing his rock-hard cock.

Kara inhaled sharply as Risk's erection sprang forward and rubbed against her bare stomach. Her hand still wrapped around him, she loosened her grip so she could stroke him, the skin gliding back and forth over his hard shaft, Risk's breaths coming out in short, ragged huffs.

"You drive me mad." He ran his hands down her sides, pushing her pants off her hips, leaving her standing in nothing but her lace panties.

"Not fair," she murmured, reaching up to unbutton his shirt.

"True." He grasped his shirt in both hands and tore it open, buttons shooting across the room, pinging onto the wood floors. With his chest bare, he grabbed the tops of his jeans and pulled them down his long muscular legs, then stepped out, leaving them puddled on the floor.

"More fair?" he asked, his body glistening in the flickering firelight.

"Much." She ran her palms down his chest and over his flat stomach. She had never stood so boldly in front of a man before—clothed or naked. How could someone as intimidating as Risk also make her feel so free, so confident?

Naked. He had seen her naked before. "Risk?"

His hands covered her butt, kneading her, his penis rubbing against her, teasing her.

"Yes, little witch." He lowered his mouth back to her breast, making her forget the question that had formed in her mind. Then his finger slid between her folds, finding her nub and stroking as she had stroked him. She wiggled against him. A sweet pressure building inside her, coiling.

"Risk," she panted, rising on her tiptoes, wanting more. Needing him inside her. Her breath coming quicker, she wrapped one leg around his waist, opening herself to him more.

"Kara, your scent—" He leaned forward, pressing the back of her leg against the couch until she fell backward. Her other leg tightened around him, pulling him down on the couch with her. A hand on each side of her head, his arms straight, he looked down on her, his eyes glowing. "You're addictive, little witch."

He leaned toward her, pressing a slow gentle kiss against her lips, then with one hand he ripped her panties from her body and tossed them onto the floor.

Risk stared down at the mound of dark curls covering Kara's sex. The center of her desire. With one finger he parted them to find the nub he'd stroked before.

Kara moaned beneath him, moved as if to grab his hand. Instead he captured both of hers with one of his, held them up above her head.

"Let me," he murmured. Slowly, he circled her with his finger, rubbing and twirling until a sharp gasp escaped her lips and her eyelids fluttered.

She was wet. So wet. His cock twitched against her thigh, begging to be part of his play.

Not yet.

He stroked her again, releasing more of her scent into the air.

Her lower lip disappeared into her mouth, her back arched, and her hips moved against his hand. She was slick; his finger slid over her softness with ease. He wanted to taste her. To feel her quivering flesh beneath his lips. She moaned, tossing her head to one side.

He could stand it no longer. He released her hands, ran his now free hand down her body, stopping briefly to caress one swaying breast. Then with a sigh, he lowered his mouth to her sex.

His senses roared.

So much to take in. His body shuddered, almost coming from the taste and smell of her alone. Kara quivered in response, her hands grabbing his shoulders, pushing him deeper into her folds.

He found her nub with his lips, pulled it into his mouth and swirled around it with his tongue. She was more than he had imagined. His nose buried in her curls, he breathed in, deeper and deeper.

His cock moved again, his seed near to exploding. Mouth still pressed against her, he panted, pressed a last kiss to her pale thigh, then pushed himself up so his hard length edged against the place his mouth had just left. Once, twice he rubbed against her, feeling her wetness.

She writhed in response. "Risk?" Her eyelids fluttered again, a flash of blue then violet.

"Open for me."

Not wavering, she spread her delicious thighs wider. He waited, prolonging the anticipation, gazing at her now open sex. Then pulling in a heavy breath, plunged deep into her.

Fast and hard, he couldn't control his need. Over and over he pounded against her.

She cried out and for a moment he paused, afraid he had hurt her.

"Again," she urged, tilting her hips up toward him.

He obliged, lifting her legs so he could move even deeper. Her breasts bounced up and down with each movement, her nipples hard. He reached down, capturing one with his fingers as he moved inside her.

"Risk," she panted, her eyes pure violet, flashing with passion and power. Heat built behind his own. He closed them, praying she didn't see the fire that lurked inside him.

She began to pant. The sound pushing Risk further over the edge. Her nails scraped along his back, her legs edging higher, letting him go even deeper inside her.

He began to shake, his own release near. She cried out. Her muscles tightened around him, squeezing. His eyes flew open as his own orgasm hit, his seed spilling out, his body shuddering to completion. With a cry, she joined him, her arms clutching his shoulders, her body quivering and shaking beneath him.

The after waves of her orgasm still shaking her body, her heart still pounding, and her muscles still quivering with her release, Kara reached up to press her hand against Risk's face. His eyes closed, he turned his face to place a soft kiss into her palm.

A little buzz of electricity tickled against her palm. Startled, she stared up at Risk, but he just pressed a second kiss to her palm, and lowered his head to press another to her cheek. She sighed. He thrilled her, made her feel alive and safe at the same time. Something Kelly would probably say was impossible. Her sister was always on the hunt for the next big hair-raising adventure, saying it made her feel alive. Safe equaled dull for Kelly.

But then, Risk was far from dull. Kara smiled, brushed her fingers through his blond hair.

He shifted, moving her onto her side so they were curled against each other, his bare skin warming her more than the fire that snapped and popped in the hearth.

"Risk?" she asked, her head nestled against his chest, her hand clasping his arm that was draped about her waist.

"Temptation?" he replied.

Her lips curved. Temptation. She liked being someone's temptation. "The night you found me, and took me back to your cabin…"

His chest tensed behind her.

"I…I woke up naked. Why?"

With a low laugh, he relaxed back against her. "You needed sleep, little witch. Would you sleep with your clothes on?"

She raised her eyebrows. Oh. "So, nothing…?"

"Happened?" He laughed again, cleared her hair away from her ear, and whispered in her ear. "Will you so easily forget what we just did?"

"Never." With a purr, she turned in his arms so she faced him, and unable to believe her good luck, reached her hand to caress his face again. God, he was beautiful. Full lips. Chiseled face, and hazel eyes that seemed to change color by the second. Her world would be perfect, if she could just find Kelly—or when she found Kelly.

Murmuring a word she didn't understand, Norwegian she guessed, he caught her hand in his and lowered his lips to her palm again.

This time the crackle where his lips touched her was undeniable. Kara pulled back, still unsure of the sensation. Risk froze.

"Did you feel that?" she whispered.

He closed his eyes, nodded his head. "Your power. I think you've found it."

Her power. She did have powers—or the ability to store and release power. However it worked, she had it. She pulled her hand back, scraping her fingers along the rough stubble on Risk's chin as she did, and stared at her palm. Powers. Could she use them to help find Kelly?

She glanced up at Risk, excitement bringing a smile to her lips. "Do you know what this means?"

Risk pushed off the couch, grabbed his jeans and pulled them on. "Yes, I do."

Kara sat up. Not even bothering with her own clothes, she bounded to her feet.

Risk strode across the room, picked up a poker and stabbed at the fire.

"Kelly. This means maybe I can find Kelly. I just need to learn how to use them." She tilted her head, peering at Risk. "Are you sure your boss wouldn't—?"

He spun, the poker knocking a smoldering log from the hearth with his movement. "I told you no. Lusse is no help to you."

The log crumbled, a piece rolling off the brick and onto the wool rug that lay beside it.

"Risk." Kara stared at the smoking log. The smell of burning wool filling the room.

He stared back at her, his muscles bulging, the poker hanging at his side.

"Risk," she yelled.

He blinked, glanced down at the smoking rug, and cursed. Dropping the poker with a dull thunk, he grabbed the glowing log and tossed it back into the hearth. Then smothered the remaining embers with his shirt, which lay a few feet away.

Kara ran to his side and grabbed both his hands in hers. "Are you okay? Are you burned?"

He stared down at her, his gaze unreadable.

"Risk, did you hear me?" Kara flipped his hands over, running her fingers over his broad palms. Not a burn in sight. She heaved out a breath. "What were you thinking? You could have hurt yourself."

He stared down at his hands, clasped in hers, then laughed without humor. "I could walk through Muspelheim unscathed, little witch. It isn't fire I fear." He glanced up; a tinge of uncertainty colored his gaze.

A frown furrowed Kara's brow. What had happened? Had she done something wrong? She opened her mouth to ask, to gain reassurance, but he pulled his hands from hers and strode to the couch to retrieve her clothing.

"I need to leave for a while," he said.

Kara's mouth snapped shut. He was leaving her.

"I have to check on Lusse," he continued. "Wait here. I'll come back."

Kara tilted her head, studying him. There was no sign

of anger in his demeanor, more sadness and resolve. Just a man who needed to check in with his boss, nothing else. It was unfair of her to expect him to forget everything for her, wasn't it?

He padded back to her side, and pulled her T-shirt over her head so gently Kara barely felt the shirt being tugged into place.

She stood there, letting him, enjoying his touch even while she mourned his leaving.

With the shirt on, he pulled her long hair through the neck opening too, letting the length trail through his hands until it tumbled down her back. "We'll sift through what we've learned, and we will find your sister."

With that said, he tilted her face up with one finger and pressed a soft kiss to her mouth.

Kara stood there, telling herself it was fine. He had to leave. He'd be back, and until then she had all kinds of things to sort out herself.

Risk left Kara standing with her back to the fire, her jeans held in front of her, her legs still bare. He had to leave. Needed space to think about what was happening to him—what his newfound fears for Kara meant, what her powers meant. How he could keep her safe and use her to separate him from Lusse at the same time.

The answer was simple—he couldn't. He would have to choose. His freedom or Kara's safety. There was no way to have both. But there was still Lusse to deal with. She wouldn't give up her hunt for Kara now, not knowing she was half of a twin set. And there was Kara. She wouldn't desert the hunt for her sister.

He could perhaps convince Lusse that Kara was dead—

especially given a bit of time, and he could disappear from Kara's life, make sure Lusse never again caught a whiff of her—somehow. But his disappearance wouldn't stop Kara from looking for Kelly. She would go it alone without him there to protect her.

No, he had to come up with another plan. Give Lusse enough information to buy him time, return to Kara just long enough to find her sister—then return to Lusse forever.

He shimmered into Lusse's foyer this time, a small room separated from the rest of Lusse's residence by sizzling sheets of power. He waited, knowing one of her guards would announce his unexpected arrival.

Within seconds he heard the tap-tap of her heels coming toward him. Lusse greeting him herself? She must be eager.

"Risk." Lusse waved the wall of energy aside like a beaded curtain. "Do you have news?"

Lusse was lovely as always, her silver hair held up with diamond clips in the front and left to cascade down her silk blouse in the back. Today she was dressed for riding in leather pants and polished boots. She held a riding crop casually in one hand. "I was heading to the stables. Perhaps you'd like to tag along?" She smiled with no trace of anger or malice.

Risk returned her smile, his blood pounding in his veins. What game did she play now? "Of course."

She stepped forward, the riding crop raised in front of her, and tapped him on his chest. "But you must change first. Can't be strolling through the snow like that, can you?"

Risk glanced down. His chest and feet were still bare. He paid little attention to what he wore except to blend in the human world and when forced by Lusse.

"Bader," she called.

The servant appeared beside her, clothing draped over one arm and a pair of fine leather shoes in his hands.

Without a glance at either of them, Risk stripped off his jeans and pulled the fresh garments on. Everything was of the most expensive design and material. Risk didn't have to be a fashion expert to discern that. The shirt lay close to his skin, outlining the taper of his waist, and the pants were snug against his legs without confining his movement. For some reason, Lusse wanted him dressed like her equal instead of her chattel.

"Fabulous." She ran her hand down his sleeve, squeezing the muscle underneath as she did. "You should always dress like this, Risk. Your fascination with that hideous woodsman garb, I just don't understand."

Risk endured her touch, refusing to respond to her gibe. After circling him once, studying him from all angles, she slipped her arm through his and waved aside a second wall of energy. "To the stables then, don't you think?"

Resisting the impulse to tell her the silk trousers she'd chosen for him wouldn't hold up for long in the snow that carpeted her dimension, he matched his step to hers and walked out into the biting cold.

Stark mountains shot up from the landscape to their left; to their right a small path wove through the trees, leading to the stables and kennels. As the leather sole of Risk's shoe hit the glasslike pathway, foreboding shot through him.

The kennels.

"Did you not want a report?" he asked, his tone casual.

"Of course, but what's the rush? I'm sure you've been keeping your word to me. Watching the witch—searching for her sister." She patted his arm, only the slight narrowing of her eyes giving Risk any warning as to her true thoughts.

"There was a clue," he commented.

The path curved revealing the stables and next to them the kennels.

"A clue?" She paused.

Snow fell over the tip of Risk's shoe. He ignored it, instead turning so they faced the mountain backdrop. "Another witch was found—dead."

Lusse frowned. "Drained?"

Risk hesitated. How much to tell her? But Kara was right, Lusse might know something that would help them find her sister. "No, burned. The human police thought she was the victim of lightning, but there was no entrance or exit point for the energy."

She tapped her riding crop against her leg. "Did you sense magic?"

"Yes."

Lusse lifted the crop to her chin and stared out over the vista.

Risk watched her, looking for a sign of her mood. Interrupting her could have painful consequences, both for him and anyone else who crossed her path tonight.

She turned to him, a calculating look in her eyes. "This may be good news—very good news indeed."

"You have heard of such a thing?" he asked.

She slipped her arm back through his. "Magic is very complicated. Not every practitioner is as gifted as I."

She paused.

Knowing the expected response, Risk replied, "None, Lusse. You are the most powerful witch of all time."

She patted his arm, letting him know his response was on mark. "But others beside witches practice magic."

Risk raised an eyebrow. "You mean like...?"

"The forandre, like you and your kind, possess a primitive magic that allows you to shift between your forms."

A bland smile curved Risk's lips. Lusse would kill to be able to harness the power to shift forms like hellhounds, garm and the other forandre. Of course, Lusse would kill for her morning cup of cocoa.

"The gods, of course, reek of magic." Lusse's nails scraped against Risk's sleeve. "But..." She took a breath, exhaling slowly through her delicate nose. "What you've described makes me think we are dealing with an amateur, someone incapable of focusing her power unaided. Someone I can beat." She laughed and patted his arm again.

"But if this being is so weak, how can she have destroyed the witch I saw and hold the twin witch?"

Lusse turned her head, her hair snapping with the gesture. "Are you comparing *me* to a mortal witch?"

"No, of course not." Risk bit the inside of his cheek. He needed real information not assumptions colored by her ego. "So, the burned witch...that was caused by...?"

Her lips thin, Lusse slapped the riding crop against her thigh. "I don't know that you need to know that."

Risk waited, to push her now would guarantee her silence.

She flicked her gaze to his face. "But since I am feeling so generous today, I'll tell you. A familiar. She is using them to focus power she can't control alone."

"Focus power?" Risk prompted.

Sighing, she turned them both back onto the path, heading toward the kennels. "Those less adept at the handling of magic often have focus problems. They might be able to pull the energy they need for a spell, but either not enough at one time to get the results they want, or the power splinters, flying around, each piece no more than static.

"They use a familiar as either a battery of sorts, storing up power so they can gather it in bits, or like a convex lens that focuses their energy rather than light."

The path they were on split, a gravel section breaking off and leading to the kennel door. She paused, her foot hovering above the walkway. "Would you like to visit your son? I've heard he's doing quite well."

Risk tensed. Venge. What had she done to him? Keeping his face neutral, he replied, "Whatever you wish."

She tilted her head as if considering. "As long as we are so close, it would be rude to just walk by, don't you think?"

Risk gave a slight nod of his head. "Of course." And followed her onto the gravel path.

Determined to get all the information he could while her seemingly mellow mood held, Risk continued their earlier conversation. "And the witch being so completely burned. Does that indicate anything? Any added danger?"

She laughed. "Just more ineptitude, I'd guess. But don't worry, alpha. Just lead me to the thief who has stolen my witch."

Sensing this was as far as he could push her, Risk let the conversation drop and followed her into the kennels. Cells lined the walls of the first room. Blue energy crackling floor to ceiling guaranteed anyone trapped inside would stay inside—even a hellhound in hound form. Today the cages were all blessedly empty.

With a wave, Lusse gestured for him to follow as she walked down the aisle between the cells and pushed open the door that led to the next room.

The space was dark, the smell of anger and discontent thickening the air. The center aisle continued, flanked by a row of cots on each side. Lusse flitted through, pausing to pick up a discarded bloodied bandage, which she ran through her hand like a satin ribbon.

"Where can they be?" She spun to face Risk.

He knew very well where the hounds would be if not in the kennel—the pit. And…his stomach twisted…if Lusse was this carefree, Venge had to be the center attraction.

"Could they be?" She flitted to the end of the room where doors led out to the viewing area over the pit. "Why yes. There they are." She glanced at Risk over her shoulder. "It appears we are in luck. Your son is exercising."

His face grim, Risk followed her out onto the dais carved from one mammoth stone.

Chapter 9

Kara sat in front of the dying embers, her arms wrapped around her knees. She wasn't sure which of today's events to analyze first. So much had happened in so little time. Some amazing. Some horrifying.

Risk fitting in the amazing, if somewhat unsettling, part.

It was great to have someone in her corner, especially today. Kara couldn't believe she would have survived the visit to the morgue if he hadn't been there to lend her strength. Then after, back here... A shiver of pleasure danced up her spine.

She wasn't exactly the most sexually active woman in the world, but she'd had her turn at hurried sessions in the back of a car, and less hurried but just as unsatisfying sessions in a few short-term boyfriends' apartments. But she had never experienced anything to prepare her for Risk.

For the first time sex made her feel strong instead of vulnerable and exposed.

And it wasn't just in her head—she had physical evidence that she actually was stronger. She held out her hand. Power. She had powers. What could she do with them?

She twisted around until her knees were under her and placed her empty whiskey glass on the warm brick beside her. Holding out her arm, she concentrated on zapping the glass to dust.

Nothing, not even a tingle.

Frowning, she picked up the glass and moved a few inches closer. After lowering her shoulders and rolling her head from side to side, she tried again.

Nothing.

Damn. Kara stared at the glass. If she couldn't even crack cheap barware, she'd never be able to use her powers to save Kelly—once she found her.

Think. Think. Think. What had she been doing when her powers had first appeared?

Stroking Risk. Her lips curved at the memory. God she hoped he hurried back. How could she so thoroughly miss someone she'd just met?

Concentrate. Risk wasn't here, and she needed to do this alone, anyway.

So, maybe not what she was doing, but how she was feeling. Could that be the key?

Sitting back on her heels, she let her mind drift back to the moment. Risk on top of her, his warmth seeping into her. Feeling appreciated—worshipped almost—safe, and most importantly strong.

Her eyes closed, she dropped her head. Let the feeling wash over her. She was strong. Confident. Nothing could stop her. Breathed in. Her lungs expanded. She could feel the energy flowing into her body.

Smiling, she opened her eyes, held out her hands and blasted the whiskey glass into tiny shards.

With a laugh, she jumped to her feet. She did it. She had powers and she could use them.

Twenty feet below where Risk and Lusse stood lay the pit—a steep-walled hole with no place to hide and no way to escape, until the fight was deemed over by Lusse or whomever she gifted with that power in her absence.

Today the pit was slick with mud, oil and blood. Five hounds in human form circled another armed with nothing except his balled fists.

Venge. Risk's son.

One of the attackers, Sigurd, a burly man Risk recognized from his own time in the kennels, picked up a staff and gestured to the other four. Venge spun, attempting to keep all five within his view. Two dove for his feet, knocking him to the ground, while the other two grabbed him around the wrists, pinning them into the mud.

Lusse laid her hand on the icy metal railing in front of them. "Oh, that doesn't look good. Does it?" She tilted her head toward Risk.

He gripped the railing. Heat raged through him, melting the ice under his hands.

Below them, Venge twisted away from one of the males holding him, then swung his now free fist into the nose of the second. Blood splurting from his face, the second attacker loosened his grip on Venge's wrist. Free, Venge sprang to his feet.

Risk's grip loosened a bit in response.

"Hmm," Lusse murmured.

The leader, Sigurd, signaled for the others to step back, then feinted to the left. As Venge turned to protect his right side, Sigurd arced the staff down, striking him across the neck.

Chuckling, the leader hopped back and yelled something to his companions.

They were goading Venge, trying to make him lose control. Risk moved closer to the railing, his gaze frozen on his son.

"Forandre rules. He changes, he's dead," Lusse commented with the casual delivery of a weather report.

Forandre rules meant a shape-shifter had to stick to his weakest form—in other words human. It also meant to win, all the other hounds had to do was taunt Venge to the point the beast in him took over. For many hounds this took little more than seconds.

"How long have they been fighting?" Risk asked, trying to match Lusse's tone.

"Hmm? You know I have no use for time—unless I'm waiting for someone." She gave him a calculating look, then pulled a slim watch out of her pocket. "But since I *was* curious when you might pop in, I happened to take note of when the festivities began. Let's see…" She made a show of mumbling under her breath and counting off on her fingers. "It must be close to eighteen human hours now."

"You put him in there as soon as I left?" Surprise caused Risk to ask the question, though his logical mind knew it was a mistake.

Fortunately Lusse seemed unfazed. "Why yes, I guess I did. He's held up quite well, all things considered. How long did you make it?"

Weeks. Risk had endured weeks of the torment. But he had been older, more in control of his urges, and he hadn't already been weakened by a fight with his father and who knew what other torture from Lusse. She'd done Risk the favor of putting him in fresh. Just to prolong the pain, Risk suspected.

"I really wasn't sure how Venge would do, but with his bloodline, I hoped he'd make it at least a few days. It would look bad if my alpha's son fell in the first day, don't you think?"

Below them, the burly leader took another swipe at Venge with his stick. Venge leaped, somersaulting over it and landing on his feet.

"See, he has days left in him. Perhaps he'll be finished up when you return with my witches." Lusse turned her eyes, focused with deadly intensity on Risk.

So this was her game. Force Risk to hurry his hunt with the threat of his son being destroyed at any second.

Some games Risk wasn't willing to play.

Slipping off the worthless shoes she'd forced him to wear, he catapulted over the railing and landed in crouch on the rutted ground below.

Cold mud squished between his toes, his fingers also sinking in the muck. He ignored it, concentrating instead on the six males in front of him. The leader, Sigurd... Risk's mind spat out the name...stepped back, widening the circle and pulling Risk into their midst.

Risk smiled.

Sigurd palmed his staff, his brows lowering. "I thought you were off playing lapdog, alpha." He made the title sound like an insult. An assessment Risk shared.

"And you got bored waiting for my return?" Risk nodded toward Venge. The boy's only acknowledgment of Risk's notice was a tightening of his jaw.

"What's your interest?" Sigurd spun the staff like a deadly windmill in front of himself.

Risk shrugged. "My interest. My business." He glanced around. "But don't you think you should even things up a bit?"

Sigurd laughed. "You have been gone too long."

Risk cocked his head. "No? Fine. If you don't want to call more hounds to assist you, why should it bother me? A quick slaughter is always better. I have places to be."

Sigurd's eyebrows shot up, but as Risk circled toward him he lowered his staff and matched Risk's approach.

"What about her?" Sigurd motioned to where Lusse stood watching.

Risk kept his eyes trained on his opponent. "As long as there's blood—she won't care from what source."

"Good with me." Sigurd raised the staff and swung out with the first blow.

"Not with me." With a roar, Venge threw himself across the circle and plunged into Risk's side, knocking him into the mud.

Late the next morning Kara took a taxi to the Guardian's Keep. Risk had very considerately left his Jeep for her, apparently taking a cab wherever he had gone, but Kara needed to retrieve her own car. Driving Risk's Jeep would have just meant leaving his vehicle in this less than savory section of town. After paying the cabdriver, she slammed the door and hurried toward the bar.

After her last visit here, she didn't want to spend any more time loitering around outside than absolutely necessary. She was focused on learning something about Kelly's disappearance. She wrapped her hand around the worn metal door pull, and stepped inside.

The Guardian's Keep was less intimidating in the daylight, and dirtier. Kara scuffed a discarded cigarette butt off her shoe—much dirtier. The overhead lights were dingy with dust and dead insects. The floor so sticky with spilled beer, a little sucking noise announced each of Kara's steps.

But she was here, and with the sun filtering through two grimy windows, she could see it was just an old rundown bar with nothing overly nefarious in sight.

Her newly found powers giving her confidence, she squared her shoulders and walked toward the dark wooden bar that ran along the left side of the room. The same bartender who'd refused to answer her questions a few nights earlier was clicking away on a computer tucked out of sight under the counter.

She strolled toward him and knocked her fist on the wood. Strong. Confident. That was her.

Eerie, almost clear, blue eyes glared up at her. She took a step back.

He gave her a quick startled look, then as if sorting something out, shook his head and continued clicking.

Kara used the time to study him more closely. The other night she'd been too busy scurrying away in fear to really size him up.

He was tall, not as tall or broad in the shoulders as Risk, but definitely in shape. His pectorals had seen more than one set of chest presses. Even the back of his neck as he bent down to flip off the computer screen showed cording. And, with the exception of his eyes, dark. Dark skin, dark hair—he looked back up at her—dark mood.

"You need something?" He raised one brow, his gaze skimming her body.

Inhaling through her nose, Kara mentally recited her mantra—confident, strong. "I was here the other night. I'm looking for my sister. She looks just like me, except..." She paused. She had been about to say stronger, but that wasn't true anymore, right? She squared her shoulders. "She looks just like me."

"Can't help you." He picked a glass out of the sink and placed it on the drain board.

"But..." Kara bit her lower lip. He had to know something. He had to. "I know she's been in here. I found this with her things." She opened her palm to reveal the matchbook.

"You found a matchbook and you think that means she's here? Look around. You see anyone?"

Kara glanced over her shoulder at the almost empty bar. One man sat in the booth she'd occupied on her last visit. His hooded sweatshirt pulled up over his forehead and an ashtray full of butts in front of him.

"I didn't mean now." She replied, her exasperation showing. Good. Maybe she needed to get mad. She let the emotion grow. "I'm not asking you to do something crazy like..." She wiped her hand over the bar, her palm coming back stained with brown goo. "Clean. Just tell me if she was here—two weeks ago."

He folded his arms over his chest and cast her an assessing gaze. For a moment she thought her act had worked, then he said, "Go home." He strode to the other end of the bar and started sifting through what looked like receipts of some sort.

Damn it. Concentrating on the small pile of paper beside him, she held out her hand and prayed. Get his attention.

A small wind stirred around her, shifting her hair. Then a skittering feeling ran down her arm—like a cockroach scurrying for safety. Kara fought off a shudder.

Why didn't tapping into her power feel as good today as it had earlier? Ignoring the nagging thought, she focused on her task.

A muttered curse rewarded her efforts. She snapped open her eyes to see the bartender turn a slightly singed paper in his hand. A deadly expression on his face, he strode toward her.

As threatening as he looked, Kara's gaze was frozen to the paper in his hand. A wispy trail of smoke snaked from a hole the size of a quarter. That was it? That was all the power she could muster? What happened to exploding bar glasses?

"How'd you do that?" Leaning across the wood, the bartender shoved the paper under her nose. "This place is off-limits. Only protective—" He glanced over her shoulder to the man in the booth, then turned back and fixed a glare at her. "None of this." The paper in his hand twitched. "How the hell did you…?" He muttered then, seeming to collect himself, he lowered the paper, and placing both hands flat on the bar, got right in her space.

"Go home. I don't know what your hellhound's thinking letting you wander around like this—but tell him the guardian said to keep you away. Bull-headed little witches have a habit of disappearing around here."

Then without another word, he flipped up a hinged section of the counter, strode through the doorway next to the bar and disappeared in the dark hall.

Kara stared after him, her eyes wide. *Bull-headed little witches have a habit of disappearing*. Was he threatening her? Had he taken Kelly? Swallowing the bile that had collected in the back of her throat, she pushed away from the bar and forced herself to follow him.

The air in front of the door was still—unnaturally still. Stuffy without being hot, like an old attic no one had stepped into for a hundred years. Her mouth dry, she sniffed, halfway expecting the smell of mothballs and dust to greet her.

Nothing, not even the stench of cigarettes and old beer that drenched the rest of the room.

The doorway looked normal enough. No obvious signs of danger, death or mayhem, but something didn't feel right. Her heart sped and her hands shook. There was something just wrong here.

Wrong. Like Kelly being missing. That was wrong. Giving herself a mental shake, she held out her hand toward the open doorway. Nothing happened.

She laughed. God, she was being so silly. It was just a door—probably led to the restrooms. Running her hand over her forehead, she stepped through the doorway and right back into the room she had left.

What the hell. She looked around. The door was now behind her. How did that happen? Mumbling to herself, she turned around and rapped her fist on the door frame. The solid sound of her knuckles knocking against wood assured her she wasn't completely losing it. Or was she?

She stepped back to analyze the doorway again. Hairs on the back of her neck stood up, accompanied by the crawling feeling of someone watching her. As casually as she could, she cast a glance over her shoulder. Studying her from behind a half-smoked cigarette was the creepy little man in the stained hoodie.

Kara resisted the embarrassed laugh that tickled the back of her throat.

So some vagrant, probably lit up on heavens knew what, saw her talking to herself, walking through a door that led nowhere. No reason to be embarrassed. Probably an hourly occurrence for him. Still, she was feeling a little uncomfortable in the Guardian's Keep right now. Not that it was ever welcoming.

And she had learned some things. The bartender definitely knew something about witches and their disappearances. Then there was his odd comment about a hellhound. That certainly warranted at least an Internet search—and chatting with Risk.

And she didn't think the bartender was coming back anytime soon. She peered past the doorway into the darkness. No sign of anything—just a murky blackness. She should check again, though, right? She should. She really should.

Balling up her fists and screwing up what courage she had, she took a deep breath and stepped through the doorway again. This time she landed on the front step of the bar.

Damn. She glanced up, her heart pounding loudly in her chest. The blue-gray sign of the Guardian's Keep swung above her head suspended by two chains. The creak of the metal links against each other and the damp feel of air laden with unshed snow assured her she was truly back outside.

She spun, her hand on the cold metal doorknob before her rational mind caught up with her. That doorway beside the bar was taking her nowhere. Or worse, it might take her anywhere.

A sudden gust hit the sign above; the chain let off a squealing complaint. Kara jumped, falling forward and knocking against the closed front door. She leaned there for a second, her breath escaping in quick huffs.

That door could take her anywhere. The thought seeped into her brain. She pressed her forehead against the cold wood. Believing these things wasn't easy. But she had to—if she blithely walked through that doorway again, she might land anywhere—northern Siberia, Mars, hell... She rapped her head against the door softly. Point was, it could most certainly be someplace she couldn't easily escape.

Right now, her Honda was parked a short walk away, waiting to be coaxed into life. A lot smarter choice than tempting whatever had control of that doorway. Even knowing the logic of leaving, she hesitated. Leaving felt like failure. She was fed up with failure.

She curled her fingers into her palm and shook her head. Time to pack it in and go find Risk. Standing out here would get her nowhere. There was no shame in getting help to sort it all out.

Her arms wrapped around her for warmth, she gazed across the parking lot where she'd encountered the dogs before. The sun blared down on her providing little heat, but plenty of cheerful light.

No sign of any dogs today, she assured herself. Just a few empty feet of asphalt and snow, then she'd get in her Honda, say a few mantras and cajole the machine into taking her home.

Nothing bad could happen in the face of such glorious sunshine. After one last glance around, she trekked toward her car.

Risk fell to the ground with a grunt, Venge's arms wrapped around his waist. Lusse, still on the dais above them, waved the bloody bandage like a hanky.

The bitch.

Risk muttered an oath and shoved his hands onto Venge's shoulders, trying to push him away. The boy wouldn't budge.

His heels dug into the mud, Risk fought for leverage. Venge held tight. Without changing, Risk doubted he could break his son's hold. And he wouldn't change—too much was riding on him now. Kara, her sister, and his son, whether Venge realized it or not.

Muscles straining to keep Venge from shifting his grip from Risk's waist to his neck, Risk addressed his son. "This is what she wants. You. Me. All of us fighting. It only strengthens her control. She feeds off it. Steals our energy to use against us later."

Venge wedged his legs back underneath himself and burrowed his head into Risk's rib cage, pushed them forward through the mud. The oily, bloody gunk caked into Risk's hair, and chunked over his shoulders onto his stomach. But Venge's change in posture also gave Risk a new opening.

Forcing the back of his head deeper into the gunk, Risk curled his feet toward his body, catching Venge in the gut and sending his son flying over his head to land with a splat in the mud.

Shaking the goo from his body, Risk stood up. Venge lay on his back for only seconds before flipping himself upright—into a crouch. Rage poured out of him.

Risk's own anger peaked in response. Clenching his fists, he tamped down the emotion and looked around for the other males. All five stood behind the power grid that separated spectators from participants. For the first time, Risk noticed the viewing area was full. All of Lusse's hounds had turned out for today's little event.

Satisfied that at least the fight was solely between him and his son—at least until Lusse decided to interfere—Risk lowered into a fight stance.

"You are playing into her hands. You're smarter than that—or should be." He flicked his hand, sending a black glob soaring into the crisp blue sky.

Venge snorted, and took a step closer.

Risk matched his move, his feet slogging sideways through the mud. His foot hit something solid. Without letting his gaze drop from Venge, he ran his bare foot over the object, round and hard. Sigurd's staff.

"Why so angry?" he asked, moving again until he was centered over the stick.

Venge lowered his eyebrows, his hands curling closed in front of him.

A sharp breeze cut through the ring, shooting the evidence of Venge's emotions straight at Risk. Anger, determination and the first whiffs of power.

Risk was losing him. Venge was on the verge of changing.

There was only one way to stop him. Defeat him first.

Mumbling words of regret that his son wouldn't appreciate, Risk dropped to the ground, yanked the staff through the inches of mud that covered it, and bits of muck flying like a swarm of locusts, pole-vaulted across the fifteen feet that separated them. With a roar he landed an arm's reach from his son.

Venge stared back at him, his eyes turning crimson. Before Venge's change could go further or Risk's own hellhound nature could manifest, he raised the pole and cracked it across his son's face.

Venge crumpled to his knees, his face frozen in disbelief. Blood streamed from where Risk's staff had struck, making a trail down Venge's forehead into his eyes. Eyes that glimmered red for one second. Then noiselessly, Venge dropped into the mud unconscious.

With a growl, Risk flung the staff across the rink and into the grid. The pole exploded, sending chunks of wood and mud splattering around the arena. The hounds behind the grid stood silent, all eyes filled with assessment.

Had Risk helped Venge or just endangered him more? The other males knew Risk's trick. Knew he could have killed Venge outright or simply allowed him to change—a death sentence by forandre rules. Would they now see Venge as an easy mark? Realize his tie to Risk?

Risk strode to his son's unconscious body. Time to add to the act. Confuse them if nothing else. Arms raised to signal his victory, he lifted his bare foot and used it to smash his son's face firmly into the mud.

Chapter 10

With a roar, Risk stepped around his son's prone body and stared up at Lusse. She leaned over the railing, the bandage in her hand waving in the breeze. Her eyes sparkling, she dropped the bloodied cloth. A flick of her hand diverted the wind, directing the strip to Risk's feet.

Nodding in acknowledgment, he bent to retrieve her favor then strode to the ramp that led out of the pit.

"I don't remember giving you permission to leave me." She slapped his arm lightly with the riding crop.

"But the fight met with your approval?" He held out the bandage she had tossed him.

"Very entertaining, and very enlightening." The expression in her eyes turned calculating.

"Then I should consider my efforts rewarded." He turned to look out over the arena.

Enlightening. Had his performance at the end of the match failed?

"So, Sigurd is still in charge of those in need of exercising?" He bit back a laugh at the term. Exercising. More like exorcism, but in reverse. Lusse's goal was always to bring more demon into a hound, not relieve them of what they had.

"You would know, if you spent more time behaving like the alpha, rather than playing with the humans. Of course, I could change that couldn't I? Cut off your contact with humans altogether?"

Risk tensed, then forced his muscles to relax. "But who would bring you your witches?"

She tapped her chin with the crop. "Sigurd? Venge—when he's done a bit more exercising?" She stepped forward until her body pressed against Risk's back, the leather tail of the riding crop tickling his ear. "I smell her on you, you know. I may not have the nose of a hound—but you reek of witch and sex."

Risk stared blandly down at the ring. Sigurd strode out into the mud then signaled two other males to remove the still-unconscious Venge.

"I only did as you asked—used my talents to gain her trust."

"Is that what you did?" Lusse murmured.

Sigurd left the ring and began striding up the ramp; the two males dragging Venge followed close behind.

"Of course. What else? And it worked. I learned of the other witch."

"The dead one—the focal tool." Lusse pulled back. "I might know where to find our witch thief, or least who can lead us to her." She turned, pressing her back against the railing beside him. "Have you met any garm, in this little human world of yours?"

Risk frowned. Garm, a wolf forandre, were not friends of the hounds. Not that hellhound's had any friends. But as hunters they were the natural enemies of garm whose only passion was to protect and guard—no matter who or what they had to destroy in the process.

"I don't search out garm too frequently."

"To find my witch, you may have to. Garm guard the portals. I suspect our thief has tucked herself away somewhere I and others can't sense her attempts at improving her powers. Which means it has to be one of the protected worlds—one that can only be reached through a portal.

"Find a garm, and you will find the portals," she concluded.

"Any garm?" Risk asked.

Lusse sighed. "There's a pecking order of some sort—not all garm have the strength to keep the portals controlled, but find one and he will surely know where to find a garm that does."

The strong scent of testosterone warned Risk that Sigurd and the other males had arrived. Widening his stance, he fixed a disinterested expression on his face.

"Your whelp," Sigurd announced as the two males rolled Venge across the stone dais.

Thinking his old nemesis had learned Risk's connection to the boy, Risk's gaze shot to Sigurd, but his eyes were squarely on Lusse.

"Yes, my whelp." Lusse tilted her head toward Risk.

Venge shifted, his head raising for a second, then plunking back onto the rock.

"Did you have to shame him so thoroughly, my alpha?"

She looped her arm through Risk's. "It will make keeping him alive in the kennels all the harder, I'm afraid."

As was Risk.

Venge stiffened.

Risk stared at his son's beaten form, before switching his gaze to Lusse. "Perhaps he should be caged."

"Caged?" Lusse's eyebrows shot upward. "You surprise me. I thought perhaps you had some affection for the whelp."

"Only thinking to save your investment. As you have pointed out, he comes from good bloodlines. It would be a shame to lose him before he had a chance to show his merit."

"But the cages? That's so cold."

And safe. It was the one place Risk knew the other males wouldn't be able to get to his son.

Placing her hands on her hips, Lusse surveyed the group. "I think I just might. And after our conversation, I realize you deserve a reward of some sort."

Risk's throat tightened. He could not even guess what Lusse might consider a reward.

"You're on the trail of finding my witch—and who knows when you find the garm what other treasures you may uncover.

"I'm going to offer you a little prize. You bring me back the two witches you've promised me and I'll give you four—" she motioned to the males on the dais with them "—of my hounds in return."

The lines around Sigurd's mouth deepened. His companions stood completely still, only their eyes darting from Lusse to Risk giving away their shock.

Risk could do little more than mirror them, surprise holding him captive.

She laughed. "A hound owning other hounds. I don't think it's ever been done."

A shuffling sounded from where Venge lay. He looked up, his gaze locked on Risk and his eyes glowing red. Sigurd stepped forward, his staff poised above Venge's head.

"He's coming around," he stated.

Lusse tilted her head at Risk. "The cage?"

Risk gave her a short nod.

"To the cage," she announced gaily, then with a laugh, she slipped her arm back through Risk's. "Shall we ride?"

Risk followed her back through the kennel, ignoring the bellowing rage of his son behind him.

Why had she parked so far away the other night? The trip from the Guardian's Keep to Kara's car stretched out in front of her. Even in the bright daylight she was beginning to get that itchy feeling. As if someone was watching her, or sneaking up behind her.

She wouldn't give in to the fear. She would just stop, stand solid and prove to herself nothing was behind her. Lowering her chin, she spun, her hands ready to shoot out whatever power she could muster.

Nothing but an empty parking lot covered in newly fallen snow greeted her.

See; nothing. She turned back toward the street.

The dull whoosh of feet brushing over damp pavement froze her in midstride. Almost immediately an arm smacked against her windpipe, momentarily cutting off her air, and something sharp pricked her neck.

"Don't move, witch," a gravely voice mumbled. "I got me a stunner." Blue lightning flashed in the corner of Kara's eye.

"I don't want to use it, you understand. I hear tell it hurts right bad, worse than the knife." He gouged her again. Kara pulled back, but her body was wedged against his. Her movement brought her face closer to his. The stench of stale beer, cigarettes and motor oil assaulted her. She twisted her head again, causing the knife to tear a thin trail across her skin. Her knees bent and her eyes flickered closed against the pain.

She was such a fool. Why had she thought she could handle this?

"Careful, bitch." He chuckled. "I got that right this time. According to the Guardian you been bedding down with the dogs. Not that there's anything wrong with that, mind you." He laughed again, a high-pitched almost hysterical sound.

Dog, hounds. What was with this talk of her and a hound?

She angled her neck in an attempt to put space between her and the blade. "I think you have the wrong person. I don't like dogs."

"Don't like dogs. Well, that makes two of us." He pulled her backward, her heels making parallel trails through the snow.

What did he want? The knife. The bar. It was all too similar to the scene that had flitted through her head when she'd touched the witch in the morgue. Was this what had happened to Kelly?

He reached one of the cement barriers that marked the parking places, and stopped, apparently deciding his best route from here.

"We got about twenty feet between us and the Keep. You think you can be a good little witch and cooperate? 'Cause if not, I'm gonna have to..." Blue flame sizzled next to Kara's face. "Hurts like the dickens, and it freezes all your powers. That's the downside for me. Hard to get top dollar when you can't perform."

A snowflake drifted from the blue sky and landed on Kara's nose. She loved snow—or used to. Now she wondered, would she hate it as much as she hated dogs?

"So, whatcha say? We got a deal? I get my fix and you get a pain-free trip through the portal."

Another bigger flake plopped onto Kara's eyelash, then fell, a tiny shock of water into her eye.

Funny. She wasn't much in a deal-making mood. His arms held her around the biceps, but her hands were still free and with her elbows bent she should be able to use them to shoot whatever power she had over her shoulder and into his face.

She inhaled, thought of Risk, and prepared to fight. Her elbows bent almost of their own accord as energy thrummed into her.

"Aw, no. You oughtn't to do that." Blue flared again. Heat seared the side of her face, and the smell of her own hair singing burned her nose.

She wasn't ready. She could feel it. She needed more time, just a second or two.

No time to think. Screwing her eyes tight against the threatening blue light, she willed all the energy she'd stored down through her arms and out her raised hands.

The man behind her yelped. Jumping sideways, he dragged the knife from her neck to her shoulder as he moved. The stunner snapped and burned a path through her hair. Then Kara was free.

But she couldn't run. Couldn't do anything except stand there panting as if she'd finished a marathon in record time.

Her assailant crouched a few feet away, his knife clutched in his fist and his stunner on the ground by his feet.

With narrowed eyes, he picked up the weapon. "Can't be easy. Can it? God forbid I made an easy score now and again." He rolled a switch on the side of the thing and held it out toward her. "Now see this is going to hurt." Shaking his head, he scrambled to his feet and limped toward her.

Kara stood there, her breathing slower, but her power drained. She didn't know how she knew her resources were empty, but she did. She might as well be holding off a grizzly with an unloaded revolver.

Lusse tilted her face to the falling snow, the tiny flakes catching on her silver lashes, and tumbling onto her cheeks where they lay unmoved.

Risk fisted his hand around the bloody bandage. He didn't have time to be playing games with Lusse. His son was safe for a while at least, but Kara was alone back in the human world where some thief was hunting witches. And he had new things to consider, like Lusse's promise of a gift of the other hounds and her information on the garms.

"How many portals do you think there are?" he asked.

Blinking, she lowered her face to look at him. "How many? I don't know. The gods and the garm are very hush-hush about all that."

"So how does someone know to go to a portal in the first place?"

Air exploded from her mouth. "They just know."

Her toe tapped against the path. "Perhaps it's time for you to get back."

Risk couldn't agree more. With a nod, he took a small step backward and shimmered away.

* * *

Kara staggered backward, stumbling over a cement barrier and falling onto her butt. The man limped toward her, the blue flame of his stunner barely visible against the early afternoon sky.

She groped behind her, coming up with nothing more than a handful of snow. Desperate, she threw it at him. Hissing, it struck the flame and evaporated into steam.

"Now that's not gonna help any." He bent down, his knee pressed into her chest, one hand wrapped around her neck. "If you hold still, I'll zap you in the arm. They say it don't hurt as bad there."

Kara flailed upward, her closed fist making contact with the side of his head.

"Shit. That hurt. I'm gonna have to quit being nice to you." A wild glint in his eyes, he pulled back the hand holding the stunner.

The flame sped toward Kara's face. She reached up her hand to block it. Her arm collided with his seconds before a loud roar shook the ground beneath them.

The man on top of her fell off, his eyes wide and his face slack. "I wasn't hurting her. You tell him, witch. I wasn't going to hurt you, was I?"

Rubbing her arm, Kara scooted her body back, away from her crazed attacker.

"I'm not looking for trouble. Just stopped by for a drink. That's all," the man blathered, his eyes fixed on someone or something to her side, out of her vision.

A growl rumbled toward her. The hairs on her arm shooting up at the sound.

It couldn't be. Not again. Not the dogs.

* * *

Risk saw the man leaning over Kara as soon as he materialized onto the Guardian's Keep parking lot. She struggled as the man moved closer, then jerked again as what looked to be a weapon flared next to her skin.

Rage poured through Risk.

Without pause, he released the iron controls he kept on his hellhound nature—stretched his neck and curled his fingers toward his palms. It took only seconds for the magic that was a part of him to complete his change.

His clothing fell to the ground. Silver hair hung over his eyes. Snarling, he shook it away. His eyes darted, seeing twice in this form as in his weaker human shape.

The pavement was wet and cool beneath his pads. He flexed his broad feet. His muscles ached to run, he ached to run, to feel the air blowing through his fur, to see the blur of cars, houses, trees as he raced after prey. He held his nose to the breeze. Cocked his ears, letting in sound inaudible to both humans and mundane dogs.

His prey was here. He could smell him. Hear him.

He turned his massive head toward the scent of desperation and sounds of struggle.

Kara threw up her arm trying to defend herself. Risk didn't have to see or smell her fear, he could feel it. His muscles tightened, his lips curling away from his teeth.

The man muttered something, then, his glowing weapon gripped in his fist, slashed down toward Kara's wide eyes.

Risk roared, his anger filling him with heat.

Hunt. Kill. Destroy.

He leaped across the parking lot.

* * *

The massive animal stood six feet away, its paws braced apart, its head lowered, lips pulled back revealing shining canines. His glowing eyes were fixed on the man now crab-walking away from her, the stunner still gripped in her attacker's hand sizzling and popping as he dragged it through the snow.

"She didn't tell me, she belonged to no forandre. Bad enough I got to deal with the garm and that other. I wouldn't be poaching on no hellhound's territory."

The man was talking to the dog as if it could understand him. Kara pushed herself backward until her body collided with the side of the Guardian's Keep. The dog seemed focused on the man. Could she escape—run for it? Leave the nasty little man to fend for himself?

She pressed her fingers to her closed eyelids. God help her. It was tempting. She wasn't sure what the man had planned for her, but she knew it hadn't been good.

The stunner spit and steamed as it knocked against a hunk of ice dropped some point in the past from under a bar patron's car.

That thing was wicked. She owed the vile man nothing.

Curling her feet up under her body, she balanced on the balls of her feet and waited for an opening.

The dog took a step forward, his head swinging toward the man. His mouth opened to release a howl that sent chills racing down her spine.

She bit her lip until she tasted blood.

Death. That was the sound of death, and not a pretty one.

Damn her for her weakness, but she couldn't do it. She couldn't leave. Sensing she had only as long as it took the dog to complete his glass-breaking call to make her choice, she raised shaking hands and held them, palms out, toward the dog.

Power. She needed power. Again she concentrated on feeling strong, in control.

Heat tickled her palms, then crept up her arms. Strong, she was strong. In a surge, the energy exploded into the rest of her body, filling every molecule. She breathed power, opened her eyes and could see power.

The dog was surrounded by red bands of undulating energy that grew darker and more angry as his howl continued. The man, his legs curled into his chest, emitted nothing more than a light yellow haze.

What had Risk said about witches? They pulled power from those around them? Was she pulling power from the dog that she now was going to use against him?

Her hands outstretched, she swallowed hard. She could do it. She could kill this dog, steal its life as easily as that other dog had stolen Jessie's. Send it to hell.

Eyes trained on the baying beast in front of her, she breathed in, then released all the power waiting inside her.

Chapter 11

Risk lowered his head, his death call complete. His prey was curled into himself, not even bothering to run. The hound in Risk mourned such an easy kill.

Run, Risk urged his prey, using the telepathy only available to him in his hound form.

The man's gaze shot to Risk, then behind him. A glimmer of hope flickering in his eyes.

Risk turned, suddenly realizing the shift in the air. Energy was draining from around him, streaming toward the building behind him—to a lone figure crouched at its base.

Kara.

Before he could form another thought, two parallel streams of blue fire shot toward him. He dropped, the energy crackling as it passed over his body.

Kara had attacked him.

For a second his mind spun. Had he been right when he

saw her collapsed inside that circle? Had she been trying to trap him then? To kill or capture him now?

No, even with his mind clouded by his beastly form, he knew that wasn't true. Realized she had no idea he and the dog she feared were one.

The line of fire over him died. Next to the building, Kara teetered to her feet. She was breathing hard, her knees and arms shaking. Bracketing her body against the bar building, she closed her eyes.

What was she doing? Risk pushed himself to his feet, preparing to go to her. Then he heard it, the whoosh of energy being sucked from around him, from him.

She was stealing his power—to use against him. It shouldn't surprise him. It was what he had told Venge Lusse did—and it was, but Lusse was more like a sponge sopping up the excess. To suction power the way Kara was attempting took ritual and concentration even Lusse couldn't manage with no preparation or tools.

And it ended with only one outcome—death for the target and power lust for the initiator.

Power was surging into Kara. Stronger this time, quicker. Her heart pounded, her body pulsed as if she were at a rock concert, the bass driving against her over and over.

She flipped her eyelids open, watched the red energy flow over the parking lot, welcomed it with her arms held wide.

What she could do with such power. Find Kelly. Save herself. Never be afraid—make others afraid instead.

No, some tiny part of her objected. Not that. That wasn't what she wanted.

Another wave of energy rippled into her. She closed her eyes savoring the warmth, letting herself soar.

Heady. She could get lost in this feeling, addicted. Exist on nothing but power.

"Kara," Risk's voice snapped inside her head. "Kara. Break the connection. Stop the pull. You can't handle it—it's too much. You won't survive."

Kara frowned. Risk. What was he doing here, trying to stop her fun?

She needed to feel strong. Deserved to feel strong.

Another current pulsed against her. She arched her back, opening her chest, letting the power pour into her.

Too much? It would never be too much. She would drain the dog, the man, then anything that even hinted of magic.

She would drain the world.

"Kara," the voice was more urgent now. "Kara you have to stop. You'll kill yourself, and kill me. Who will save Kelly then?"

Kill Risk? She wouldn't kill Risk or herself. She blinked; his words made no sense. And where was he? Her view blurry, she looked around the parking lot—nothing but the dog and the man. No Risk.

"Kara, look at me," the voice said again.

She tilted her head—the man? Was he playing a trick on her? No, as she stared at him, her attacker flipped to his knees, then with one backward glace, broke into a run, leaving his knife and stunner behind.

He escaped. Damn him—taking his power with him, measly though it was, it was her power now. She narrowed her eyes, her arms shooting out in front of her. She would stop him. Teach him not to take what was hers.

"Kara." It was a yell now, and so loud, Kara jerked in response. "Look at me. Look at what is happening to you."

Kara turned her head, scanning the lot, her gaze finally

falling on the dog. He looked weaker now, his head hanging lower, his tail drooping between his legs.

"Kara, look at me."

The dog. The voice was coming from the dog—no, her head. The voice was in her head, but the dog was responsible.

"Risk?" she murmured, her hands falling an inch.

"Kara." He was tired. She could hear it. Feel it.

"What happened? What's wrong?" she asked.

"The power. Let it go, Kara. You can't handle it."

She stood there, the power whipping around her, through her. Her hands trembling with her desire for more.

"It will destroy you. Make you want nothing but more."

More. She did want more.

She stared down at her hands, turned her palms toward her, unintentionally breaking the connection.

A groan sounded from across the pavement. She looked up and saw Risk, naked, crumpled onto the snow.

Dear God. What had she done?

She ran to him, sliding and falling along the way, but picking herself up and continuing until she collapsed by his side.

She pressed her hands to his bare chest, felt the movement of breaths and the reassuring warmth of his body.

He sighed, his hand reaching out to cup her cheek, his thumb brushing along her cheek. "Blue. Your eyes are still blue."

Then he took her hand in his, pressed his lips to her palm and everything around her began to shimmer and shift.

Kara's living room flickered around her, as if she were caught inside a TV with choppy reception. Then with a low soothing hum, the world smoothed and she found herself on the singed rug in front of her fireplace and draped across Risk's naked body.

She placed her palm over the hole where the ember had fallen just hours earlier. The wool pile was rough and crunchy, the fist-sized spot of wood floor exposed beneath it cool to her touch.

"Risk?" She blinked, her head fuzzy from the influx of power and her strange trip home.

He slid his hand up her arm. "You're okay," he murmured.

She nodded and sat up. "What happened? How'd we get here? The man, the dog, then you? I was pulling in power, and it felt good." A shiver raced over her. "Too good."

"Dangerous," he said, his eyes tired.

"But…?" She didn't know what to ask first…where to even begin.

"You first. Tell me why you were at the Guardian's Keep, everything that happened there."

"Are you okay?" she asked. He hadn't moved more than his arm since they…she glanced around the room…arrived back at her house.

"Just a little drained." A mocking smile tilted his lips. Then he brushed a lock of hair back from her face. "I'm fine. You talk."

Kara hesitated, not convinced he was okay and unsure where to start with her own adventures.

He squeezed her hand and gave her a nod.

Still not convinced he was all right, she took a deep breath and began talking. "After you left, I went to the bar." She edged a look at him. He had told her to wait.

He frowned.

"I talked to the bartender. He was…difficult. And weird,

well, not him so much as what happened there." She told Risk about following the bartender through the doorway and finding herself back where she'd started. "Then I tried again and this time I was outside the bar."

Interest flashed through his eyes.

Kara rushed on, the reality of what she was describing unsettling her. "And then this nasty little man attacked me, snuck up on me somehow. He had a knife and this other thing. He called it a stunner. Then the dog came, and I was pulling the power, and then—" She stopped abruptly not sure what else to say.

Risk pushed himself onto one elbow. "What about the bartender, did he say anything?"

"To go home. Then some gobbledygook about telling my hellhound the guardian said to keep me away. Oh, and he said bull-headed little witches had a habit of disappearing around there." Kara knew she was speaking too fast. She snapped her mouth shut, stared at Risk for a second, then continued more slowly. "That bar has something to do with Kelly and her friend, I know it." Relieved she had gotten the story out, she folded her hands in her lap.

"He called himself the guardian?" Now sitting upright, knees bent, Risk leaned forward, his eyes intense.

"Yeah, Guardian's Keep, the guardian. I guess that's what he was talking about." Her gaze wandered over Risk's bare chest and arms. The late afternoon light leaking through the front window caught in the silver hairs on his forearms.

Lost in thought, he rested his arm on his knee.

He was so comfortable in his nudity, almost as if he noticed no difference from being fully clothed.

His thigh brushed against Kara's arm. Her anxiety melted as heat pooled in her core.

"I need to go." He stood.

"Wait." Kara pressed her hand to his shoulder. He couldn't leave yet.

He stared at her, waiting.

"Uh, what about the dog?" She threw out the first question she could latch on to. "Do you think that's the hell-hound the bartender mentioned? Have you ever heard of a hellhound?"

His eyes went from alert to guarded. "Hellhounds were used by the gods to hunt souls of the evil. Until the wild hunt was deserted, that is."

"The evil? But I'm not evil." The word hit her in the chest, memories of the power flooding into her and the thoughts of leaving her attacker to face the dog alone, of killing him and the dog. "Am I?" she added, her voice quiet.

"No." He tilted her face to his, brushed hair away from her eyes. "You are not evil."

"Then why—"

"Hounds used to run in the wild hunt, but that was a thousand years ago. Now they…they exist however they can."

"So?" Kara was completely lost.

"So, you aren't evil." He wove his fingers into her hair, massaging her scalp.

Kara pressed her head against his hand and closed her eyes. His fingers kneaded their way down the back of her head, stopping at the nape of her neck. She tilted back her head, a soft moan leaving her lips.

"What else did the garm say?" he asked.

Her eyes fluttered open. "Garm. What's a garm?"

A line cut between his brows. "The bartender."

"He's a garm?"

His hand still pressed to the back of her neck, he pulled her toward him until she fell, cradled in his arms. Brushing his lips over hers, he whispered, "Perhaps."

Kara rested her palm on his firm chest. His heart beat a steady rhythm against her hand. Risk lowered his mouth, and captured her lips, his tongue slipping inside. He smelled vaguely of smoke and man, and Kara wanted nothing more than to curl up against him forever, forget everything to do with magic, hellhounds, and vile little men with magical stun guns.

"You're beautiful and innocent. No amount of power could turn you into Lusse," Risk murmured against her ear. Pulling her hair back, he trailed kisses down her neck.

Lusse, his boss. Kara frowned at the mention of another woman when they were in such an intimate position, his erection pressing against her side emphasizing just how intimate.

Holding her in his arms, he twisted to a kneel, then released her body, letting it slide slowly down the length of his. When she was kneeling in front of him, he ran his hand from her thigh, over her buttocks and up under her shirt. His hand burning into her bare skin, he lowered his mouth to hers again.

She placed both hands on his hips, skimming the indentation of muscle over his abdomen with her thumbs. His tongue plunged into her mouth with new intensity.

Her back arched, pushing her pelvis against his erection. Murmuring something against her lips, he pushed his hands under her shirt and released her bra. His hands cupped her breasts, his thumbs rolling her nipples until she wanted to scream from anticipation.

Her eyes closed, she threw her head back. Risk pulled her shirt and bra over her head, and lowered his lips to her nipple. Muscles deep in her body clenched.

The world pulsed around her. Her hands wrapped around his lowered neck, she straightened and opened her eyes. It was happening again. She could see the power throbbing around them, violet and red blending together, forming a cerise mist that tinted everything.

She sighed, her mind accepting what only days earlier would have startled and confused her, but it felt so right—her power and Risk's blending to make something so beautiful.

Risk's power. Red.

The dog had been surrounded by red.

A cold chill crept up Kara's back. No. It was impossible. Risk couldn't be…

Risk's hand slid down to the front of her jeans. The purr of her zipper moving downward, pushing her to speak.

"Risk, why did the bartender say that about the hell-hound?" she whispered.

Risk froze, his fingers brushing the mound of hair covering her core.

"I mean like I belonged to it or something. And then the man, the one who attacked me, he was talking to that dog." She ran her fingers over his chest, willing him to say something rational and easy to push aside.

Cool air touched her nipples, damp from Risk's kisses. She suppressed a shiver. Why wasn't he answering?

"Risk?"

His head was bowed, his eyes lowered.

Unease crawled over her.

He pulled his hand from her jeans and reached for her shirt. "Kara, we need to talk."

Kara could only stare at him. Her mouth forming a silent *no*.

Risk pushed Kara away from him, afraid to tell her what he knew had to be revealed with her pressed against his body.

Her eyes were round with dread, but she took the shirt he retrieved from the floor with steady hands.

She could handle this, he told himself—learning he was a hellhound wouldn't matter. Even knowing he had been sent to bring her back to Lusse in what amounted to a death sentence and that he still was bound to obey Lusse, to retrieve not only Kara, but now Kelly, too, she could accept that. Understand, that together, they could beat Lusse at her own hunt—somehow.

She had to.

But how to tell her? Deciding on the most direct approach, he stood. "Watch me," he ordered.

Her eyes filled with uncertainty, she curled her knees toward herself and watched.

"Don't move," he added, then shimmered to his cabin. There he quickly grabbed a pair of jeans. Now was not a time to be naked with Kara. She was too tempting and too much rode on how she took what he was about to tell her.

Telling himself, all would be well. He returned to her living room.

Kara still sat on the rug, her eyes staring blankly out into the room.

"What are you?" she asked, not moving her gaze. "I know you're not a witch—you would have told me."

"No, I'm not a witch. I'm a forandre." A place to start. The full truth would come. He lowered himself to the floor a few feet away from her. "You know I said I work for a witch?"

She looked at him then, nodding.

"It's more than that. My parents sold me to her when I was eight."

Her eyes showed her shock. "Your parents sold you? How can that be? Is that legal…" she paused, her mind obviously working to sort through the possibilities "…anywhere?"

He laughed. "It's more than legal. In my world, especially at that time, it was considered an honor. Every family wanted one of theirs to be bound to a great power—a god or if they were strong enough, a witch. And Lusse is the strongest." He glanced at her, thought of how she had drained away his power in the parking lot with an ease Lusse had never possessed. "Or was."

"So, you're bound to this witch. What does that mean, and what is a forandre? What does she want from you?" Kara pulled her knees tighter, as if shielding herself from the answers.

Three questions. Risk chose the first. "It means I can't escape her. I belong to her. If I try to ignore what she asks of me, she can starve me, torture me, whatever she wants and no one will stop her. If I try to escape…" He reached up and grabbed the silver chain at his neck. "She calls me back. I am bound to do her bidding."

Kara's brows lowered, her full lips falling open. "That's awful. How long has it been?"

"Five hundred years."

Five hundred years? Kara blinked. "But that means you're…immortal." That was too much. Magic okay, doorways that took you back where you started maybe—but the virile man she'd made love to…five hundred years old? No. That was impossible. She looked at Risk, waiting for him to correct her.

"Not immortal."

Kara let out a breath.

"But close."

She inhaled through her teeth. "How close?"

"Forandre can be killed. It's just hard for anyone besides another forandre or a god to do it."

"What about old age?" she asked, not even sure her lips were moving—the world she had just been dropped in was so surreal.

He shrugged. "My father was eight hundred when I left. I don't know if he's still alive or not." His fingers curled into his palms.

Kara stared at his balled fist. "So, thirteen hundred years old?"

He flicked his hands open. "Maybe, maybe less. He could be dead by now." He swallowed hard, stared down at his fingers.

A band constricted around Kara's heart. Five hundred years Risk had spent bound to another person. His family cut off from him, possibly dead. At least she'd had her parents until she was out of high school, an adult—and then Kelly…

"How do you keep going?" she asked, longing to go to him, to comfort him, even though he'd made no indication he wanted that. But something kept her planted on the rug, something in his posture telling her more was to come.

He frowned. "I didn't think I had another choice, until recently."

Kara tilted her head. "So, you think you do now?"

He nodded. "I do, but there's more I have to tell you."

She pulled her lip into her mouth.

"You asked why the hellhound wanted you." He flexed his fingers. "He was sent to hunt you down. To take you back to the witch he's bound to. So she could drain your powers to bolster her own."

"He…it is bound to a witch? Like…you?" Pieces of conversation, snippets of events from the last few days began tumbling through Kara's mind. Then one by one they snapped into place and Kara looked up, her hand covering her mouth. "No."

"Exactly like me," Risk responded.

Kara stared at him, trying to imagine the man who had stroked her so gently, made love to her as no one ever had before, made her feel stronger than she ever thought she could…tried to imagine him as the snarling beast of her nightmares. "But you can't be…I mean…It's a dog. You're a man."

"Forandre. A shape-shifter."

Kara jumped to her feet, her hands held out in front of her. "You were the dog in the parking lot—the one who attacked me?"

He shook his head. "No, I was the second hound. The one who saved you from the first."

Kara's mind was whirling. "But you were there to…?"

"To capture you for Lusse. It's true."

"But you've never hurt…" She let the word trail off. She could see the hideous truth in his eyes.

"And Kelly? Is that why you wanted to find her, too?"

He nodded. "Twin witches are very rare. Legendary. Lusse wants you both, but I also hoped you could…you might be able to break her hold on me."

Kara stared at him as if she'd never seen him before. He'd never wanted to help her. He just wanted to use her and Kelly to save himself. "And after we helped you?"

His held out his hands. "I don't know."

Chapter 12

How could he not know? Kara knew—thought Risk knew. Even though she hadn't said the words, hadn't even let them form in her mind—she knew.

She loved him.

How could he stand there and stare at her telling her he didn't know?

Maybe she had fooled *herself* more than Risk had fooled her. Maybe his ability to shift into a beast straight from her nightmares wasn't the only thing she had been blinded to. Maybe she was nothing more to him than a means to an end—chattel to deliver to his boss or a tool to use for his own benefit.

Could she even believe his story now? How did she know that his family had sold him, that he was really bound to some witch, or that he was the dog. Each piece was more fantastical than the last. Wouldn't she be a fool to believe any of it?

"Show me," she ordered. "Turn into the dog."

"What?" He looked at her, brows lowered.

"Change. I want to see for myself that you really are that dog."

"Kara." He held out one hand and took a step toward her.

She raised her own hand, palm out. "Stop. Either change or leave. I don't have time to sort through all this right now, to worry about the man that I—just change or get out." Her voice cracked at the end. This was the only way. She had to know at least part of his story was true.

Risk stared at Kara standing there, her face firm, but the slight quaver in her voice and the pheromones rolling off her giving away her fear.

If he changed here in front of her, what would happen? Would she accept him for what he was, or run—never able to accept his demon half?

Her best friend had been killed by a dog, a mundane stray, and she still bore the scars. How could she possibly accept Risk after actually witnessing his change?

He dropped his hand. It didn't matter. He couldn't do it. It was hard enough to stand here and see the uncertainty in her eyes. Revulsion. Terror. To see those after the softness and concern she'd shown moments earlier would be more than he could bear.

Lusse was right. Just this short touch of a human existence, a human relationship, and he was weak. Open to a hurt he'd never even known existed.

"I can't," he replied.

Relief, confusion, anger, and finally, resolve flowed across Kara's face.

"Then leave." She pointed toward her door.

Risk hesitated for only an instant, then turned and headed to her door. He couldn't even bring himself to shimmer. Even that small natural act brought more strongly to mind the differences between them and the unforgettable fact that at his core, he was in her eyes a monster.

Kara watched Risk drive off. She didn't know why he bothered with a car at all. She'd seen his power to dissipate like mist, then reform miles away. She'd apparently experienced it herself. That at least explained her journeys from the bar to his cabin and her house.

Why keep the Jeep?

What did it matter? She pulled the drapes closed with an angry whoosh. He surely had his reasons. None of which were important to Kara.

Her arms folded over her chest, she sat down on the couch. The couch where she and Risk—

No. She wouldn't think about that.

Risk had lied to her, over and over. Making her believe he wanted to help her, that he cared about her.

Okay, he hadn't said the words, but— She picked up a pillow and shoved her fist into its middle.

That was enough.

As far as the rest of it, maybe he was the dog, maybe he wasn't. Kara wasn't sure how she felt about that. She had hated dogs for so long, feared them. To think the man she'd made love to was… She laughed. God. The entire thing was insane. That she might even contemplate a relationship with such a being was beyond ludicrous.

But it was Risk, a tiny voice in her head reminded her.

She squished the square pillow into a ball and buried her face in it.

Why now? Why did he have to drop this on her now? When she had a real lead to finding Kelly. When things were looking up in her life.

Why couldn't he have just gone on pretending a little longer?

She jerked her face away from the pillow. Damn it. Was that all she wanted—pretense? Was she that pathetic?

Dropping the pillow onto the floor, she stood up.

Okay, so Risk didn't love her. So she'd come close to making a fool of herself and endangering both herself and Kelly. She hadn't. She'd made Risk leave.

Now she was alone—no worse off than she'd been before. Better off. She was wiser, knew about her powers, knew the key was at that bar.

She could do this by herself. She didn't need Risk.

No, that same tiny voice murmured, *but you want him.*

Risk drove as fast as the Jeep would go, the doors and undercarriage rattling as if pieces would fly off at any moment. He'd left when Kara had asked him, but he couldn't walk away.

Lusse wouldn't let him, but that wasn't all. It was Kara. He couldn't desert her. She might want nothing more to do with him, but he had to do what he could to make sure she was safe.

Maybe if he didn't bring her and her sister to Lusse, Lusse would kill him. Of course, that would solve nothing. Lusse would just send another hound to hunt them down—maybe Venge.

Risk whacked his fist against the steering wheel.

There had to be a way out. Kara might never accept the reality of what he was, but there had to be a way to save her from Lusse and whatever else was stalking witches in her world.

Gravel and dust flew from the back tires as he took the turn that would take him through the portal and to his secret escape.

He'd found the doorway centuries earlier. The worlds were littered with portals, most of them just like this, leading to one small pocket of alternative reality.

No one bothered guarding a portal like this—unless it was the being that claimed the patch of world on the other side. But the portal Lusse'd described—one that a forandre as powerful as a garm would protect—that had to be something else entirely.

Lead either to a number of worlds—or one claimed by a very powerful being.

A powerful being who even right now could be stalking Kara.

Another taxi ride brought Kara back to the Guardian's Keep. She slammed the cab's door and strode to the bar's entrance.

This time she wasn't leaving until she found out who had her sister. Ignoring the sign swinging overhead, she yanked open the door and placed her slush-covered boots firmly inside. Take no prisoners. Take no flak. That was her new motto—at least for tonight.

The bar was busy again—as it had been the first night. Every table and booth was full, all but two bar stools occupied.

The same uncooperative bartender stood behind the bar, his gaze traveling over the crowd.

Staring down a cocktail waitress who swung past her, tray loaded with drinks, Kara forged a path toward one of the empty stools.

"Whiskey. And information." She dropped a twenty onto the wood.

The bartender picked up the bill, wadded it into a ball and set it back in front of her.

"Go home." He grabbed a bottle from under the bar and filled the glass of a man sitting nearby.

Kara tugged off her leather gloves one finger at a time. "I'm not leaving. I know you know something."

"Do you?" He shrugged and swept some change off the bar into his waiting palm.

Kara stared after him, her resolve still strong. "And I know there's something funny about that door over there," she called.

"Really?" He cocked his head at her, then slapped an ashtray down in front of a soup-kitchen reject a few feet away.

Kara pursed her lips. She would not be put off. Not this time. What was it Risk had called him?

"Garm," she muttered.

"What was that?" He turned, spilling cigarette butts into the ice.

"Garm. You're a garm." She'd surprised him that time. Her lips curved upward.

He stared at her for the count of five, long enough that Kara felt the need to shift in her seat, but she didn't. She held her place, and kept her gaze solid.

Finally, he shook his head. "You don't know anything."

He went back to gathering dirty ashtrays, his tapered back straight.

Kara exhaled, her shoulders dropping a fraction. He had to tell her something. He had to. She stared at the balled-up twenty, willing her brain to come up with a plan.

The bartender glanced back at her and sighed. After grabbing a glass and a bottle of whiskey, he strode toward her.

"It's for your own good," he muttered, sloshing the liquid into the glass three fingers high. "Not all that go in come back out, and none of the witches."

Her face still lowered, she peered up at him.

He sighed again. "I tried to warn the other one, but she…" he let out an exasperated grunt "…was worse than you. Stomping around, making sure every magic-hungry thug within three worlds knew what she was. Know what it got her?" He leaned forward, his ice-blue eyes spearing Kara. "Nothing." He shook his head, his hand caressing the neck of the whiskey bottle.

"At least she hasn't come back out yet. May mean she's still alive, but for what? Nothing good going on down there. That's as sure as a wolf's howl." He picked the bottle up and slammed it under the counter.

"Anyway, once the toll's been set and met, there's nothing I can do to stop it."

A new patron slid in between two stools and signaled for a drink. With a scowl, the bartender grabbed the bottle of whiskey and turned to leave.

"Wait," Kara called. He was talking about Kelly, she knew it. Finally, someone had started talking to her. Kara couldn't let him get away now.

He paused.

"A toll? You said there's a toll, how much is it?" Kara

didn't have a lot of spare cash, but she and Kelly owned their small house outright. It had to be worth a decent sum.

He laughed, a you-have-to-be-kidding sound.

"For you? Not much. Witches don't pay the toll."

The patron waiting for his drink picked up an empty bottle and banged it on the counter.

The bartender shot him a killing look. The man dropped it and scurried away from the bar.

Muttering under his breath, the bartender turned to walk away.

Kara threw herself across the bar and wrapped her hands around his forearm. "Wait. You said witches don't pay the toll. I'm a witch—I can prove it." She released his arm to free her hands.

"You have no more sense than the other one. Do you know what kind of beings are in here?" He grabbed both her hands in one of his, then just as quickly let go.

Kara placed her palms flat on the bar and glanced around. The bar was lined with men and women interchangeable with the one who'd attacked her earlier—dull, lifeless, even their clothing lacking in color as if they were trapped in some old sepia-tinted photo.

The bartender recaptured her hand and squeezed until she thought a bone might pop. "Desperate. That's what kind. Doesn't matter if they're forandre, giant or dwarf. Or even demon or god. If they're here, they're desperate, and that makes them the most dangerous of their kind."

Kara stared down at his hand. His darker, larger hand made hers look delicate, defenseless. But she wasn't. She looked back up at him. "Well, I'm desperate, too. And from what I hear, I was already one of the most powerful of my kind."

The woman sitting closest to them edged sideways—away from them and the tension thickening the air.

Kara waited, her heart beating in her ears. Would he call her bluff? Was it a bluff? She had no idea exactly what she would or could do to get what she wanted anymore.

Brows lowered, he pulled his hand away and crossed his arms over his chest. "Not my job to save you. You want to know why witches don't pay the toll, can't pay the toll? 'Cause witches *are* the toll.

"You want to go where the stubborn little bit like you went? Do what she did. Announce to any of these fine customers what you are, and they'll happily stick a knife to your neck and escort you through the doorway."

Kara's eyes darted down the bar.

The bartender picked up her drink and set it back down with a bang. "But don't do it here. I don't need a fight breaking out tonight." He pushed the glass toward her with one finger. "Oh, and don't plan on coming back. As I said earlier, a jaunt through that doorway, is a one-way journey—at least for witches."

He strode away.

Kara edged her eyes from left to right. Giants, dwarves, demons, gods? Could anyone in this dreary place be a god? She picked up her glass, the amber liquid sloshing out onto her hand. She didn't believe in a god or gods, remember? At least she thought she remembered thinking that sometime in the past.

Of course, what had she believed in the past? She couldn't remember.

From behind her, breath as cold as an icicle scraped over her skin; a tinny voice whispered in her ear, "I'll help you out."

"No, let me." A second voice oozed over her like fog.

Kara whirled, looking for the source of either voice. No one was near her. In fact even the woman who had edged away from Kara earlier during her argument with the bartender had left.

The entire bar was empty except for Kara and the bartender. From the other end of the bar, he gave her a sad smile. "I warned you."

"Where did everyone go?" Kara asked.

He jerked his thumb toward the front door. "Waiting. They know I won't put up with trouble in here. They're out there."

Kara pulled a black vinyl-covered chair under one of the windows and stepped onto it. Using her balled fist to clean a place through the grime, she stared out into the growing dark. There were a few loiterers, a man with a ball cap flipped backward, a woman dressed in velvet and high-top tennis shoes, but in general the street was empty. Just an occasional whirlwind of snow dancing across the parking lot.

"You won't be able to see most of them. Not if they don't want you to. They're all different, except that desperation thing I mentioned, but they can all hide well enough you won't know what's got a hold of you until two, or more, of them are fighting over you."

He picked up a dirty ashtray and dumped the butts in the trash. "Good news, though. This toll has conditions—you don't arrive alive, you aren't worth nothing."

Kara hopped down from the chair before her shaking legs forced her down.

"Course, a lot of them aren't that smart. Wouldn't be the first time one of them missed a detail like that."

Kara bent at the waist; her hands gripped around the top of the chair and she filled her lungs with air. He was just trying to scare her.

She glanced around the empty bar.

Besides, there was no turning back now.

Risk pulled his Jeep into the lean-to behind his cabin and shimmered inside to grab a shirt and boots. He was already regretting the time he had wasted driving up the road, but his power to shimmer another mass didn't extend to something as big and inanimate as the Jeep. And when he'd first driven off, he hadn't been thinking of his hunt—just of Kara and the image of horror in her eyes.

This human weakness had to stop. The best way to save Kara was to stop thinking of her as a woman and start thinking of her as just another witch he had to retrieve.

Dressed, he pressed his palms against the rough stones of his fireplace and concentrated. He would go to the garm, force the wolf forandre to let him pass, and retrieve Kara's sister. After that he would… His mind grasped for a solution.

He smacked the rock with his closed fist; a chunk of stone smashed against the floor. He picked it up, let the sharp edges dig into his palm.

There had to be a solution, and he would find it, but for now he would just concentrate on the first step in his plan. Time to intimidate the garm.

Focusing on the area outside the bar, he prepared to shimmer. The first tingles had started crawling up his arms when he heard it—the eerie peel of Lusse's horn.

Damn the witch. She was calling him back again.

Chapter 13

Risk arrived in Lusse's parlor again. She was sitting in her velvet chair flanked by Bader, who held the horn, and Sigurd. The other hound shot Risk a challenging stare.

Risk ignored him.

"Lusse," Risk said, a tinge of his impatience leaking into his voice.

"Risk?" She arched one brow.

He breathed in. This was not the time to antagonize her, not when he was so close to finding Kara's sister. He curved his lips into a smile. "I hadn't expected to see you again so soon."

She tapped white-tinted nails on the arm of her chair. "Is my call a problem?"

He stepped forward. "Of course not. I was just on my way to confront the garm."

"So, you found him." She tilted her head toward Sigurd.

"Sigurd suggested perhaps you were getting sidetracked. He heard…rumors."

Where had Sigurd been that he would be hearing anything involving Risk's activity in the human world? "I didn't realize Sigurd was so trusted."

She tipped just the ends of her lips upward. "Yes, well, it's always good to have a backup plan, don't you think? With Venge…detained. I needed another option. Sigurd stepped forward."

The other male crossed his arms over his chest.

"No need. I will question the garm as soon as we are done here."

"And the witch?" Lusse asked.

"Safe. I'm sure it won't take me long to retrieve the sister," Risk replied.

"But what will you do once you've retrieved her?" Sigurd asked, dropping his arms to his side, his chest expanding.

"Did you need anything else from me before I go capture your witch?" Risk asked, his gaze on Lusse.

Lusse twisted in her chair, her eyes drifting over the two men. With a smile, she turned back to Risk. "Don't you have an answer for Sigurd?"

"Oh." Risk angled his head. "Did he ask something?"

Bader clasped the horn, his hands turning white from the effort.

Risk's gaze jumped from the old servant to Sigurd. "I apologize. Did you say something?"

Sigurd clenched his jaw, his eyebrows lowering. "You heard me. Talk is that the witch you were sent to find has a new pet. A hellhound."

Risk kept his face still. "Of course, I've been with her. How else could I use her to find the sister?"

"Or maybe she's using you. I can smell the humanity on you." Sigurd curled his lip.

"I'm surprised you can smell anything over the stench of your jealousy." Risk turned his gaze to Lusse. "I'm close. If you have no objection, I'll—"

With a roar, Sigurd changed from man to beast.

Kara straightened. "Why can't I just pay the toll myself? With myself?"

The bartender picked up a towel and rubbed a glass dry. "'Cause I'm the guardian. I get the basics from the things on the other side of that doorway, what they want. I decide the details and what I want. And detail number one is no witch is giving herself up.

"You want to get through that door? Show enough balls to deal with one of them—" he pointed to the wall behind her "—out there. I guarantee you, desperate as they are—they've got nothing on what's beyond that door." He twisted his finger to point behind him.

Kara stared over his shoulder toward the dark doorway to which he'd gestured. Where did that thing lead? "Is it h-hell?" she asked.

He snorted. "No such place, at least not like you're thinking of. Besides, in this case it isn't the place you need to fear, but what's living there, and how bad he wants out."

"Is it—"

He held up one hand, interrupting her. "We're hitting those details again. I'm done. Time for you to pick your fate."

Kara walked to the front door and placed her hands against the chipped paint. She could do this. She had to.

"You want, I can call that hellhound of yours. He can get you out of here."

Call Risk? Kara didn't even bother asking the bartender how he would do it—it didn't matter. Shaking her head, she placed her hand on the doorknob.

The door burst open before she could even turn the metal ball. Her hooded attacker from earlier fell inside, his knife clattering onto the floor beside him.

The bartender walked to the end of the bar to scowl at the new arrival. "We're closed."

Her attacker looked up at the bartender then pushed himself to a sit. "I lost something here earlier. Had to leave in a bit of a hurry. Just stopping back to see if I could—"

Kara stepped out of the shadows and the man froze. Using the heels of his feet, he scooted backward. Eyes wide, he held up one arm as if to ward her off. "I didn't hurt you none. Don't be turning your hellhound on me."

Kara glanced from the man to the bartender, whose frown darkened.

She squatted onto the floor next to the man, and grabbed his foot as he made a move to put more distance between them. "I want you to take me through the doorway."

His mouth fell open, revealing twisted, yellowed teeth. "No."

With a light smile, the bartender shrugged and reached for another glass.

"It will be worth your while. I promise," Kara urged.

"Even a giant's cauldron of gold won't help me if your hound gets me first." The man successfully jerked his foot from her grasp, curled his legs into his chest and glowered at her.

"What about two cauldrons? I'm really valuable," she replied.

"Two?" The man's gaze darted to the bartender.

The bartender shook his head. "I just know the toll, not the reward or price once you fill it."

The man edged forward, his eyes darting from side to side before settling on Kara's face. "What makes you think you're so valuable? That Jormun will pay more for you?"

The bartender made a hissing noise between his teeth. "No names, Narr."

Narr tossed another cautious gaze around the empty room. Then reached out to grab Kara around the wrist. "What's your talent?"

Narr's rough hand bit into Kara's skin, and he smelled of old beer and sweat. But he was a helluva better bargain than whatever waited for her outside the Guardian's Keep.

"I'm a twin. A twin witch. And this…" she glanced at the bartender and lowered her voice "…Jormun you mentioned. He already has my sister." At least she thought he did, and was willing to gamble her own life on that belief.

A small intake of breath signaled Narr's excitement. He rubbed his hands together, glee shining from his eyes. "So, he needs you more than the others."

He pulled his ratty hoodie close around his face and mumbled to himself. "Should be worth an extra cauldron, but—" He tightened his grip on Kara's wrist. "What about the hound? I don't want to be messing with no hound."

"He's not here is he?" she asked.

"Don't mean he won't show up. Forandre." He narrowed his eyes to stare at the bartender. "They're a territorial bunch."

Kara licked her lips and tried to ignore the pain shooting through her arm from his viselike grip. "He shows up later, you tell him I asked you to do it. Tell him it was you, or them." She shifted her gaze to the front door and whatever lay waiting for her outside.

"Yeah. Yeah. That's true enough. Barely made it through the desperates myself. Be like I'm doing a good deed. He'd see that, right?"

The bartender grunted.

Kara nodded. "Exactly."

Dear God, let the man take her through that doorway before Risk showed up.

Sigurd stood in front of Risk, four broad feet planted firmly apart, his head lowered, and his lips pulled back in a snarl.

Risk watched him through narrowed eyes. Hound against human was an unfair fight, but Risk would be damned if he would acknowledge the other male's challenge by changing, too.

"This is why you can never be alpha, Sigurd. It has nothing to do with me. I'm not your competition. You taunt me for having too much humanity. You don't have enough. You can't think when the bloodlust is on you. In your hound form it's even worse, isn't it? Can you even follow what I'm saying to you?"

The black hound stepped to the side, circling Risk.

"Confused aren't you? So what if you kill me like this? It won't gain you anything. The others will know you were weak. That you had to change to gain the courage to face me."

The black dog growled deep in his throat.

Risk stared him down. This wasn't like Sigurd. Yes, he was jealous of Risk, hated him, but he wasn't this stupid, and he would never attack Risk in front of Lusse unless he'd been encouraged.

Sigurd wasn't his problem here. It was Lusse, as always.

This time he needed to address her, head-on. He spun

on his heel until he faced her, Sigurd still in his line of vision, but barely.

"What are you trying to do, Lusse?" he asked.

She flicked her gaze from her nails to Risk. "Me? You know what I want."

"I'll bring you your witches, but I can't do it from here. Release me, so I can finish the hunt."

She placed a fingertip against her bloodred lips. "The witches. Yes, I want the witches, but I also want to know my alpha is dedicated to me. After the stories…" She glanced at Sigurd, who shifted his weight slightly from side to side. "How can I trust you haven't lost your strength? You tell Sigurd humanity gives logic during bloodlust, but we both know that's a lie. Humanity offers nothing but doubt, hesitation, weakness."

She tapped her finger against her lips. "I think I'll prove it right now." She flicked her hand toward Sigurd.

From the corner of his eye, Risk saw the hound lunge. He raised his arm, blocking the gaping jaws headed for his throat.

Sigurd's teeth sank into his forearm through muscle all the way to bone. Gritting his own teeth against the pain, Risk shifted his gaze to Lusse.

"Oh," she added. "Forandre rules. Each of you in your weakest form, and didn't you just admit for Sigurd that was hound?"

Damn the witch.

Narr glanced around the bar again, his hand tugging Kara's wrist close to his chest. He gave it another tug, pulling her in, close to his face. "This isn't a trick? You won't fight me?"

Forcing herself not to turn her head away from the sour

smell of his breath, Kara shook her head. "No. No trick. I'll go now."

"Yeah, now is good." Narr grinned and jumped to his feet with surprising agility. His fingers still wrapped around her wrist, he tugged her toward the bar. "I got my toll, garm," he announced.

The bartender stared at them for a second, his expression unreadable.

Narr stepped closer and slapped her arm against the wood. "I got my toll and I'm demanding passage."

The bartender narrowed his eyes. "Demanding, Narr?"

Narr cringed slightly, but held his ground. "Don't be getting all beastie on me. I know the rules. I got the toll. You have to let me pass."

The bartender growled, but flipped open the hinged portion of the bar and stepped beside them. "Unfortunately, you're right. But don't be expecting any favors from me when her hound comes hunting."

Narr shot Kara a nervous glance. Afraid the bartender might still talk him out of taking her through the doorway, she patted his arm with her free hand. "Don't worry. He isn't *my* hellhound."

The bartender laughed.

Kara changed her pat to a stroke. "And if he does come looking for me, just tell him what I said."

Narr nodded and took a step forward. "We're ready, garm."

Sigurd pulled his massive head left then right, trying to tear the flesh from Risk's arm.

Just a week earlier Risk would have taken Lusse at her word and let Sigurd rip out his throat, but now there was too much at stake. Too many other lives depending on him—lives he now had to admit, at least to himself, he cared about.

Sigurd clenched his jaws tighter around Risk's arm. His eyes were crazed and glowing red against black fur.

He was slipping quickly into the bloodlust. If Risk hesitated, Sigurd would surrender completely and Risk would have little chance of escaping to find and save Kara's sister.

Murmuring a quiet apology for using what he knew was an unfair fight move, Risk pulled back his hand and shoved two fingers into Sigurd's glowing eyes.

With a howl, the hound released him. Blood streaming from his eyes, he pawed at his injuries. Knowing Lusse would be satisfied with nothing less than a full knockout—if not a kill—Risk stepped forward; his knee flying upward with the motion, he caught the dog under the chin and sent him flying backward.

Not waiting to see if the other male would rise, Risk closed the space between them and pinned him to the ground. As the giant beast struggled to get his back feet into position to kick Risk off, Risk wrapped his good hand in the chain around Sigurd's neck and twisted.

Sigurd's head swung, his jaws open and one tooth scraping Risk across the cheek. Sweat beaded on Risk's forehead as he twisted the chain tighter.

"Pass out, Sigurd, you slow-witted cur. I'm not your enemy. Lusse is and you're giving her everything she wants," he muttered against the dog's ear.

Whether the dog heard him or just couldn't continue, Risk couldn't tell, but all fight seemed to leave the beast. Spittle leaking from between his jaws, tension left Sigurd's limbs and he collapsed on the floor beneath Risk.

Lusse pushed herself out of her chair and strolled over. "Well, that was rather disappointing, wasn't it?" She looked at Risk, her lips twisting.

"You got your answer. I'm still the strongest you have." Risk shoved Sigurd's body away and stood.

Her arms folded over her chest, Lusse tapped the toe of her riding boot. "Fine. You proved yourself for now. But when you find the second witch—I want to know immediately. Or the lock on Venge's cage might just work itself loose."

She lifted one of Sigurd's paws with the top of her foot then let it flop to the floor. "I'm sure if Sigurd isn't recovered, one of the other hounds would be more than happy to challenge the whelp. Especially if word of his lineage just happened to leak out."

Without another word, Risk spun and strode from the room, shimmering midstep.

Shaking his head, the bartender reached behind the bar and pulled out two luminous straps, like the plastic ties police used on drunken crowds except shiny and somehow much more dangerous looking.

"What are those?" Kara asked, her gaze darting to the silvery strips in his hand.

"Part of the process," the bartender replied as he motioned for Narr to hold out her hands. With a deft movement, the bartender wrapped a strip around her left wrist, then slipped the second through the first and around her right. With a snap, the two tightened like industrial rubber bands, locking her wrists against each other.

Kara pulled. Even though she couldn't feel the bands

against her skin, her wrists didn't budge. "Why do I need these? I'm going freely," she asked the bartender.

"It's part of the—"

"Rules," Kara finished for him.

He frowned. "They insure you won't attack anyone as soon as you arrive."

Kara spread her fingers and bent back her hands as if she were making a shadow puppet of a bird flying. She could still use her hands, or at least as much as she needed to for magic. She smiled.

The garm pushed her hands down. "Don't be getting hopeful. They don't just hold your wrists. They bind your magic. With these on, you couldn't light a candle soaked in whale oil."

Kara's hands slapped together and her head dropped. She stared at the round toe of the bartender's black military boot. How would she free Kelly when she found her, if she couldn't use her magic?

"We doing this?" Narr grumbled, grabbing her by the elbow.

"I'm ready. How about you, witch? You still determined to get through this doorway?" the bartender asked.

Kara looked up. The garm watched her, his blue eyes appraising. Meeting his blue gaze with her own, she replied, "I'm ready." Access to her power or not, she was going to find Kelly.

"All right." The bartender stepped behind the bar, fiddled with his computer for a second, then looked up. "They're expecting you."

Narr took a step forward, jerking Kara with him.

"Witch," the bartender called.

She turned her neck to see him.

"Keep your nose down and your ears up. And remember…"

Narr took another step toward the doorway; Kara leaned back to hear the garm's last words.

"In the other worlds, things aren't hardly ever what you think they are."

Narr tightened his grip on her arm. "Gotta go. Them outside'll be getting restless."

With a nod, Kara took a deep breath and strode into the murky darkness in front of her.

Chapter 14

The sound of water whooshed around Kara. It was dark, hot and humid, like a rainforest at midnight. Only the thin strips around her wrists showed, pearly lines that bounced with her steps.

"They're near. I can smell 'em. You smell 'em?" Narr whispered in her ear.

With Narr by her side, Kara could smell little else. She bit her lip and lowered her face to her shoulder, wiping a ribbon of sweat away. "Who…what are they?" she whispered back.

"You'll see soon enough. The drop-off's up ahead a bit. Just walk fast. I don't like spending no more time than I have to out here." With that, he grabbed Kara's bicep and pulled her along.

* * *

Risk materialized in the Guardian Keep's parking lot. Energy throbbed around him, the air heavy with the scent of greed and desperation.

Something brushed against him, whispering in his ear, "Go home, little doggy."

He turned, his hands grasping for whatever taunted him. A laugh danced across the icy ground.

A woman dressed in a short green velvet jacket and purple high-top tennis shoes dropped a cigarette butt into the snow and stepped on it. Her gaze fixed on Risk, she muttered a curse and turned to leave, gesturing to something or someone Risk couldn't see.

"What's happening here?" Risk called.

She paused, then turned, her head cocked. "Nothing now that you've arrived."

Something trailed over Risk's face, caressing his torn skin. A cold wind whipped around his body, spraying snow and tiny ice shards into his eyes. The voice he had heard earlier chortled nearby.

Rubbing the ice from his eyes, he looked at the woman. "Is this your doing?"

She shrugged. "My daughter. She's disappointed you arrived and stopped our quest."

Risk tilted his head. "What quest would that be?"

The woman pulled a fresh cigarette from her pocket. "Bounty. We hunt bounty. There's a good one for bringing in witches, but I guess you know that."

Risk shimmered across the lot, materializing inches from the woman. His fingers flicked out to grab her cigarette and snap it in two. "What witch?"

She looked at him with dead eyes. "Any witch."

Risk stared at her, still not sure what she was or what powers she held.

"Maybe your witch," the woman added, a new cigarette appearing in her hand.

Risk reached out, intending on grabbing her, but she stepped back, disappeared for a second then reappeared. "I don't have to talk to you, hound. We all know what you are. We've seen you here panting after that little witch."

Risk flexed his hand, grasping nothing but air.

She smiled, then pushed his hand down with her own. "But because I have a weakness for lovers, I'll tell you. Your witch is surely gone. She's been inside too long and Narr's in there now. If Kol hasn't kicked them both out in the snow by this time, he's let them through."

An icy band clamped around Risk's heart. "Through to where?" he demanded.

She raised her finger in a tiny no-no motion. "You'll have to ask Kol about that. I don't piss in a garm's pasture." Stepping back again, she held up her arm. "Time to go."

As the wind twirled around her, she stepped off the curb and into the street. A thin bony tail trailed from under her velvet jacket, swaying to and fro with her steps.

Trolls.

Risk rubbed his hand over his face. This bounty on witches must be great, if trolls were out with the sky barely settled into darkness.

He stared at the swaying sign above the door to the Guardian's Keep. Now he knew he was at the right place—there was a garm inside and it sounded as if he already had Kara.

Not bothering with the niceties of walking or opening a door, Risk shimmered into the bar.

A yellow light shone ahead of them. Kara shuffled along, her fingers gripping Narr's grimy sweatshirt, sweat streaming down her face into her eyes.

"Ssstop," a voice hissed.

"I have the toll," Narr replied, his voice shaking. With one hand he reached behind himself, grabbed Kara and shoved her in front.

Blinded by the sudden light, Kara blinked. Featherlight, something flickered across her face.

"Ssshe looks like the other one," the voice said.

Kara's breath caught in her throat. *Kelly.* He was talking about Kelly. She squinted into the light, willing her eyes to adjust.

Four round yellow spotlights shot out at her from the darkness, a thin black vertical line making them look like cat eyes, but they didn't blink. They held steady.

A wisp of panic curled inside Kara's chest. What kind of creatures were they?

"She's a twin," Narr's voice boomed from behind her, causing Kara to jump.

The foul little man was getting bold just as Kara's bravado was failing her. Maybe because he thought he would escape soon.

His words seemed to excite whatever bore the spotlights. They leaned together, whispering.

Kara glanced around, looking for any clue as to where she was. With her back to the spotlights, she could make out shapes and movement around her. Fluorescent green streaks sped past her on both sides. Kara shivered, but held out her hands toward them.

"Can't touch them," Narr whispered in her ear. "They's on the other side of the tube."

"The tube? Where are we?" she asked.

"Jormun's," Narr replied.

Like that should explain everything.

"Who—?"

An exasperated sputter flew from Narr's lips. "Garm's right, got no business hanging out at the Guardian's Keep, don't even know who Jormun is."

Kara waited, sensing the little man wouldn't be able to resist being the smart one.

"Midgard Sea. That's where you are. Them streaks are fish."

The Midgard Sea. Kara searched her memories of high-school geography for any mention of Midgard. She came up empty.

"We're on the bottom of the ocean?" she asked.

"Bottom, middle. Don't know. Don't know that there even is a bottom," Narr muttered, as another streak of green sped by.

"Ssstep forward," the voice ordered.

Her hands clasped in front of her, fingers intertwined, Kara took a small step.

"Not her, you."

Narr's fingers wrapped around her arm. "This is it. Once I get my bounty, you's on your own."

Kara swallowed and nodded her head even though she doubted the man could see her in the gloom.

The pressure of Narr's hand on her arm disappeared. The scuffle of his feet against the floor telling her he'd moved toward the lights. As he got closer, she could see him, a squat dark silhouette against the yellow glow.

There was mumbling and hissing. Then Narr turned and scurried back toward her. "Good luck, witchy," he called, his sleeve brushing against her as he hurried past.

His footsteps seemed louder as his speed increased, then suddenly silence.

Kara pressed her clasped hands to her lips. He was gone and she was alone except for whatever creatures stood waiting for her behind the glowing lights.

Risk glanced around the darkened bar, his fists clenched at his sides, his jaw tightened. The place was empty.

Knowing the garm wouldn't have gone far, Risk strode to the bar, shoving a stool out of his way with his foot.

The stool teetered, then fell with a loud clunk onto the floor.

"Are you always this late, hound?" The bartender from the night Risk had first entered the Guardian's Keep stepped through a door next to the bar.

Risk narrowed his eyes. Garm. With the bar empty, and his senses not focused on prey, he could smell the pungent pine of wolf.

"Where is she?" Risk asked through gritted teeth.

"She?" The garm walked to a display of glasses and removed one. Not taking his gaze from Risk, he picked up a bottle of liquor and filled the glass.

The aroma of whiskey wafted across the space.

Fire flickered inside Risk. Kara's drink.

He narrowed his eyes. "Where did you send her?"

The garm laughed and slid the glass down the length of

the bar toward Risk. "I didn't send her anywhere. Your little witch did this all on her own."

The glass stopped a few inches from Risk's hand.

"Where?"

"Can't say, unless you have the toll." The garm leaned back and crossed his arms over his chest. "You got another witch to spare, hound?"

Risk lunged across the bar, his fist balling into the other forandre's T-shirt. "Send me to her."

The garm's gaze dropped to Risk's fist, then over to his torn arm. "Challenging me won't get you your witch. Even if you could win, you can't operate the portal." He raised his eyes to meet Risk's glare. "Remove your hand, or I'll ban your ass from my bar."

Risk stared at him, the desire to smash the garm against the mirrored wall behind the bar almost overwhelming.

"Hounds," the garm murmured. "Inbreeding makes you weak, a victim of your own nature."

Risk's pulse throbbed in his neck, fire building to a roar inside him. His fist tightened.

Kill. He wanted to kill—consequences be damned.

"Choose, hound. Bloodlust or logic? I'm almost out of patience."

Bloodlust. Sigurd.

Risk inhaled a shuddering breath. Was he as weak as the male he'd left unconscious on Lusse's floor?

His mind shot to Kara—how would she see him?

Beast. Fear. Repulsion.

His body shaking with the effort, he straightened his fingers and released the garm.

"That's a good dog." The garm grinned at him, revealing white, even teeth.

Risk's hands flexed. "Send me to her."

The garm leaned back, his elbows resting on the shelf holding the liquor. "No can do. Not without the toll."

Impatience boiled through Risk's blood. Maybe Sigurd had the right of it. Maybe some things called for bloodlust.

His hands pressed against the bar, Risk took a step back. He had to get through the portal, and the garm's games had worn through three seconds after Risk had landed in the Keep.

But, he knew the garm spoke the truth. Risk had no way of operating the portal without him. Or did he? Remembering his battle with Kara's protective circle, he eyed the dark doorway next to the bar.

The garm rolled his head from side to side, as if the whole thing was boring him.

A high-pitched whistle sounded from under the bar. Cocking one brow, the garm strolled over and bent down to tap on a computer.

Risk inhaled a breath filled with stale beer and cigarettes, and shimmered. Materializing six feet in front of the doorway, he lowered his head and charged.

The garm glanced up, just as Risk plunged into what appeared to be empty space. The air around him melded until he was moving but against a force, like running into a trampoline. Then with a snap, he went flying backward, straight toward the brick wall of the Keep.

Cursing, he shimmered again, landing in a crouch beside the bar, his breath heaving.

"Cute," the garm commented. "Next time lose the shimmer."

Risk raised his lip in a growl.

With a chuckle, the garm turned his back to Risk and

strode to the doorway. Two seconds later, the man who Risk had seen holding a knife on Kara in the parking lot trotted through the door, a scroll clasped in his fist.

"Back so soon?" the garm asked, a half smile tilting his lips.

"I wasn't exactly waiting for an invite to tea," the man replied, stroking the paper in his hand.

"And you got what you hoped for?" the garm prodded.

"Yep. She wasn't lying. Once they saw how much she looked like the other one, they didn't bother hemming or hawing. Paid right up." With a grin, he looked up—directly at Risk.

All color drained from the man's face, leaving him a dirty pasty white.

Risk straightened, his arms held loosely at his sides, his eyes fixed on the man who had just traded Kara for whatever he gripped in his hand.

"Where is she?" he asked, his voice barely louder than a whisper.

The man took a step back, his empty hand held up in front of him. "Now, don't be getting excited. She told me you weren't—"

Risk narrowed his eyes, his nostrils flaring.

"She, she told me to tell you she made me take her. Damn near threatened me. Kol, here, he can tell you." He shot a nervous glance at the garm. "That's right, isn't it?"

The bartender leaned against the bottle shelf, an amused smile on his lips.

Risk took a step forward.

The man shoved the rolled paper inside his sweatshirt and edged toward the garm. "You don't want it getting out the Guardian's Keep isn't safe to do business at, do you, Kol?"

The garm shrugged. "Can't say it matters much to me."

Risk smiled, his hand reaching out. The man spun and sprung like a cat to the top of the bar. Cursing, Risk lunged, snagging the man's tattered hood and jerking him back to the ground.

He leaned down and growled in the man's ear. "Tell me who has her and how I get to her."

The man glanced around, his brow lowered to a stubborn set. "Ask the garm."

Risk twisted the man's hood around his fist, pulling the material up around the man's neck until he sputtered for breath. "I asked you."

The man glared back.

Risk's hand shot out and wrapped around his throat. He might need the garm, but he didn't need this little thief.

He squeezed. The man's heels kicked against the floor, his face turning red, then white.

The garm leaned over the end of the bar. "How's that working for you?"

Risk glowered back.

"You know, you'll catch more bees with honey. Or in Narr's case, by taking his honey." His gaze shifted to the zippered opening where the man had slid his scroll earlier.

The man's eyes bulged, his lips ringed with blue.

Wishing he had his hands wrapped around the garm's neck, Risk flung the man away. Then while the thief lay panting on the floor, Risk reached in his shirt and yanked out the paper.

"Back," Narr muttered, holding up a weak hand.

Risk patted the scroll against his palm. "Where is she and how do I get there?"

"Gotta pay the toll." The man coughed, his hand pressed to his throat, his eyes focused on the rolled piece of paper.

Risk snarled. He was fed up with games.

"A witch. You gotta have a witch. Garm has to let you through if you do. Part of the portal rules."

Risk glanced at the garm. The other forandre lifted his head in a short nod of acknowledgment.

A frown cut across Risk's forehead. "Who's buying them? And for what?"

Narr glanced from the paper in Risk's hand to the garm. The bartender pushed away from the counter and strolled to the other end of the bar. His back toward them, he began stacking glasses.

"Jormun," Narr whispered. "Don't know what for, but he's been going through a cauldron of them. Every bounty hunter in all nine worlds been bringing in witches. Getting to be hard pickings anymore."

Risk sat back on his heels. Jormun. What was the outcast son of Loki trying to accomplish with these witches?

"Garm," he yelled. "Does he tell the truth?"

The bartender turned, his jaw set. "Greed and dim-wittedness may haunt Narr, but I've never seen him lie."

Dropping the scroll on Narr's chest, Risk shimmered out of the bar.

Perched on a boulder outside his cabin, Risk stared into the forest. The air was cool, but not biting. The scent of pine reminded him of the garm. He adjusted his bare feet on the smooth stone.

He had to return to Lusse. It was the only way to save Kara and her sister. He needed a witch to get into Jormun's realm.

Before Kara, he would have simply tracked down an

unknown witch and used her to buy his way into Jormun's, but he couldn't do that any longer. Couldn't surrender an innocent, even to save himself or Kara.

A raven landed on a nearby branch. The sun glinted off its blue-black feathers.

For better or worse, things had changed. Risk had changed. Now he had no choice but to go forward and hope everything worked out somehow.

Life bound to Lusse had been unbearable before meeting Kara. Now, after knowing her, touching her, a lifetime separated from her would drive him mad more surely than even the bloodlust that ruled so many hounds.

The raven pointed its beak up to the sky, its raucous call splitting the air.

"Risk?" Lusse turned on one foot, a box of chocolates balanced in one hand, her eyebrows raised in surprise.

Risk tamped down a small surge of satisfaction at surprising the witch for once.

"I know where the twin is," he announced.

"Ah, good." Lusse lowered herself into her chair. "I did tell you to stop by before you went to retrieve her, didn't I?" She flipped the lid off the candies and speared one with a fingernail. "So, you are concerned for the whelp." A frown flitted across her face.

"Of course not," Risk replied, adding a tinge of surprise to his own face.

Lusse held up the chocolate and studied it for a second before switching her gaze back to Risk. "Good, because I've been considering selling him. In fact, the potential buyers could be arriving any time."

Anger twisted Risk's gut. If Lusse was flaunting such news, it had to bode ill for Venge.

Choosing his words carefully, he said, "I didn't know you ever gave up a hound. He's well, isn't he? Capable?"

She shrugged one shoulder and grasped the candy between her teeth. After swallowing it, she replied, "Still in his cage and possessed of a foul temper. I tire of his tantrums. But the sale was just a passing fancy, perhaps I won't."

In other words, she would wait to see which choice tormented the other males most.

Risk shoved his concerns to the back of his mind. Venge was safe for the moment; besides, if Lusse was with Risk in Jormun's realm she wouldn't be able to wreak havoc here.

"I know where the witch is, but I need your help to retrieve her."

"Really?" Consternation and pride warred for Lusse's expression. Dropping the candy box onto her lap, she huffed out, "Explain."

Risk told her what he had learned from the thief at the Guardian's Keep.

"Jormun?" Lusse prodded the inside of her cheek with her tongue. "What is he up to?"

"I wondered the same, and I'm sure there are those who would pay well for the knowledge," Risk prompted.

"Gods even," Lusse murmured to herself. "How many witches did the thief say Jormun had taken?" she asked.

"No count, but he acted like the number was dangerously high for the survival of witches."

"Well, we can't have that, now can we? What would *I* hunt?" Lusse laughed. Turning pensive, she ran a finger over the tops of a line of chocolates. "And the portal…how is it guarded?"

Risk frowned. What was she thinking? "I only saw the garm."

She tilted her neck, her mouth twisting to the side. "Hmm."

"There is no getting past him without paying his toll. I tried. And he has the power to shut down the portal. Then I…we'd never get your witch."

"And I'd play the role of toll." She flipped her gaze toward him.

"A pretense only," Risk assured her.

"Of course." She pursed her lips, her eyes focused on a spot behind him. Glancing back at him, she asked, "And you think he'd believe that? That you have control of *me*?"

Risk filled his lungs with air. "I don't know that it will matter. From what I understand, garm are ruled by their dictates. Once the guidelines have been set he won't vary from them."

"It's possible. Garm are an unimaginative sort." Her finger pushed into the top of a chocolate, releasing an eruption of sugary syrup. "I have been feeling a little penned in. It's been what, four hundred years since I left here?"

She picked up an untouched candy and popped it into her mouth. "Yes, a little trip to the Midgard Sea sounds divine. I can hardly wait to see what Jormun has been up to."

With a peal of laughter, she stood up, the box of chocolates tumbling to the floor. "Yes. A trip. I think I'll even pick up a few things while I'm out."

With another laugh, she swept from the room.

Chapter 15

Footsteps shuffled toward Kara, the round yellow lights growing larger. She swallowed and clasped her fingers more tightly together.

Something danced across her face again. This time followed by an excited hiss.

"Jormun will be pleased," a new voice said.

Dry hands grabbed her arms and pulled her forward. Her captors spun so they and Kara faced forward, the yellow beams now clearly lighting the passageway in front of them.

Kara kept her gaze straight ahead, not ready to see who or what held her arms.

They stood in a hallway, constructed from what appeared to be a gigantic tube with just enough flat area forming the floor for her and the two creatures flanking her to walk side by side. The entire tunnel was transparent revealing what Narr had said was true—they were submerged deep inside some ocean.

The escort on her right swung his beam slightly outward revealing a large school of hideously fanged fish swimming by.

A shiver rippled through Kara's body. What was Jormun that he chose to live here?

Something flicked against Kara's hair. She bit her lip, refusing to look for the cause. She was fine. She was on her way to finding Kelly. Better she didn't know right now the complete reality of her situation.

Ahead a translucent wall blocked their path. Her companions began hissing and speaking in some language she couldn't understand, but based on the tightening of their grip, she guessed they were excited.

The one on her left released her to step forward. Her other captor's twin beams shone ahead revealing the back of a bald head, and what appeared to be a normal if somewhat short-legged and slim form.

Kara let out a puff of air. Not so bad.

The captor in front pulled a stick from his black jumpsuit and swung it into the doorway like a gong, three times. His body swayed side to side with the motion. He paused for a second, his arm dropping slightly, then pulled back and repeated the process twice more.

There was no answering sound, but vibrations of what Kara now recognized as power pounded against her, making it impossible for her to breathe or even think.

As the last vibration faded away, the wall thinned and her captor shoved her forward, through the opening.

She fell, landing on her knees in a room much wider than the hallway, but curved and with the same rounded walls. She glanced up, startled to see a blue sky dotted with fluffy clouds overhead. Had she gone through yet another portal?

Her guards shuffled forward, only their feet visible to her from this angle.

"Stand her up," a voice boomed.

Kara was jerked from behind, landing on unsteady legs. Upright, she could see she was still in some kind of hall, but more what she imagined from a medieval castle than the tube she'd just walked through.

Fine rugs covered stone floors, and tapestries depicting dragons and large serpents devouring unsuspecting knights adorned the walls. And the ceiling…she peered at it…still appeared to be the sky on a warm summer day.

Shrugging off a sense of surreality, she searched the long room for the source of the voice.

Far in the back, stretched out on a bed of pillows, lounged a giant of a man. "Bring her forward," he yelled.

One of her companions prodded her from behind. Squaring her shoulders, Kara walked toward the man she assumed was Jormun. He was entirely hairless—from his bald head to his face to the V of skin exposed by his voluminous shirt.

"Far enough." He held up one hand, rings on every finger. He studied her for a second, then reached into a basket to retrieve something alive and wiggling. "Report," he ordered, then dropped the hapless animal into his wide-open mouth, swallowing it whole.

Kara's stomach flopped. She closed her eyes and breathed slowly through her nose, the thick moist air offering her no sense of calm.

When she opened her eyes, one of her guards had left her side and now kneeled next to Jormun. He gestured and nodded, then following Jormun's gaze, turned to look back at Kara.

Kara's heart slowed, her mouth going dry. Her captors weren't odd-looking humans. They were… She licked her lips. Snakes. Humanoid, but still snakes.

Two giant yellow eyes shone back at her, and as the creature talked more with Jormun, his slitted tongue flicked in and out of his mouth. His skin was white, but too white, and with a greenish cast. Long body, short legs and arms—like a science experiment gone terribly wrong.

The guard still lurking behind her gave her a tiny shove. Kara turned her head, giving herself a glimpse of him, too. The hair on the back of her neck flew up and a shudder shook her body. Same eyes, same tongue.

Swallowing the bile that had crept to the back of her throat, she placed one foot in front of the other and trudged toward Jormun.

"Twins?" Jormun lurched upright, his eyes filled with interest.

The snake-man beside him hissed something in reply.

"Good. Good." Jormun motioned for Kara to come closer. "How are your powers, witch?"

A drip of perspiration fell into Kara's eye. She blinked, refusing to be demeaned by raising her bound hands.

Jormun rested his meaty arms on his bent knees, his gaze glued to her face. "Bring her closer." He motioned with one hand.

The snake-men nudged her in the back of her knees until she crumpled forward, her hands in front of her keeping her face from colliding with the stone floor.

As she struggled to right herself, Jormun grabbed her

chin with strong fingers and tilted her face up. "Amazing," he muttered, his gaze meeting hers.

Clapping his hands together, he leaned back. "She's perfect. Take her to her sister."

Kara's heart leaped. *Kelly*. Kara had done it. She'd found Kelly.

The snake-men shuffled forward, bodies bent and stubby arms ready to tug her to her feet.

Not waiting for them to touch her, Kara hopped up and held out her hands.

Part one was accomplished. Now she just had to get her and her sister out of here. She squeezed her eyes against the image of the burned witch she'd seen at the morgue.

They might not have much time.

Risk stood on the doorstep of the Guardian's Keep, Lusse beside him, her cape flapping in the wind. The witch held up her hand to adjust the bottom of her white leather glove.

"Is this it?" She raised a brow. "Really, garm take no pride in their surroundings, do they?" Huffing out a breath, she jerked the door open, leaving Risk to follow behind.

The garm stood leaning against the mirrored back of the bar. At their appearance, one eyebrow shot up.

"Back so soon?"

Risk glanced around. Two men seated near the door watched them with undisguised interest. Risk bared his teeth, turning their interest quickly back to their drinks.

Three tables were occupied, but neither the troll he'd met outside nor the thief who'd transported Kara were present. Just as well. Risk was not in the mood for renewing old acquaintances. Once he was sure no one in the room posed a threat, he replied to the garm. "I've brought the toll."

"Her?" The garm shot Lusse a disbelieving look. The witch stood feet apart, hands on her hips, obviously assessing the other occupants.

"Her," Risk replied.

The garm paused for a second, then shrugged. "Fine. Bring her over." He walked from behind the bar to stand by a doorway, two thin straps in his hand.

Risk walked to Lusse, then gestured toward the garm.

With a bored sigh, she sauntered to the doorway. "This is the garm?" she asked, her gaze roaming over the bartender's muscled body.

The garm crossed his arms over his chest, his eyes narrowed.

"You here alone, garm?" she asked.

The bartender glanced at Risk. "You ready?"

Risk nodded, the hair on his arms rising. Lusse stood with her hands still on her hips, studying the garm the way a cat studies a mouse.

"What powers do you have?" she asked.

The garm passed a questioning glance to Risk. "She your toll or not?"

Risk placed a gentle pressure on Lusse's elbow, urging her forward. She turned her head with an annoyed snap, but moved closer to the doorway.

"She has to wear these." The garm held the thin straps over his open palms.

Lusse laughed. "Jormun's idea?"

Ignoring her, the garm twisted a strap into a circle and leaned forward to slip it over Lusse's wrist.

She stepped backward, pulling her hunting horn from

inside her cloak. "Lovely bauble, though it is. I don't think so."

Before Risk or the garm could react, she tipped the horn to her lips and blew.

The air around Risk began to shimmer.

The garm vaulted over the bar, reappearing with a silver bar in his hand, just as five hellhounds in human form shimmered to solidity behind Lusse.

With a smile, Lusse held out her hand and blasted a stream of white-hot power toward the portal.

Not waiting for the impact, Risk somersaulted across the floor, knocking two hounds down on his way.

Lusse's line of energy crashed into the portal, screeching against the protected doorway like metal on metal. Bits of stray power sprayed across the room, striking patrons as they fled. The sounds of cursing, tables crashing and feet pounding toward the exit filled the space.

Risk stayed in a crouch, the fingers of one hand splayed over the dirty wood floor. The energy in the bar shifted, signaling the arrival of more hounds. At least six, Risk guessed, but his gaze stayed locked on Lusse.

Crazy power-hungry witch. What was she doing? She was going to lose any shot he had at saving Kara.

His fingers curled into a fist, rage washing over him. Kara. She was risking Kara. He would not lose her now. Not just so Lusse could play whatever game she had chosen.

His eyes blazing, he stood up and stalked toward the portal. Without pausing to consider the consequences, he reached out and grabbed Lusse by the shoulders.

Eyes narrowing, she turned her head toward him and murmured, "Stupid hound."

With no other warning, Risk sailed backward, crashing

into the wall behind him before he had any thought to shimmer. The chain around his neck constricted, cutting into his throat. He grasped at it, struggling for air. The chain only pulled tighter, matching its resistance to his own.

"Who is ruled by the bloodlust now, alpha?" Two black boots stepped into the gray ring that outlined his diminishing circle of vision.

Still struggling with the chain, Risk rolled to his side and glared up at Sigurd.

"You can't beat it. Haven't we all tried enough?" The other male stared down at him, his eyes dispassionate. "It matches its force to yours. The harder you pull, the more tightly it constricts. Won't kill you, but you'll be laying here for centuries—long after your little witch is dead."

Risk's fingers hesitated, some tiny rational part of his brain telling him Sigurd was right. There was no fighting Lusse. To try now would only put off finding Kara more. His fingers trembled, instinct warring with logic.

Sigurd nudged him with his boot. "Your choice." Then shifted his gaze to where Lusse stood, both hands now extended, parallel lines of energy crackling from her hands toward the doorway. Her body shook with the effort, her cape swaying as she moved.

The garm stepped forward, the silver bar held like a bat in his hands.

"Capture him," Lusse screamed, her voice cracking.

The garm swung, the bar striking the closest line of power. His muscles trembling, he held the bar into the stream. Energy bounced against it, bending like light on a mirror. The stray force shot upward, burning through the dingy ceiling tiles and out through the roof.

Bitter night air poured into the bar.

The garm couldn't hold her off, not without destroying the bar, and what would happen to the portal then? Shut down? Risk's only hope of saving Kara gone?

But Risk couldn't fight Lusse; he'd proven that to himself yet again. But maybe… He stared at the sweating garm, the bartender's brows lowered in concentration, his muscles bulging with exertion. Risk couldn't fight Lusse, but maybe he didn't need to. Maybe he could use her own ego against her.

Relaxing his fingers, Risk willed his body to accept the bondage of the chain.

Six hellhounds swarmed onto the garm, knocking him to his knees. The bar dropped with a clank on the floor, releasing Lusse's stream of power back toward the portal.

The garm raised the bar again, striking a dark-haired attacker in the head. The male faltered, but another surged into his place. Two males grabbed at the bartender's wrists using their weight to pull his arms down.

If they subdued the garm, Risk's plan would be lost.

He unfolded his fingers and concentrated on thoughts of Kara relaxed in his arms, blue eyes gazing up at him, her fingers stroking his arm. A smile curved his lips, a sense of peace settling over him.

With a clink, the chain loosened.

Risk pulled cold air into his lungs and swung his eyes back to the battle.

The garm was covered by Lusse's males, all but Sigurd answering her call. From beneath the squirming mass, a howl rent the air.

The garm. He was changing. Leaving Risk with only one option. With a roar, he released the hold on his beast and began to transform, as well.

* * *

The great room curved and narrowed into a narrow tube, exactly like the hallway Kara had entered through. Glancing at the glowing fish as they swam by, she wondered if Jormun's entire home was like this—one long curving tube that bloated out occasionally. A vision of a giant snake digesting its rat dinner filled her mind.

A hiss escaped her lips at the thought. The lead snake-man turned to her, surprise on his face. Giving him a bland smile, she concentrated on what lay ahead—and not just in this tunnel.

She and Kelly had to escape. Her hands were still bound. Were Kelly's? Could they somehow convince Jormun to release their powers? Even if he did, and they managed to escape to the portal, could they pass back through?

Panic clawed within her, crying to get out, past the calm she'd enforced on herself since leaving the bar with Narr. If only Risk were here. Even if he didn't love her, he would help her free Kelly, right? Surely the witch he planned to turn them over to couldn't be as bad as…

They entered a new section of tubing, this one lined on the right with shimmering doors. The side of the tube with the doors was more opaque, smoky. Without pressing her face to the glass there was no way Kara could see what lay beyond the doorway.

They passed the first door and the second, but as they approached the third, the snake-man slowed.

Her heart pounding, Kara waited as her escort pulled out his stick and banged on the door. The barrier thinned, and he grabbed Kara by the arm and shoved her through the opening.

A brief image of a brightly lit room constructed of the same curved translucent material was all she got before something struck her from the side. Her feet flew from the ground. Then after a second of panic, she landed with a thump onto the hard floor.

She lay there, her breath knocked out of her, the hip she'd landed on aching.

"Oh, my God. Kara, is that you?" Her sister, naked, swung from a black rope above her.

Mentally cursing, Kara stared up at her. "You're nude."

Kelly yanked the rope free from the pipe it was draped over and dropped to her feet. Panic written across her face, she padded toward Kara, the rope still clutched in her hand.

"Are you all right?" Kelly balled the rope, which Kara noticed was really a black jumpsuit like the snake-men's. Not waiting for a response, Kelly placed the makeshift pillow under Kara's head.

"How did you get here? It was the bartender, wasn't it? Did he search you out? Lure you to that bar with a promise of helping me?" Kelly mumbled a few curse words and fidgeted with the placement of her pillow.

Not sure how to answer her sister's tirade and still shaken from her fall, Kara could do little more than blink at Kelly.

"He acted all 'no involvement,' but he has to be the heart of the problem. He's always there. No one would get through without him—he made that perfectly clear." Kelly's eyes thinned to tiny slits. "I destroy that bar, and I destroy the market." She slammed a closed fist into her palm.

As Kelly ranted, Kara levered herself to a sitting position and looked around. They were sitting in yet another transparent tube, or maybe *capsule* was a better descriptor. A capsule that clung to the side of the larger tube she'd walked through with the snake-men. On one side was the main tube, although obscured by the smoky coloring, on the other dark ocean. The ceiling and floor both revealed nothing but miles of water.

She stood up, walked to the end of the space and cupped her hands to the glass. Pressing her eyes in the opening she'd made, she peered out into the water. Separated from them by a few feet of water appeared to be a second capsule, but unlike their own it was dark inside.

"What are you doing?" Kelly leaped to her feet. "You hit your head pretty hard."

Kara squinted, hoping to catch a flash of movement in the neighboring tube. "Is there someone else here?" she asked.

Kelly stared over Kara's shoulder, her gaze growing distant. "There was. On both sides, but they disappeared, and never came back." Turning on her heel, she picked up the twisted jumpsuit and jerked it on.

Looking back at Kara, she said, "We have to get you out of here."

Kara blinked. Get *her* out of here? "You mean *us*." She stared at her sister, realizing they hadn't even exchanged a hug.

Kelly waved her hand. "Yeah, us. Listen, we need to talk. I don't know how you got down here, but I'm sure you're pretty scared and confused right now.

"I know it doesn't look like it, but I've been working on a plan, and I think I can get us out of here." She put her arm around Kara's shoulder. "You just have to try and not panic, okay? Things here are pretty…odd, but just try not to lose it. Can you do that?"

Kara glanced into her sister's caring blue eyes. Felt the warm pat on her shoulder.

God, she really had been a mess before, hadn't she?

"I think I can manage," she replied dryly, pushing past her sister to study the room more.

Kelly frowned, but before she could continue, the doorway began to vibrate.

"They're back. Damn." Kelly tugged on the material of her jumpsuit. "There's no time to get back in position."

Kara stared at her. This was her plan? Knock a snake-man down then run naked into Jormun's hall? What then?

Heaving out a sigh, Kara moved to stand in front of the door. Whatever was coming through, she might as well greet it head-on.

The door finished its waving, revealing the green-tinged snake-man carrying some kind of tool, like a screwdriver. A jumpsuit was folded over his arm.

He stepped inside, his eyes pinpointing Kara then Kelly before he did so. Then with a wave of his stubby arms, he gestured for Kara to step forward.

Shrugging, she complied. They hadn't done anything horrible to her yet.

He gestured again, telling her to hold out her hands. She complied and he slid the tool under her straps. A quiet zip and her hands were free.

The snake-man nodded, and Kara bent down to scoop up the plastic strips. With a smile, she handed them to him. He dropped the jumpsuit at her feet and backed out of the room.

Once the door was set back to solid, Kelly stomped forward. "What was that? This isn't a game. I know I said not to panic, but you have to realize this is serious, too."

Kara huffed out a breath and bent to pick up the jumpsuit. "I guess they want me to put this on." She held it out in front of her. "Should I?"

Kelly folded her arms over her chest. "Yeah. It seems

to have some kind of body-temp regulator. Without it, I sweat like a prostitute at bible study."

Not bothering to reply, Kara peeled off her pants and shirt.

"Kara," Kelly began. "I'm really worried you aren't taking this seriously."

One leg in the jumpsuit, Kara paused. Kelly's attitude was getting annoying. "Because I'm not freaking out? First you tell me not to panic, then you lecture me because I'm not." She shoved her other leg into the suit. The material formed to her body with a snap.

Kelly blanched. "I… You don't understand." Her face took on the I'll-take-care-of-everything expression Kara used to depend on.

"I understand plenty. Maybe more than you. You're a witch. I'm a witch. There are things roaming the world I don't understand—men who make you love them and then turn into bone-crushing beasts, men who shove a knife in your throat and try to drag you through a portal to another world, snake-men who seem to be the most polite of any of them."

Kara glared at her sister. "Yeah, I understand plenty."

It was Kelly's turn to blink. "You know we're witches?" Kelly's eyes rounded with disbelief.

"Yep, and the news didn't send me crashing to my knees." Kara ran her hands down her backside, smoothing out ripples in the material. The jumpsuit was surprisingly comfortable. She was instantly at least ten degrees cooler, and as tight fitting as the suit was, she didn't feel confined at all.

"Kara?" Kelly stepped forward. Her hands on Kara's arms, she turned her until she could stare in her eyes. "What's my favorite food?"

"What?" Kara asked, her voice rising in disbelief.

"The scar on my pinkie, how'd I get it?"

Kara shook her head. "Have you lost your mind?"

Kelly took a step back, her eyes narrowed. "Answer me."

Kara sighed. "Anything with ketchup. It's disgusting. And Tommy Sullivan bit you in the first grade. You ripped the head off his Transformer and flushed it down the toilet—or maybe that's why he bit you. I get confused."

Kelly bit her lip, her brow furrowed. "It is you."

Kara glanced around her new home again. No chairs. This conversation on top of her trip through the portal was exhausting her. She needed to sit.

Seeing no alternative, she plopped on the floor and leaned against the curved wall.

Kelly was still watching Kara as if she expected her to morph into a crazy at any moment.

Considering everything that had happened to them, her sister was being smart.

Patting the floor beside her, Kara said, "Sit. I'm okay. I've just learned a lot in the past two weeks.

Kelly slid down the wall to sit beside her. "I guess. You hardly seem like the same person. You're so confident."

"Really?" Kara tilted her head. That was nice. Her sister, a woman who would scare Rambo, thought she was confident. "Thanks."

"You're welcome."

They sat there for a few seconds, staring out into the dark water of the Midgard Sea.

"Where should we start?" Kelly finally asked.

Kara tapped her nails against the floor. "I don't know. There's a lot to tell you." She thought of Risk and how she'd made him leave. She'd love to tell Kelly, get her reassurance that Kara had done the right thing—or even better, that it would all work out, but that was a conversation for a normal world, and…another glowing fish, this one orange, swam by…this was anything but normal.

She clunked her head against the wall behind them. Suddenly she was very, very tired and not just physically. "You start. What do you know about this place?"

For the next hour, Kelly told her everything. How she'd been practicing magic since puberty. She'd first discovered her powers when she'd fought the dog off Kara and Jessie, but it had taken years to really understand what that meant and search out others like herself.

"There are lots of us. I've met just a few in person, but there's a whole community on the Net."

"I…" Kara paused. She needed to tell Kelly about the woman in the morgue, but how?

"Then witches started disappearing. It was only a couple at first, but it started being more, and all of them were seen in certain areas. One area in our town."

"The bar," Kara commented.

Kelly nodded. "Yeah, the bar. A friend and I discovered the connection just a few weeks ago. We were watching the place, and then she disappeared."

A school of fish brushed past the wall. Kara curled her nails into her palms.

"Kelly…" she began.

"So, I knew it had to do with that bar. I went down there and *tried* to talk to the bartender. He was an ass. Wouldn't help me at all. Then some woman dressed in velvet and high tops of all things dropped a net on me—a net!

"And it was weird, too. I couldn't do anything but lay there. It was like I just didn't care. I could see what was going on around me, but… Anyway, the bartender twisted those plastic straps on my wrists, Miss Hightops dragged me through that doorway, and bam, here I am in weirdo world.

"I've tried to watch for Linda, but I haven't seen her." She exhaled, her shoulders slumping.

"Kelly," Kara tried again. "I think I know—"

Power pulsed through the tube, vibrating through Kara's body and robbing her of her breath. "What was that?" she panted, pressing her hand to her chest.

Kelly cast her a sidelong look. "Weirdo world, remember?"

The next second the lights shut off, leaving them in complete darkness. Kara slid her hand toward her sister.

"Just watch," Kelly whispered. "They do it every night, or at least I think it's night. I've kind of lost track of time."

A strange hissing started, then light returned except from behind them instead of overhead. Kara twisted her body, looking over her shoulder.

The smoky wall had turned clear. Lining the tube behind them was snake-man after snake-man, their eyes glowing yellow and pointed out toward the sea.

"What are they doing?" Kara asked, her voice low and shaking.

Kelly's hand clasped hers, warm and reassuring. "I'm not sure, but I think they're worshipping."

"Worshipping what?" Kara asked, heart thumping loudly in her chest.

"That." Kelly squeezed her hand. "Look at the water."

Kara turned. Pressed against the side of their capsule was a gigantic wall of green scales.

"What is it?" Kara's voice quavered.

"I'm not sure, but I think it might be their mother or something," Kelly replied, her voice low.

"It's alive?" Kara's eyes rounded, her hand closing more tightly around Kelly's.

"Oh, yeah. You can see it move. I even saw its head one night."

As Kara watched, the green wall moved up and down, swaying slightly against the water.

"So, it's a snake?" she murmured.

"Granddaddy of them all."

They sat in silence for a few moments, the sound of the snake-men's hissing almost hypnotizing.

"You know," Kelly murmured, her thigh pressed against Kara's. "I didn't used to think I was afraid of anything."

Kara twined her arm through her sisters. "That's funny. I used to think I was afraid of everything.

Chapter 16

Risk rolled to his feet and turned back toward the battle.

Another howl, then the garm stood in wolf form. Black with a sprinkling of gray around his face, he shook, his hair fluffing out to make him appear even larger. The males on top of him scattered. Feet splayed, lips pulled back in a snarl, the garm swung his head from side to side in a clear warning to any challengers.

Risk had to move fast, before the other hounds changed and an all out forandre war began.

"Garm," he bellowed mentally. One major benefit all forandres in their nonhuman form shared was the ability to speak telepathically. This privacy was essential to Risk's plan.

The garm ignored him, his blue eyes scanning the room for the next attacker.

With a growl, Risk pulled back on his haunches and leaped, landing four feet from the snarling garm.

The garm turned sideways, his tail stiff and the hair on his neck raised.

"Garm," Risk repeated.

"Call them off, hound," the garm said in Risk's head. "Nothing gets past here without my permission."

"Grant it." Risk moved with the garm's movement, the two of them traveling in a slow circle.

The garm barked out a laugh. "You think I'll let you through now?" He motioned with his head toward Lusse, who still stood hands outstretched, power pouring from her. "She's an idiot. She'll never break through."

"Maybe, but she's an idiot with power. If you don't play her right, she'll make Niflheim look like a spring romp through the woods."

The garm scoffed again.

"And isn't she worthy of the toll?" Risk asked.

The garm shook his head. "She isn't under control, that's a requirement."

"Yours or Jormun's?"

The garm growled.

"If Jormun wants witches, he'll want Lusse. She's drained more witches in her immortal life than wolves have fleas."

"Ha," the garm replied. "Is that how you grovel?"

Risk snarled. "I don't..." He let the words fade off. He was in the garm's territory. Circumstances in which a forandre could never submit. But one of them had to.

"Attack him," Lusse screamed.

The witch was getting tired. Risk could smell her frustration. The other males who had been standing back waiting for Risk to make a move stirred.

"Hold," he yelled at them. Then for Lusse's benefit, he lunged toward the garm, snapping at his neck.

The garm danced backward, his wolf eyes narrowing. "I can't beat you with your witch and your pack here, but I can shut down the portal. I can move it. You'll never find your twin witch—the one you sniff after."

"You're right. I want to save her. Let me through with Lusse, and I'll grovel. I'll turn my head and let you rip out my throat—just let me save Kara and her sister first."

The garm paused, his tail dropping an inch. "For witches? Stubborn witches who ignored all warnings? Who are too distracting for their own good? I didn't want to send them to Jormun, you know. I tried warning both of them away—but they were stubborn." The last came out as a growl.

"Let us through," Risk urged again.

The garm glanced around, his tail lowering more with his indecision. "It's too late. If others hear the witch..." he shifted his gaze to Lusse "...challenged me and got through, I'll have a parade tromping through here, thinking they can best me, too."

"No one will know," Risk pledged. "Why should they? I brought my toll."

The garm hesitated, the hard edge in his eyes softening. Then Lusse screamed out again, "Kill him."

The garm's gaze narrowed.

"Sigurd. If Risk won't kill him—you do it, and you will be alpha," she bit out, her arms shaking, sweat trickling down the side of her face.

Sigurd roared. The air rippled with new energy as the hound changed.

Risk moved so his back was to the bar, the garm on his left and Sigurd, shifting quickly, on his right.

"Scared, alpha?" Sigurd asked, his toes flexing as he settled into his canine form.

"Back down, Sigurd," Risk growled.

Sigurd lunged forward, his teeth brushing Risk's fur.

"This is the pack you command?" the garm asked with a snarl of disdain.

Risk stared at the other two forandre, both willing to rip out his throat to get what they wanted.

What they wanted, Risk repeated to himself.

"Sigurd." Risk swung his body, blocking Sigurd from lunging again. "You want to be alpha? Fine. I submit."

Sigurd lowered his head, a hank of hair falling into his eyes. "Submit? You'd never submit. I saw you in the pit, when Lusse declared you alpha."

"That was before," Risk replied.

"Before?" Sigurd shifted backward, his eyes moving from Risk to the garm.

"Before I had something to lose," Risk said.

Sigurd paused. "The witch?" he asked.

"Yes." And Venge, but Risk didn't want to reveal their connection yet.

"What's the price?"

Risk opened his mind so both the garm and Sigurd could hear his reply. "The garm will let Lusse and I pass, but in exchange, you have to guarantee no word of what happened here escapes the bar."

Sigurd glanced around. "The hounds aren't a problem, but what about the others? The patrons who ran out of here?"

Risk stared him in the eyes. "You'll figure something out."

Sigurd lowered his head in thought. "And Lusse?"

Risk growled. "If all goes well. She won't come back."

Sigurd laughed, his tail twitching to one side. "And I'd still be alpha?"

"I won't challenge you, and Lusse's other offer…" Risk

stared at Sigurd knowing he'd realize Risk meant the ownership of the other hounds "…will be void."

Sigurd tilted his head in consideration, then glanced at the garm. "And you, wolf?"

"You keep your part of the bargain I'll keep mine—but with one more restriction." He shifted his gaze to the group of males behind them. "No hounds in my bar—ever."

Sigurd tilted his head. "As if we'd choose to come here."

"Swear it, or no deal."

A growling rumble escaped Sigurd's throat. "Sworn." After giving the garm one last hate-filled glance, he turned his head back to Risk. "Anything else?"

Risk glanced at Lusse, then back at Sigurd. He had to ask one more thing. "Once we're through I want you to free the whelp, Venge."

Sigurd raised a canine brow. "He is yours."

Risk leveled his gaze. "Agree?"

"He'll still be bound to Lusse, you know that."

Risk nodded. "As I said, if all goes well, she won't be coming back."

The three males turned to stare at the witch, her face pale with exertion, curses streaming from her mouth.

With one last nod, Sigurd stepped out of his way, and Risk moved to her side.

Within seconds, the portal opened and Risk shoved Lusse, still cursing, through the doorway.

Lusse fell forward. Risk quickly stepped in front of the witch, keeping her from landing on the floor.

She shoved off his back and righted herself.

"What happened?" she heaved out, her hair disheveled and her breath coming in angry puffs.

"We did it. We're through the portal," he murmured to her.

Risk scanned their surroundings. It was dark, raven's-breast black actually, but with his hellhound vision, he had no problem making out where they were.

"It's a tube, I think." He stepped forward, leaving Lusse leaning against the now solid doorway they had entered through. "It isn't long and there's another door ahead."

"What do you mean *tube?*" Lusse shoved her hair away from her face and unhooked her cloak. "Why is it so hot? I despise heat."

Risk pressed his nose against the tube wall. "We're in a passageway, but it's round, like a tube. I think the walls are clear, but I can't tell what is on the other side."

"What a waste of time. Let me." Lusse pulled back her sleeves and held up one hand. *"Lyse."*

A faint glow bubbled in her hand, like the dying embers of a campfire. Lusse stared at it, the glow just enough to light her shocked face.

"What did you do to me?" She swung toward Risk, the power in her hand pinging off the sides of the tube like BBs.

How Risk wished he had the ability to drain her powers, but not now. Now he needed her to be strong—strong enough to tempt Jormun.

"It's nothing. You're just tired after battling your way through the portal." He prayed this was true. "No one has ever done that before," he added, hoping to cut off her anger.

Lusse fisted her palm and pulled it to her breast. "True, and Sigurd now has the garm, right? No one except the gods can claim ownership of a garm." She smiled.

"And you," Risk prompted her.

"And we are near Jormun?" she asked, her hand relaxing to press against the tube's curved wall.

"Very near." Risk padded forward, leaving Lusse to fend for herself. The witch wouldn't take offered aid easily, and he had no real desire to ease her journey.

He reached the end of the tunnel and turned to look for her. She struggled along, trailing her cape and tugging her gloves from her hands. "What now?" she asked, coming to a halt beside him.

"Another door," Risk said. "It's guarded. Can you feel the energy?"

She shot him a scathing glance. "Of course I can. Your only advantage here is your hellhound sight, and that I'm a bit worn. Don't be getting any ideas, alpha."

"Never, Lusse." Risk sat back on his haunches. "What is our next step?" Risk waited. It was important that Lusse feel confident when they arrived in front of Jormun. Let her think she was in control.

Lusse dropped her cloak and gloves, then lowered herself on top of them. "We wait. My powers will rebuild and I will blast our way in, or someone will open the doorway before then. Either way, I'll soon learn what Jormun has been up to."

His body rigid beside her, Risk turned his gaze to the doorway.

Let Sigurd and the garm keep their parts of the bargain, he prayed, or he might be stuck in Jormun's realm with Lusse forever.

Chapter 17

A sharp pain shot through Kara's shoulder. Blinking, she sat up. It was bright again, and the hissing had stopped.

She rubbed her shoulder then her neck. She must have fallen asleep sometime while the giant snake was still twined around their capsule.

Something flopped against her leg, causing her to jump. Just Kelly's hand, lying limply across Kara's thigh. Kelly always had been a bed hog. Moisture welled to the back of Kara's eyes. Thank God she had found her.

Moving to the side, she carefully lowered her sister's hand to the floor and stood up.

Within seconds, Kelly rolled to her feet and landed in a fighting pose, legs braced apart, one fist guarding her face, the other ready to strike.

"You'll make a wonderful mother some day," Kara drawled.

Still in attack mode, Kelly didn't reply.

"Kelly." Kara waved her hand in front of her sister's face.

Kelly tilted her head, her expression softening. "Sorry. I'm a bit on edge."

Like she needed to explain her state of mind to Kara.

Kara watched as her sister shook out her arms and then proceeded to twist her body into a series of yoga moves. "Kelly?" she prompted.

Concentrating on a point somewhere out in the Midgard Sea, Kelly didn't reply.

"I need to tell you something," Kara continued.

Kelly twisted her body into a triangle position, then stood. "Tell."

Kara took a deep breath, her eyes focused on her sister's face. "Maybe we should sit."

Kelly stared at her for a moment, then turned and walked to the other end of the tube.

"Kelly?" Kara called after her, surprised.

"Don't say it," Kelly replied.

"Don't say what?"

"What you've been trying to tell me since you got here." She turned, the pain on her face shooting through Kara like a spear. "You know something, don't you? Something about Linda—why I haven't seen her here. Why those other capsules are all empty now." She walked to the wall and pressed both palms against it. "I don't know what happened to all of them. I don't think I want to know."

Her black jumpsuit clung to her body, emphasizing the line of tension running down her back. "That's terrible, isn't it? Not wanting to know? Being…afraid."

Kara took a step toward her sister, her hand raised to reassure her.

Kelly spun, her eyes bright with anger. "I was so stupid. That bartender told me I was when Linda and I went in there the first time, but I didn't listen to him. I talked Linda into going back—to keep looking." She stood there, her body shaking, her eyes staring unseeing ahead of her. "And now…" She looked at Kara. "She's dead, isn't she? I killed her."

Kara stared at her sister, the strong one—the one who had saved her over and over and who now stood shaking at the thought of her failure—and dropped her hand to her side.

It was Kara's turn to be strong.

"It wasn't your fault. Everyone makes their own choices. Just because you believed it was the right thing to do—going back to that bar. It doesn't mean Linda didn't want to, as well. It doesn't mean whatever happened to her wouldn't have happened anyway." Kara stepped forward and heaved out a breath. "They are hunting us. If it hadn't been Linda, it would have been another witch, eventually all of us. You were right. We have to stop this—stop them."

Kara held out her hand, palm up. "We're going to stop this."

Risk's ears flipped forward; the sound of hissing came from the other side of the doorway. Someone was coming.

"Lusse." He turned to the witch who sat with her chin resting on her knees, her eyes faraway and swimming with dark plans. "They're coming."

She smiled. "Good."

Now was when Risk needed her to play along with his plan, but she couldn't know he was manipulating her.

"What is our plan?" He projected the question into her mind.

She shrugged. "My power has almost returned. I'll blast the guards and take what I want."

"The witches?" Risk asked.

"Yes, and whatever." She flicked her gloves in the air.

"But…" He let the thought trail off.

"What?" she snapped.

"Nothing, just, it would be a shame if we left before you had a chance to learn all of Jormun's secrets."

Lusse twisted her mouth.

"Maybe there is a way to spend time in Jormun's world without him suspecting your goal. You can blast your way free and steal the twins whenever you like."

She tapped a finger against her lip. "Yes. He wants witches, doesn't he?"

Risk nodded. "The most powerful."

A smile split Lusse's face. "And who is more powerful than I?"

"No one," Risk murmured, praying it wasn't true.

"Exactly. There must be some way to gain his trust…" She slapped her glove against her palm. "What was it that garm insisted on?"

"A toll," Risk murmured telepathically. If Lusse would cooperate, perhaps he could arrange a simple exchange.

Her nose wrinkled. "I won't pretend to be a toll."

Tension wove through Risk's body.

"But we can pique his interest other ways. A challenge." She clapped her hands together. "I've heard Jormun can't resist a challenge. And since he was exiled by Odin he can't have had any worthy opponents. We challenge his witches to a battle. He won't be able to resist." She laughed. "That will get us in to see Jormun, but I'll need you to stall for time a bit, keep him busy some way—until I've had a chance to let my powers completely renew."

The doorway began to pulse.

Lusse stepped forward until her thigh was pressed against Risk's side. Reaching down with one hand, she snagged his chain. "And remember, alpha, I still own you. The power of this chain is no less here than it is in my realm or the humans'. If you attempt to escape me, I'll throw your son in the pit and lock you in a cage for eternity."

The doorway vibrated again.

Risk lowered his head in a silent nod.

Two strange hairless beings greeted Risk and Lusse as the door's power shield thinned. Their huge eyes glowed yellow, and thin silvery tongues flicked out of their mouths, brushing against Risk's fur and Lusse's cheek.

She swatted at the intrusion.

"Lusse," Risk spoke in her head. "Remember your plan."

She frowned, but stood still, letting the creatures analyze them. They leaned together, their heads almost touching, hissing and waving their short arms toward Risk. After their consultation, one stepped forward, his tongue again flitting out of his mouth to dance over Risk's face.

Risk froze, his hackles raising. When the tongue returned again, he raised his lip in a warning snarl.

The creature hopped backward, and the two engaged in another round of excited hissing.

"What are they?" Still in his hound form, Risk was able to keep his question audible only to Lusse.

"No idea," she replied, not bothering to lower her voice. Her arms crossed over her chest and an impatient huff escaped her lips.

Risk inhaled, trying to identify the beings. They smelled of heat and moisture, like the tube, but stronger, and something else. Something that made his hellhound nature want to grab them by the neck and shake, something unnatural.

"They aren't natural," he murmured in Lusse's head.

"Really?" She cocked a brow, her head tilting as she studied them in return. She held out a hand and waved it slowly toward them. "You're right." Excitement cracked her voice. "They are made."

"By the Great One." One of the creatures stepped forward. His yellow gaze dropping to Risk. "What type of creature are you?"

Surprised they could speak, Risk glanced at Lusse. She waved her hand in a circular motion. Get on with it.

"Forandre. Hellhound." He projected his reply so both the creatures and Lusse could hear.

More hissing, then one of them asked, "You change, like the Great One? Is your other form serpent?"

Risk's lip curled at the thought. "Human."

The creatures looked at each other and nodded. "We didn't think there was another as strong as the Great One," the second creature replied.

"Change," the first demanded.

Risk narrowed his eyes. His ability to shift between hound and human was not a circus trick to be performed for others' entertainment.

Beside him Lusse shifted, her exhaled breath telling Risk she was impatient to get on with their quest.

"Yes, yes, shift," the second creature chimed in, his long body bouncing slightly with his excitement.

Gritting his teeth, Risk considered their request. He was strongest in his hound form, but his strength would do him no good trapped in this waiting area. And there were benefits to being human—like being addressed as an equal.

With an annoyed growl, he shook his body out and willed his form to change. The magic that allowed his transformation swelled from within him, shifting his form from hound to human in mere seconds. Risk stretched, pushing himself to his full height, the heat and humidity of the tube rolling over his naked skin.

The creatures stepped back, their huge eyes glowing even more brightly. "Ah, he did it."

"Yes, yes." The second creature clapped his hands together. "Big."

"Not as big as Jormun," the first chastised.

"No, no. Jormun is the greatest," the second agreed.

Lusse whipped her cape around her arm with an impatient snap. Risk touched her arm lightly, reminding her of her plan. If antagonized, Jormun's front guard might choose to leave them in the portal's entrance tube.

Her lips thin, she waited.

"And this one?" The creature gestured toward Lusse. "She is your toll?"

Lusse opened her mouth, but before she or Risk could reply, the creatures continued, "Too late. Jormun has no more need of such. So sorry, forandre." With an awkward bow, the pair turned to leave.

"Halt," Lusse ordered.

The creatures glanced back, their tongues flickering out of their mouths.

"How can he not need me?" Lusse swept her arm down the length of her body. Her hand fisting.

The creatures looked back at Risk, confusion on their faces. "Your toll wants to serve Jormun?"

Lusse stepped forward. "I am not a toll. I'm a challenger. I challenge Jormun's new witches."

Risk lowered his brows. Lusse's arrogance was intolerable to him; he could only imagine how the creatures before them viewed it. "Doesn't Jormun want the most powerful of witches?" he asked.

Lusse smiled, her hand relaxing.

"He has them," the creatures replied, their faces still twisted in confusion.

"Impossible," Lusse spit out.

Before she could continue, Risk jumped in. "How does he know? Has he pitted them against the strongest of their kind?"

The creatures glanced from Lusse to Risk, then turned back to face each other. "How did you get here? The garm grants only those with a toll passage."

"I blasted my way through, then enslaved the little wolf," Lusse replied, a bored tilt to her lips.

The creatures glanced a question at Risk.

He nodded, hoping the garm did nothing on the other side to give away his lie—and that the garm didn't trap Risk here in Jormun's realm when he learned of it.

After a few more seconds of hissing, they turned back. "We will consult with Jormun. Wait."

With a snap, the door closed again, leaving Risk back in the moist darkness, an angry Lusse at his side.

She barely had time to huff and declare her outrage at being left before the doorway thinned again, and the two mutant creatures reappeared. The first carried a black piece of cloth, which he handed to Risk with a bow. "For your comfort, Jormun thought you might prefer to be clothed."

Risk pulled on the outfit—a black jumpsuit identical to what the two creatures were wearing.

With Risk dressed, the two ushered Lusse and Risk out of the narrow tube and into a brightly lit grand hall.

A man, at least a foot taller than Risk, stood in front of a convex window looking out at the sea. When he heard them approach he turned, clapping his hands together. The sound echoed through the room.

"A hound." His dark eyes lit with delight. "I haven't encountered a hound since…" His eyes darkened. "For what feels like a millennium. Do you still hunt with the gods?"

"The hunt is dead," Risk replied.

Jormun folded his arms over his massive chest and peered down at Risk. "So, now you hunt…witches?"

Risk angled his head. "Not all of us, but yes, that's been my life."

"Hmm. And this one, you claim can outpower the pair I have? They are twins, you know. Identical."

"So we've heard. That's certainly rare, but this witch has unequaled power."

Jormun stepped back to analyze Lusse, who met his gaze with a raised brow. "She's certainly bolder than most who are brought here."

"I have nothing to fear." Lusse folded her arms over her chest, mirroring Jormun's body language.

Jormun laughed. For one interminable moment, Risk thought he was going to pat Lusse on the head. Instead he stepped back and studied Risk.

"You have my interest. What bounty do you request?"

"No bounty. Just a challenge." Risk nodded his head toward Lusse.

Jormun raised one brow. "Between her and my pair?"

Lusse tapped the toe of her shoe on Jormun's stone floor.

"She is stronger than she looks."

"I'm the *strongest*," Lusse interrupted. "I've spent my lifetime draining the powers of witches such as yours."

"Ah." Jormun tilted his head. "But you have nothing to offer me when I win." He waved toward the mutant creatures.

"My hound," Lusse threw out.

Jormun paused. "The forandre?" He ran his finger along the line of his chin, his eyes turning contemplative. "How do you feel about that, forandre?"

Risk froze, his breath barely leaving his chest. Would Lusse actually turn his binds over to Jormun, or was it another of her tricks—and did it matter? If Lusse lost, wouldn't it be better to be trapped here with Jormun? At least Kara would be near, at some point perhaps he could figure a way to free her, free them both.

After studying Risk for a moment, Jormun swung his massive hand, smacking Risk on the back. Risk braced his legs to keep from teetering under the giant's blow.

"It doesn't matter. I could use some entertainment and someone to talk with besides the skapt." Jormun glanced at the creatures who watched him with unmasked adoration.

"Wait," Lusse placed her hand on Risk's back. "We haven't discussed what I get when I win."

"When you win…" Amusement danced through Jormun's eyes. "Yes, let's hear your demands."

"Nothing much. Just your secrets. What you've been doing down here since you were cast into this sea." Her hand swept toward the window Jormun had been staring out of when they'd entered. "I want to learn what these skapt are, and how they were created."

Jormun's eyes narrowed, his massive fists forming balls. "No, you don't ask much."

Power sizzled around the giant, catching Risk off guard. If Lusse felt it, she showed no sign.

Jormun leaned forward until his nose almost brushed Lusse's. "Fair warning, witch. My secrets are mine, and I don't share them lightly. But…" He straightened, the power fading as quickly as it built. "Since there is no chance you can defeat my witches, I agree to your terms."

Without further discussion, Jormun left the main hall and the skapt motioned for them to follow. Tension ran the length of Risk's spine. Lusse had put him up as the prize, and made no mention of freeing Kara or her sister in the bargain.

Risk's blood boiled with anger. If only he could think of a way to leave the witch here, and take Kara and her sister in exchange. But as things stood now the best he could hope for was the twins defeating Lusse, thus ensuring he stayed here with them. If Lusse won there would be nothing gained.

Or would there? He glanced at the giant Jormun. Lusse had angered him, and he did say he wanted the most powerful witch. Perhaps there was still some way to turn this game to Risk's advantage.

Kara grabbed Kelly and pulled her into a hug. Her sister stood stiffly for a second, then relaxed against her. Tears edging into the corners of her eyes, Kara reached out and stroked Kelly's hair.

"You did the right thing. This has to be stopped."

Her face buried in Kara's hair, Kelly nodded.

"And, somehow, we'll get out of this. We're witches, right? And from what I've heard, damn powerful ones."

Kelly looped her arms around Kara's waist and squeezed. Pulling back so she could look Kara in the face, she asked, "What happened to you?"

Kara stared into her sister's eyes, the sadness hidden for a moment behind a veil of wonder.

"I don't know if you'll even believe me." Kara shook her head.

Kelly laughed. "Look around. I don't think there's anything you can tell me I won't believe."

Kara laughed, too, the moment free of tension letting her relax just a bit. "Okay, but I warned—"

A click interrupted her, and a small book-sized section of the wall slid open.

"Ah, breakfast," Kelly murmured, casting Kara a sideways glance. "You remember making fun of my ketchup obsession? Well you're about to wish you had a gallon-sized jug."

She walked across the room, to the slit in the wall. As she stood there two bowls slid through the opening.

"Yummy." Kelly grabbed the bowls and crossed back to Kara.

"What are they?" Kara asked, staring down at the brown pebbles.

"Pellets." Kelly picked up a handful and tossed them in her mouth. "You know that old saying…'tastes like chicken'? Well…these don't."

Kara popped one into her mouth and grimaced. "Should we be eating this?"

Kelly shrugged. "I tried going without the first few days, but I didn't last long. No point starving to death, and if we want to battle our way out of here, we're going to need some energy."

Kara crunched another pellet between her teeth. The taste was like old fish. She held her breath and swallowed.

Kelly shoved a handful in her mouth and wrinkled her nose. "I wish I could say they get better, but…"

The small opening clinked again. This time two foil packets appeared. Kelly tossed one to Kara. "Water."

They ate and drank in silence for a few moments. Kara's mind tripped back to Risk, wondering if he had discovered what she had done yet. Did he care? Would he come looking for her? The pellets formed a dry ball in her throat. Why would he? She'd sent him away. Unless, of course, he still planned on using her and Kelly, or turning them over to Lusse. She choked down the food, which landed in her stomach like a lead ball.

Dear God. She didn't care. Didn't care if Risk came looking for her just to sell her to the highest bidder. Right now at this moment in time, she'd give up about anything just to see him again.

"We'll need another kind of energy, too," Kelly interrupted Kara's thoughts.

Kara ran a finger under her eye, catching a tear that had formed there.

"You said you knew we are witches, but have you tried it yet?" Kelly asked, her finger poking through the pellets remaining in her bowl.

Blinking to stop any more telling tears, Kara replied, "Yeah, it was…" Empowering, invigorating, scary? "Weird," she finished.

"Weird. I don't remember feeling—"

The wall behind them shifted from smoky to clear. Kara glanced at it. "Already? I thought you said it was only once a night?"

"It is. It has been." Kelly dropped her bowl and stood facing the wall, both hands on her hips. "Oh, my God. Get a load of that."

"What?" Kara stood, the bowl still gripped to her breast.

Strolling down the tube beside them were Jormun, four of the snake-men, a blond woman dressed all in white and Risk wearing a skintight black jumpsuit.

The bowl fell from Kara's suddenly lifeless fingers, landing with a clatter on the capsule's floor. Her eyes focused on Risk, she didn't even jump.

Chapter 18

Risk strode the length of the tunnel behind Jormun and the skapt. Lusse still followed, her gaze darting from their host to his companions with a calculating gleam. Beside them Risk could make out what had to be the Midgard Sea. Schools of fanged and glowing fish flitted by the glass.

Then the scene beside them changed to monotonous gray.

"This is where I house my guests." Jormun gestured to the opaque wall, and without warning the gray dissipated like smoke, and Risk found himself staring straight into Kara's horrified eyes.

The bowl she held tumbled to the ground, and the woman next to her, her sister obviously, stepped beside her.

"My witches," Jormun announced, his arm sweeping proudly toward them. "They have yet to show their powers, but I've looked into their eyes. The potential is there, and..." He lowered his voice with something akin to reverence. "I saw violet. Can you imagine? Pure power. I'll bet your witch can't provide that."

Still staring at Kara, absorbing the way her hair folded onto her shoulders, the angle of her heart-shaped face, and the small part between her full lips, Risk heard Jormun's comment only vaguely.

"Forandre, did you hear me? I say, your witch can't boast pure power, can she?"

Shaking himself free of Kara's spell, Risk realized Jormun was speaking to him.

"Pure power is nothing but pretty. You need *real* power, power used to taking what is needed, to accomplish anything of worth." Lusse crossed her arms over her chest and stifled a yawn.

Risk blocked out the witch, instead keeping his gaze on the pair inside the adjacent room. Kelly grabbed Kara's shaking hands and clasped them in her own. Kara's eyes still rounded in horror, her face pale, she ignored her sister's attempts at comfort.

"Well, enough of that." Jormun announced. "You can see them from your own tube."

With a snap, the gray coating returned. Leaving Risk with the disturbing image of Kara's stricken face to carry with him as they walked the last few feet.

"Would you like your own space or to share with your witch?" Jormun glanced down at Risk.

The two creatures behind Lusse grabbed her by the arms and shuffled forward. Lusse jerked herself free, her hands raising to attack. Risk stepped in front of her.

"Sharing would be best," he told Jormun. The space next to Kara. He could at least watch her, know she was safe.

Jormun shrugged and waved the two creatures away from Lusse. "You'll find everything you need inside."

Lusse brushed at her arms and stared at the skapt through narrowed eyes as they waddled away. "I'll let you know when I'm ready for the challenge. Risk can entertain you until then." Without waiting for a reply, she swept through the doorway.

Jormun switched a surprised gaze to Risk, then laughed. "She may not be pure, but she's unusual, I'll give you that." Jormun stared after Lusse, a flicker of admiration spicing his gaze.

"Yes, she is." Risk studied the giant, an idea forming in his head. "She will beat them, you know."

"You think?" A line formed between Jormun's brows. "You don't think the stories about twins are true?"

"They may be true, but I don't think they take into account all that Lusse has done over the centuries."

Jormun's frown deepened.

"Of course, you didn't risk anything too valuable—just a few secrets—if you plan to keep your word that is." Risk crossed his arms over his chest and leaned against the curved wall. Jormun seemed to trust him for some reason—and certainly treated the forandre with more respect than Lusse. Perhaps he could push that advantage.

The giant snapped his gaze to Risk. "I always keep my word. It's a contract—and I expect the same from you and your witch."

"I haven't made any bargains to keep," Risk replied.

"True." Worry pulled at Jormun's features.

"I might consider entering a bargain, though." Risk tilted his head.

"How will a second contract save me from the first?"

"I brought Lusse here, right? The garm let me pass with her as my toll—ask him." Risk realized he was walking on thin ground. First he had hoped the garm wouldn't give away the lie of Lusse's trip through the portal, now he prayed the garm would protect his own reputation and declare her boasts false.

"She didn't blast her way through, like she told the skapt?"

"You haven't spoken to the garm?" Risk held his breath, waiting for the reply.

"He didn't answer my call, but seeing a hellhound was reward enough to let you two pass—for a while." Jormun nodded his head in silent acknowledgment of Risk.

Risk smiled. Jormun's words reassured him that his newly formed plan might work. "She thinks she did, but the garm knows the truth."

Jormun considered Risk's statement.

"It changes things, doesn't it?" Risk prayed his guess was right.

"Yes." Jormun smiled. "It does. By the rules of the portal anyone who delivers a toll which meets my needs can exchange that toll for a bounty—a bounty I agree upon."

Risk shifted his feet, disguising his eagerness by widening his stance.

"But," Jormun continued. "I already agreed to her challenge. I can't back out now. If she wins I tell her my secrets, if she loses I get you."

"What if we add to that bargain?" Risk asked.

"How?" Interest flickered in the giant's eyes.

"If Lusse wins, you keep her as my toll, and in exchange…" He inhaled and kept his gaze steady. "I get the twins."

"The twins?" Jormun took a step back. "No. They are far too valuable."

"But you won't need them once you have Lusse. If she beats them, she will have proven she is more powerful, and you *will* have her. She might gain access to your secrets, but you don't ever have to let her leave. Your secrets will still be safe here in the Midgard Sea."

"Ah, forandre. You are smart and powerful." Jormun pounded Risk on the back. "I will hope that the witch loses. I think you would be a much better companion."

With a nod they sealed their bargain. Risk stepped through the doorway, leaving Jormun rubbing his hands and mumbling to himself. Lusse was right; Jormun did have secrets. Secrets, thankfully, he didn't want leaked out to the rest of the worlds.

Now Risk just had to make sure Lusse beat the twins without killing them in the process.

"He made them." The words exploded from Lusse as soon as the door to their space had closed.

Eyeing the end of the room beyond which Kara and her sister's room lay, Risk didn't reply.

"Did you hear me? He *made* them." Lusse threw her hands in the air. "Do you know what kind of crime that is? The gods will do more than toss him out—they will chop him into bits and feed him to these fish that surround him." She sniffed as a purple eel-like creature slithered by their tube. "And the power. Where is he hiding his power? I could smell some on him, but nothing like what is required for this." She wrapped her hands together and stared at the doorway where Jormun's creatures had left.

"I need that power," she declared.

"You'll get it once you win," he reminded her.

"Yes, I will." Lusse walked to the end of the tube next to Kara and her sister. A wall of water separated them, but Risk could still see the pair, make out Kara's graceful movements from her sister's more determined choppy ones. "They are tempting, aren't they? They would go well with my garm."

"But they weren't part of your bargain."

Lusse tilted her head, studying the nearby tube, then snorted. "Like that matters." She glanced at him over her shoulder. "You don't think I intend to leave you here, either, do you? Bothersome as you can be, you're mine."

Heaving out a bored breath, she spun to face him. "Unless you want to be left here, get out there and befriend the idiot giant. Find out how he made those…things. Maybe I won't even need to prove my superiority. Although, it might be fun."

She glanced back at the nearby tube. "They look so fresh—entertaining. But—" she ran a hand over her bedraggled hair "—why put out more effort than's needed? Do your part. I need to recharge." Flapping her cloak, she stalked to the far end of the tube.

Risk shoved down the growl that formed at the back of his throat. As irritating as Lusse was, she was right. He needed to talk to Jormun more, get him to let Risk talk with Kara, prepare her to lose the battle that lay ahead.

"You *know* him?" Kelly still stared at the now gray section of tube where Risk had stood.

"He…he's how I found out…" Kara made a circle motion between her and her sister "…about us."

"Really?" Kelly blinked. "Is he a witch, too? Do you think that's why he's here?" She frowned. "But he didn't look like a prisoner. They've never cleared the glass like that before—except, you know, during the weirdness. And Jormun sure didn't escort me here. You?"

Kara shook her head, dread filling her with each of Kelly's words.

"It was like Jormun was showing us off. Why would he do that?" She glanced at Kara. "And who's the ice queen?"

The woman in question stepped into the tube next to them. Kara licked her lips.

Kelly narrowed her eyes. "What aren't you telling me?"

Kara shrugged. "I don't know why they're here."

"But you know who they are, what they are—*give*." Kelly stepped closer to Kara, until there was nowhere for Kara to go for escape.

"I think she might be Lusse. A witch."

"A witch?" Kelly turned to study the sophisticated blonde in the adjacent capsule. The woman, Lusse, watched them in return.

"What's with the cape and gloves? And all the white?"

"I don't know." Kara slid down the wall, facing Kelly and the tube holding Lusse. Tucking her knees under her chin, she stared blankly ahead. "I think she may be kind of…evil. She drains other witches of their powers."

Kelly spun. "And she's with the hunk because?"

Kara sighed. "He works for her. That's how I met him. He was hunting me." The words came out like an admission of guilt.

"Let me get this straight. While I was gone you got

yourself a hot boyfriend, the first in what, three years? Who just happens to work for a witch—make that an evil witch, who drains other witches of their powers. Anything else you'd like to tell me?" Kelly walked across the room, her back to Kara. "And I thought I had bad taste in men."

Kara dropped her face to her knees. She hadn't even told Kelly the really disturbing part yet. When she found out what Risk was she would never believe Kara could care for him. Kara knew her feelings for Risk sounded insane, but they were real and she couldn't let go of them yet.

Taking a deep breath, she decided to admit all. "There's more," she said.

Kelly raised an eyebrow.

"Risk isn't a witch."

Kelly waited.

"He's…he's a hellhound."

"A what?" The words burst from Kelly.

"A hel—"

"I know what you said. I just can't believe you said it."

Kara stared at the floor in front of her for a few beats. "Maybe he's here to save us," she murmured.

Kelly shot her a sideways gaze. "Yeah, there's a thought. Do you *know* what hellhounds are? What they're used for?"

Kara pressed her chin into her knees.

"They're part of the wild hunt. Gods used them to retrieve souls. And from what I've heard hounds aren't real choosy about the condition of said soul once it's retrieved. They live for the hunt, the kill. I didn't even know they could be human…" Her tone changed. "Are you sure? Maybe he was just trying to impress you."

A sad Kara nodded. "I've seen him…in his other form, I mean. Him and another one. The first night we met." She went on to explain about her encounter with Risk and the other dog in the parking lot, how she woke up in his cabin and everything that had happened between them since.

Kelly dropped down beside her. "Well, you've definitely managed to beat me on the bad choice in men contest, Sis." She pulled Kara's hand into her own. "Don't worry. You'll get over him. And there he is now."

Taking a deep breath, Kara glanced up. Risk stood at the end of the capsule, his palms pressed against the glass, and his hazel eyes focused on her.

Her traitorous heart jumping, she looked away. Should she talk to him?

"Well, at least I understand why you were able to overlook the dog bit." Kelly made a whistling sound.

Kara pushed herself up and wandered to the end of the tube, her palms mirroring Risk's pressed against the glass. His eyes were intense. Was he trying to tell her something?

"He's…hot. That's for sure," Kelly murmured, joining her at the glass. "But Kara, you know you can't trust him. He told you he was hunting you for…her, right?" She nodded toward Lusse, who had walked up behind Risk and stared at them with cool disregard.

"But it's more complicated than that and now he's here. Don't you think he *could* be here to save us?"

The door to Risk and Lusse's capsule slid open and Jormun appeared. With a wide smile, he motioned for Risk to follow him from the tube.

"No, Kara. I don't." Kelly turned, placing her body between Kara and the end of the capsule. "Did you see that? He's a guest. He's not here to save us. He works for the other side."

Kara shifted her gaze out into the Midgard Sea. Kelly

was right. It certainly looked as if Jormun and Risk were on good terms, but as the garm had warned her things here could be deceiving.

"I don't know why he's here, but I don't think it's good news for us. Don't be pinning your hopes on someone you know you can't trust. Especially when your hormones are involved." She grasped Kara's hands. "We have to do this ourselves. At some point they're going to open that door and take us away—just like they did all the others. But when they do, we'll be prepared, right?"

Kara closed her eyes, her loyalty to Kelly warring with the dream of being able to believe in Risk.

"Right?" Kelly squeezed her hands.

Opening her eyes, Kara stared into her sister's determined face. Kelly was the one person she had always been able to depend on. Kara would be an idiot to forget that now, and she owed it to her sister to do whatever she could to save her.

With an abrupt nod, she replied, "Right. What do we do first?"

With a determined smile, Kelly pulled her into a hug. "We'll be fine. You'll see. Just trust me."

Kara spent the rest of the day trying to pretend Lusse wasn't in the tube next door, and forcing herself not to look for Risk.

Hours later, Kelly was still instructing Kara on how to pull energy from the small space around them and hold it within herself.

Panting, Kara collapsed on the floor next to the bowl of pellets. If they kept this up much longer, she thought she might explode.

"Where is the power coming from?" Kara asked, gratefully pressing another water bag to her lips.

"I don't know, but it isn't enough to do much. Certainly not enough to break out of here." Kelly stared at the doorway to their prison, then turned back to Kara, a tiny frown on her face. "It gets stronger during the serpent ceremony. Unfortunately, that's also when we are completely surrounded."

"Do you think we could break out then?" Kara ran a shaking hand through her hair. Working with even this small amount of power was exhausting. Could she handle more?

"No." Kelly placed a hand on each side of their prison's door. "We would never get past those snake-men. But I'm hoping if we work with what we have, once they open that door, we'll be ready."

"You mean attack them?" Kara's eyes widened. The snake-men were strange, but so far they hadn't done anything that in Kara's mind justified hurting them.

Kelly pushed away from the door. "This is serious, Kara. It's us or them. We have to get out of here no matter who we hurt."

Kara glanced to the end of the tube where throughout the day, Lusse had been practicing her own witchcraft.

No matter how much she fought it, Kara couldn't seem to keep her eyes from turning toward the adjacent tube. Even if just looking that direction sent a dagger of pain through her center.

Bursts of light bounced around the nearby capsule, silhouetting the profile of a masculine figure. Kara hurried to the end of their prison, drawn like iron filings to a magnet.

Risk stood facing the doorway, still dressed in one of

Jormun's jumpsuits. Even this tiny glimpse of him made Kara's palms sweat and her pulse quicken. The material clung to him like a second skin, highlighting the flat plane of his stomach and the muscular bulge of his buttocks.

"Forget him, Kara." Kelly wandered up to stand next to her.

Kara swallowed, her gaze glued to the man she couldn't give up on.

Lusse strolled up behind Risk and wove her arms around his waist, then up his chest. Her face pressed to his back, she stared into Kara's eyes. *He's mine*, her gaze seemed to say. Then with a wave of her hand, a fog formed, blocking Kara's view.

"What happened?" Kelly asked, her hand reaching out to grab Kara, who wobbled sideways.

Kara blinked back the sudden moisture in her eyes. "Nothing. You're right. We have to do whatever we can to escape. We can't trust anyone except each other."

"It will be okay, Kara. I promise." Kelly pulled Kara to her in a hug. "I've never let you down before, have I?"

Kara shook her head. She could trust Kelly. Kelly would take care of everything—she always had.

Kelly turned and tromped back to the center of their room, her hands raised to renew their practice.

Kara was falling back into old habits, but…she glanced over her shoulder at the now opaque capsule next door…obviously, trusting in herself hadn't worked out.

Risk stepped forward, out of Lusse's arms. "What was that about?" he asked. While she made many suggestive comments, Lusse had never shown any real sexual interest in him or any of the males in her kennel. Risk wasn't sure if it was a basic prejudice against what she saw as interbreeding or her own sexual leanings, and he hadn't cared. It was her one redeeming quality in his eyes.

She laughed. "Your little witch over there." She pointed in the direction of the tube that held Kara and her sister. "She really is panting after you." She arched a brow. "Are you sure you don't return her interest?"

Risk stepped away. "Of course not. I needed her trust. You know that."

"Hmm." Lusse flicked out her hand, a small ball of fire forming on her palm. "I hope that's all. I'd hate to think after all these years, after all we've been through, that I couldn't trust you." She bounced the blazing ball into the air. "And Venge…I'd make sure he hated it, too." The ball landed back in her palm; with a smile she closed her fingers, smothering the sphere into smoking nothingness. She held her hand up, palm toward him, fingers splayed.

"There's something in the air here. Do you feel it? It was stronger outside this—" she glanced around their space, an expression of distaste on her face "—plastic bubble, but I can still pick up remnants here. It must be related to the power source Jormun is using to make his creatures. Have you learned anything yet?"

A band around Risk's chest tightened. Though friendly, Jormun had refused his request to speak with Kara. But Risk had no choice; he had to move forward with his plan and just hope at some point he was able to communicate it to Kara.

Time to add to his nest of lies—to tighten the noose more closely around Lusse's neck.

"I have. Jormun has been fairly free with information. He's promised to show me how he makes the creatures, but not until we prove we're trustworthy."

"Trustworthy?" Lusse pursed her lips.

"He wants to make sure the twins aren't hurt in the battle. If they're harmed they'll be of no use to him."

"Of course." Lusse shrugged. "Is that all?"

"Basically." Risk tilted his head as if just remembering something. "Except, he asks that you wear a piece of equipment, just to assure a fair fight. If I can convince you to do that, he'll trust me enough to share the source of his power with me."

Lusse frowned. "How do I know his 'equipment' won't tip the battle toward the twins?"

"I can try it on first, if you like."

Lusse tilted her head in consideration. "I still don't like it. You aren't a witch. It might affect you differently."

"True," Risk agreed. "But it's his one request."

"And you think we can trust *him?* Will he really show you the power source?"

Risk pretended to consider her question. "He will. He seems to share the garm's love of rules."

Lusse shrugged. "Perhaps a side effect of living too near the portals."

Risk fought to keep his face from twisting into a grimace. Trust and keeping a bargain were foreign ideas to Lusse.

Lusse straightened her arm, another ball of blue fire in her hand. "Tell him I agree." She glanced at Risk. "Now leave, I need to practice. Not to beat them, you understand. I just want to make sure Jormun is left with no doubt as to who is the strongest."

"I'm sure you will accomplish that," Risk replied.

As Lusse whirled the fireball down the length of the tube, Risk slipped out the doorway.

Chapter 19

"Why do you want to speak with the twins?" Jormun leaned back against a cushion, a live mouse dangling by its tail from his fingers.

"Curiosity, nothing more." Risk hid a grimace as Jormun dropped the unfortunate animal into his mouth. It was one thing to kill a beast while in his hound form and something entirely different to devour a living creature whole while human.

"Curiosity killed the cat." Jormun chuckled. "But that's right—wrong species."

Risk tapped his fingers against his thigh, the thin bracelet Jormun had given him for Lusse to wear during the battle clasped in his hand.

"Besides, I think we're almost ready for your challenge. The twins have taken it upon themselves to hone their skills. Have you seen them working in the space next to yours?"

Risk clenched his jaw. He had, and the skill and determination with which the sisters worked worried him. There was every possibility they might defeat Lusse. Funny how that used to be his goal, and now it was his nightmare.

"You're worried, aren't you?" Jormun grinned. "Don't fear, friend. Life here isn't all bad." He clapped his hand over a gray mouse as it attempted to scramble away.

"Now, I must ask you to leave. I've neglected other duties since you've arrived and some things just can't be avoided." He stood. "The skapt will escort you back to your tube."

"That's all right. I can find my way." And stop by Kara's again hoping to somehow get a message inside to her.

"No," Jormun answered abruptly. Then with a smile he softened his reply. "Not now. No one wanders free during the ceremony."

Ceremony? Risk cocked an eyebrow, but kept the question to himself. Perhaps he was about to learn the source of Jormun's power.

A skapt arrived and Risk followed him out of the hall.

As they approached the section outside where Kara and her sister were housed, an idea occurred to Risk.

"Is it a lot of work for you, waiting on all these witches?"

The skapt turned, surprise at being addressed written on his face. "Work? It's why we exist. We thank the Great One for the privilege every day."

Risk studied the skapt, trying to decide if he was one of the two Risk had met the first day. "Have you met either of these witches?" He motioned to the doorway that separated him from Kara.

The skapt frowned, his short arms hanging loosely at his sides. "Why would I?"

"You aren't curious about them? About the legends?"

"Legends?" The skapt shook his head. "Witches are nothing but tools. They don't have the power you or the Great One share."

This wasn't going as Risk had hoped. He changed gears. "But they are useful, and fascinating."

The skapt stared at him, the skapt's face blank.

This was getting Risk nowhere. "Would you like to see me change?" he asked.

The skapt's eyebrows rose. "Yes." The word came out in a reverent hiss.

Closing his eyes, Risk concentrated on transforming. Within seconds he stared at the skapt through canine eyes.

"They spoke the truth." The skapt looked as if he might fall on his knees.

Risk glanced back toward the doorway. "Do you think you could do me a small favor?" he asked telepathically.

Hands clasped in front of him, the skapt replied, "Without doubt."

After quickly changing back to his human form, Risk relayed what he needed. While the skapt scurried off to get the few supplies, Risk leaned with his forehead pressed against the glass. How he wished he could see Kara and talk with her in person, but the glass blocked all efforts—even his telepathy. He would have to depend on the skapt to carry his message for him.

And pray Kara still trusted him enough to do what he asked.

Kelly leaped forward, flinging a pebble-sized ball of power directly at Kara's head. Without thinking, Kara somersaulted out of the way and landed on her feet, her own golf ball of energy forming on her palm.

"Excellent." Kelly grinned. "No way the ice queen over there can beat us."

Kara glanced over her shoulder at Lusse, who had stopped her own practicing hours earlier. Now she lounged on a bed of pillows, her faced turned toward the door.

"What do you think she's waiting for?" Kara asked.

"Your boyfriend." Kelly shook her head. "I'd like to know how she rated those pillows." She glanced at Kara. "More proof the two of them are here as guests."

Kara stifled a sigh. She knew Kelly was right, but she wished her sister would quit mentioning it.

A click sounded from the wall.

"What's that?" Kara asked, glad of the diversion.

"Sounds like the call for kibble." Kelly sauntered to the open slot. As she had guessed, a bowl slid through the opening. "Well, this is new." Kelly pulled a folded slip of paper from under the pellets. "It's got your name on it." Frowning, she turned the paper over.

Kara snatched it from her hand.

"Don't need to be grabby," Kelly replied.

But Kara did. She knew the look on Kelly's face; she was getting ready to suggest they destroy the note unread, and Kara couldn't. It was from Risk; it had to be.

Giving her sister a quelling look, she walked to the end of the room and unfolded the note. Two words were written in a hasty scribble. *"Lose Risk."*

"Lose what?" Kelly asked, her hair brushing against Kara's neck.

"I...I don't know." Kara's fingers tightened on the paper. Not exactly the reassuring message she had been hoping for.

* * *

"Well?" Lusse greeted Risk as he walked through the doorway. "Did you find the source?"

Ignoring her, Risk strode to the end of the tube near Kara's. She and her sister stood huddled together at the other end, their backs to Risk.

"I asked—"

Risk spun, anger and impatience sending a flare of heat through him. "Not yet. Soon." He balled his hands at his sides. He had wanted to explain everything to Kara, his plan, why he was here with Lusse, that she had to trust him, and most of all that he would do anything to save her, sacrifice his own life and everything he valued just to know she was safe.

"How soon?" Lusse stood, kicking a silk pillow across the floor. "This…" She made a sweeping motion with her arms. "Is getting old."

Without warning, the lights dimmed.

"Now what?" Lusse mumbled.

The ceremony. Then the battle. And Risk hadn't got Lusse to wear the band Jormun had supplied yet. Risk wasn't completely sure what the band did, but Jormun had emphasized that it would make the transition of Lusse from free witch to his property easier—assuming she won the battle.

"Here." Risk stepped forward, the bracelet glowing in a delicate circle across his palm.

Lusse looked down her nose at the object. "What is that?"

"The equipment I told you about. Jormun's one request."

"That? He thinks that will keep me from killing his witches?"

Risk gritted his teeth. "You wearing it was his requirement for showing me the source of his power."

"Really?" Lusse tilted her head and lifted her arms. "I feel a shift right now. Do you feel it?"

Risk did, and his anxiety grew. "Will you put it on?"

Lusse glanced back at the bracelet and sighed. "Give it to me. I'll think about it." She plucked the object off Risk's palm and tucked it into the pocket of her skirt.

As she did, a loud monotonous hissing sounded behind them.

"Fascinating." Lusse's lips parted.

The wall separating their tube from the main one cleared. Standing shoulder to shoulder were the skapt, their eyes glowing and their bodies turned toward the Midgard Sea.

"What are they…" Lusse snapped her head back the other direction, toward the sea. Her inhaled breath turned Risk's attention there, too.

"I never guessed," she murmured. "I thought it was legend, allegory. Not real."

A huge undulating serpent pressed against the tube. Its body so long Risk couldn't see either its head or tail.

"You mean…" he started.

"Jormun. That is Jormun. He truly is the Midgard Serpent." Lusse rushed to the glass, her hands trailing over the smooth surface. "When he was exiled it was said he was cursed to become a huge serpent that circled the Midgard Sea, his tail clamped in his mouth. But I never dreamed…" She inhaled, excitement sending quivers down her body. "Can you imagine? A shift this huge? The power he must emit?"

"Is he forandre?" Risk asked. The skapt's reverent treatment of him was suddenly making sense.

"I don't know, but it doesn't matter. He has the power

of hundreds, maybe thousands of forandre. And to think I was happy to capture a garm." Lusse laughed. She spun back toward Risk. "The battle. When is the battle?"

His eyes still focused on the giant serpent, Risk muttered, "Soon. After…this."

"Good. Good. This changes everything. Now there is much more to gain than just a couple of sniveling witches." Picking up a pillow, Lusse hugged it to herself.

Startled, Risk glanced at her. What insanity did she have brewing now?

As the lights glowed back to life in their tube, Kara let out a breath of exhaustion. Kelly had insisted they spend the time during the ceremony pulling as much power as they could from the air.

"I know it isn't much, but it is stronger now than any other time," she had insisted.

Now that the snake-men had retreated and the serpent had sunk out of sight to return to where he lived when not being worshipped, Kara slid to the floor and attempted to nap.

The click of the food slot startled her awake. She leaped to her feet and rushed over before Kelly could beat her.

A flat tray slid through.

"Another note from doggy boy?" Kelly asked. Her arms crossed in disapproval over her chest.

"No…" On the tray were two thin bracelets, similar to the ties the bartender had placed on her wrists before she'd gone through the portal, and another note. This one was from Jormun.

It is time to perform, my little witches. Wear these bracelets to protect you from harm. Jormun.

"What now?" Kelly stalked to Kara's side. "No way."

She took the tray from Kara's hand and dropped it back on the shelf next to the slot.

"But maybe..." Images of Kelly's friend, the witch in the morgue, flitted through Kara's brain. "Maybe it's true."

"You are way too trusting." Kelly shook her head.

Kara bit her lip. "But if Jormun wanted to hurt us, why wouldn't he just do it here while we're trapped?"

"He doesn't want to hurt us. He wants to use us. You told me yourself your hound friend said that's what happened to..." She turned away, unable to say her friend's name.

Kara stared at her sister, feeling her pain, but something inside Kara said she should wear the bracelet. She knew it wasn't logical; but she just felt it. While Kelly's head was still turned, she picked one up and slipped it onto her wrist.

The slim band thinned and tightened until it was barely visible against her skin.

"What did you do?" Kelly rushed over, grabbing Kara's wrist. Kara just stared back at her. "Guess I'll find out."

"Damn." Kelly picked up the tray and tossed it across the room.

"I feel fine," Kara said softly.

"She feels fine," Kelly mumbled to herself.

Kara turned, her shoulders shaking with pent-up emotion. She was out of her element. She'd come here to save Kelly and she was just making things worse.

Kelly stared at her. "Double damn." She stomped to where the tray and second band had fallen. Shaking her head she slipped the bracelet over her foot and onto her ankle. "I'm not leaving here without you. So, I might was well share your fate."

"But?" Kara looked at Kelly's ankle.

Kelly shrugged. "Always have to do a little something unexpected—don't you think?"

With a smile, Kara nodded and stared at her own band. She could barely make out the thin raised plastic—or whatever it was. *Please,* she prayed, *let me be right at least about this.*

The snake-men came for them less than an hour later. Kara wasn't surprised. She knew those bracelets meant something.

When they arrived, they glanced at Kara's wrist and nodded. Her brows lowered, Kelly held out her ankle.

"Where are we going?" Kara asked.

"The hall." A gold-toned snake-man motioned for the twins to lead the way.

A huge ring of pulsing power was set up in the middle of the hall, the floor dirt instead of the stone Kara remembered. Jormun reclined on a floating dais filled with pillows. Risk stood next to him.

Kelly shot Kara an "I told you" glance.

Blinking back tears, Kara turned her gaze to the ring. Inside Lusse waited, her white cape rippling as if a breeze touched her alone.

How did she stay so clean and collected-looking? Even with the jumpsuit, which seemed to not only maintain body temperature, but also be self-cleaning, Kara felt worn and dirty.

The snake-man led them right up next to the energy barrier. The section faded and disappeared, forming a small doorway, just big enough for Kara and Kelly to pass through.

"What do we do?" Kara whispered to her sister.

Kelly glanced around.

Snake-man after snake-man began filing into the room, circling the ring.

"My God, how many are there?" Kara asked, her eyes rounded.

"Too many." Kelly shook her head. "I don't like this."

Kara stared at the snake-men. There had to be thousands of them squished into the space now. The row behind Kara and Kelly pressed against the sisters, nudging them closer to the open doorway.

"We can't fight our way through this many, can we?" Kara asked in a rough whisper. She hadn't wanted to hurt even one of the somehow sad creatures, but the thought of turning on this many, slaughtering them by the hundreds before there was any hope of escape, made her stomach lurch.

"No. We can't." Kelly's reply was flat, final. "We go in."

Clasping hands, the pair stepped into the ring as one.

Jormun rose to his feet; the snake-men emitting a low hiss in response. "Welcome, witches." He held up his hands. "We have had a challenge."

Kara glanced at Kelly. Her sister's lips thinned to a narrow line.

"The rules are simple. No death strike. Aside from that, last witch, or witches—" he gestured to the twins "—standing wins."

No death strike. What had Kara gotten herself into that the phrase even had to be said?

Kelly gripped Kara's arm tight. Her fingers digging painfully into Kara's skin, she pulled Kara close to whisper, "We take her out fast."

Kara's shocked gaze darted across the ring to Lusse, who stood gazing at the snake-men, a content expression on her face.

"But, it doesn't even look like she's going to fight," Kara objected. As the words fell from her lips, Lusse turned, a bowling ball–sized sphere of power flying from her hand.

"Drop," Kelly screamed, yanking Kara onto the dirt. Loose soil flew up around them, creating a cloud, shielding them for a moment.

"What were you going to say?" Kelly hissed.

"Nothing." Kara struggled to breathe, the dirt blocking her airways.

"You still think your boyfriend is here to save us?"

Kara swallowed, her throat dry and raw feeling.

Kelly grabbed her by the shoulders. "We can do this. Remember what we practiced. There's at least one hundred times the power here that there was in our tube. Use it."

A ball of blue flame landed inches away.

"Hell." Kelly pushed on Kara's shoulder, sending her rolling across the ground.

Kara landed on all fours, her chest heaving, dirt clogging her throat with each breath. Coughing, she looked up at the dais. Risk stared down at her, his hands fisted, his fingers white with strain.

"Lose," he mouthed.

Lose? The note, this was what he meant. He wanted her to lose the battle against Lusse—the witch he claimed held him in bondage. It made no sense. Kara shook her head, tears spilling from her eyes.

"Kara!" Kelly screamed.

A stream of power snaked from Lusse's hand, wrapping around Kelly's ankle and jerking her to the dirt. Kelly fell, her fingers clawing helplessly in the loose soil.

Kelly. Kara stood, all thoughts of Risk's betrayal and her own fear dissipating. Her arms held out, she concentrated on pulling power from the room. Energy flooded into her, knocking into her like a speeding train. She staggered backward, her hand pressed to her stomach.

The power whipped back and forth within her body. Raising her head, she gazed around. The world around her changed, colored, as if she was seeing through blue-tinted glasses.

Kelly flipped onto her back, her hands flying forward, her own stream of power meeting Lusse's. Her brows lowered, her mind focused, Kara held out her hand to her sister and let the energy she had pulled merge into her twin.

Kelly stiffened as the power touched her. Her head dropped against her chest for a second, as she accepted Kara's strength as her own.

Opening her eyes, she smiled, and hit Lusse square in the chest with a gleaming streak of blue flame.

Eyes round, Lusse flew off her feet, the continuing line of Kelly's power holding her six feet off the ground.

Kelly laughed, a harsh sound that scared Kara to her center. Remembering her own battle with the heady sensation of controlling so much energy, she jogged across the ring and dropped to her knees next to her sister.

"Kelly, let her down." She pulled on her twin's arm.

Kara wanted to win, wanted to escape, but if she lost Kelly to power madness in the process…

"Kelly." She wrapped her hands around Kelly's cheeks and twisted her face toward her. Her sister's eyes stared up at her wild and vacant. Keeping her voice firm, Kara repeated, "Let her down."

Without changing her expression, Kelly twisted her head back toward Lusse. The witch still hung in the air. For the first time, Kara noticed a tear in the other witch's cape, a gray tinge to her skirt and stray hairs that clung to her angry face. Lusse's face turning red with the effort, she whipped her body back and forth in an attempt to escape Kelly's energy stream.

"Kelly." Still no response. Pulling back her open hand, Kara struck her sister across the cheek. The sharp sound of impact echoed in Kara's ears.

Kelly jerked, her eyes closing then snapping back open. Pressing her advantage, Kara grabbed her by the front of her jumpsuit and shook. Kelly stared at her for one heart-stopping second then dropped her arms.

Shrieking curses, Lusse fell to the ground with a thump.

"I had her," Kelly murmured, her eyes darting side to side. "Had the power. Did you see me?"

Her hands still fisted in the front of her jumpsuit, Kara stared into her sister's eyes. "You didn't have the power. The power had you."

"Had the power," Kelly repeated.

"No, Kelly. Think. How did you feel? You weren't in control."

Kelly blinked slowly, warmth, intelligence and what Kara recognized as her sister returning to Kelly's eyes.

"Oh, my God," she muttered.

"I know. I know," Kelly responded.

"No. The witch. Move!"

Kelly rolled to the side, a power bolt splitting the ground between them as she moved.

Lusse stood six feet away, her face dark with rage, her cape and dust swirling around her. "It's my power. You pathetic upstarts." She formed an O with her hand, another short stick of power appearing in the opening. With a quick overhead motion, she pelted the new bolt toward them.

"What the hell are those?" Kelly muttered, rolling again, this time into Kara. Not waiting for an answer, she pushed to her feet and sprinted to the other side of the ring, putting distance between her and Kara.

"Over here, Cruella," Kelly screamed.

A sly smile curved Lusse's lips. "Simpletons," she said, and pulled both hands to her chest. Her eyes gleaming, she flung both arms out into a V shape, power bolts flying from each hand—one directed at each sister.

"Crap." Still on the ground, Kara scrambled to escape. The bolt brushed against her, burning through the jumpsuit and sending an icy pain shooting through her side.

Kara lay in the dirt gasping for a breath, frozen with the shock of being hit. She pressed a hand to her side; it came back red with blood.

She stared at it stupidly. Funny, she didn't feel as if she was bleeding.

"Kara," Kelly screamed.

Kara looked, her hand still palm up in front of herself.

Lusse had taken a step forward; her eyes focused on Kara, she lifted both hands and prepared to throw two more bolts—both directed at Kara.

All Kara could do was stare at her, unable to believe any of this was really happening.

Chapter 20

A scream rent the air. Suddenly, bolt after bolt of energy dug into the earth around Lusse. Kelly, a crazed look in her eyes, lunged forward, her hands a flash of movement around her head, pulling bolts from nowhere and tossing them as quickly as her arms could move.

"Leave my sister alone," she shrieked.

Lusse turned, two huge bolts gripped in her hands. Eyes narrowed, she pulled her arms back over her head and prepared to toss them, but at Kelly, not Kara.

Something inside Kara snapped. She glanced up at the dais. Risk still stood there rigid, his face grim. "Help me," she willed, her desperation pouring through her eyes.

His jaw tightening, he turned his face away.

Kara wanted to curl up in a ball, lie sobbing in the dirt until all this passed. But it wasn't going to pass, not until either Lusse or she and Kelly were declared the victor.

A whistle pierced the air, Lusse's energy bolts catapulting toward Kelly.

Inhaling, Kara pulled in more energy and concentrated on what she wanted—to save Kelly, to save herself.

Every muscle in his body clenched tight, Risk stared down into the ring. Kara was bleeding. His nostrils flared.

Her eyes huge with an unspoken appeal, Kara looked at him. Knowing he couldn't interfere, if he did it would only jeopardize their escape, he turned his face away. He felt Kara's despair, like a leaden sigh settling over him.

He couldn't help her. He had to let Lusse defeat her and her sister. It was the only way, he reminded himself over and over. The words becoming almost a mantra in his mind.

Feeling stronger, he looked back at the ring. Kara spun away, her hands upraised, her face tilted upward, exposing her delicate neck. She inhaled deeply, her hands shaking slightly as if she were holding weights that were almost too much for her to bear.

Risk tightened his jaw. She had to fight this alone—*she had to lose*.

A slight breeze stirred Risk's hair.

Jormun straightened on his bed of pillows. "Do you feel that? The twin. She's doing that." His eyes flashed with pride.

Risk leaned over the dais. The breeze grew stronger, began to move the dirt on the ring's floor, too.

Lusse blinked, then lowered her brows. With a muttered curse she heaved two energy bolts toward Kara's sister.

The wind picked up to a howl. A huge disk of power, air and dirt swirled together, forming a wall between Lusse and Kelly, and beside it stood Kara, her hands still outstretched, her body swaying with the wind.

"She is doing it," gloated Jormun, his massive hands clapping together.

Lusse's bolts slammed into the disk. Sparks sprayed as the bolts vibrated against Kara's shield. A gut-wrenching grinding sound forced the skapt backward, their tongues darting from their mouths in alarm.

"Fabulous." Jormun grinned. "Now what will your witch do?" he asked Risk.

Her face twisted with rage, Lusse began to twirl, creating her own tempest of power, but behind the shield, Kelly seemed to have tapped into what Kara was doing. She held her arms out to her sister, adding to Kara's creation.

Their disk grew bigger and bigger, forcing Lusse backward, trapping her against the boundary of the ring.

They were winning. They were beating Lusse.

Risk paced the length of the dais, watching for some sign that Lusse could still win, but the witch was fading. Her shoulder bowing as Kara and Kelly forced her into a smaller and smaller space.

Jormun clapped his hands again and shot Risk a beaming grin. "Looks like they are winning, forandre."

Not yet. The battle wasn't won or lost or…Risk shook his head. He hadn't lost his chance to save Kara yet. Fair or foul, Lusse had to win this fight.

But how? He couldn't help Lusse, even if Jormun wouldn't object, he couldn't go that far; he had to get Kara to do it herself. He had to convince her—talk to her.

The solution rocked into him; he shook his head at the simplicity. Change—he had to change, in front of Kara. She'd asked him to do it before and he'd refused, convinced it would seal her horror of what he was. But now he had no choice. It was the only way to speak with her.

Closing his eyes, he let the magic engulf him. His feet widened, his hips curved—throwing him to all fours. Sounds and scents multiplied. He could hear Kara's breathing, smell her resolve. With a shake, he settled into his hound form and opened his eyes.

Jormun stared at him, a slight curve to his lips. "You can't help her, forandre. It's her battle to win."

Or lose. The serpent shape-shifter still had no idea of Risk's true goal. His head lowered with determination, Risk padded to the edge of the dais, and opened his mind to Kara.

They were winning. And without hurting Lusse. Kara couldn't believe it was actually happening. She stepped forward, concentrating on holding the disk of power she and Kelly balanced between them. Lusse edged farther backward, her own cyclone of energy slowing, losing force with each inch of ground she lost.

"Kara." Risk's voice startled her, almost making her lose focus.

"Kara," Kelly yelled, apparently sensing Kara's drift in attention.

Kara snapped herself back, refusing to look at the dais.

"Kara, look at me," Risk called inside her head.

Kara licked her lips. They almost had Lusse. Just a few more minutes and she and Kelly would win.

"Kara, please." Sadness, desperation—emotions Kara had never heard in Risk's voice before, not even when he'd described being sold by his parents. "Kara," he pleaded again.

Unable to resist, she turned her head. The silver dog from the bar parking lot stood on the dais. A sliver of fear shot through her; her muscles clenched; her power wavered causing the disk to stutter, the edges waving, disappearing for a second.

"Kara, concentrate! What are you doing?" Kelly dug her heels into the dirt, increasing her effort to hold the disk. Sweat broke out on her forehead, lines forming on her face. Muttering, she glanced toward her sister.

Kara looked back, unsure what to do, what to think, then glanced at the dais. Kelly's gaze followed hers.

"Kara, no. Whatever he's doing to you, ignore him. We almost have her—concentrate."

Nodding her head, Kara turned her back on Risk.

"Kara, lose. You have to lose. It's the only way. Jormun wants to keep the strongest witch. If you lose, he'll let you and Kelly go free. He'll keep Lusse instead."

Her eyes huge, Kara cast her gaze toward Kelly. Her sister shot her a warning look, and nodded her head toward the disk. "Don't give up now," she seemed to say. She pushed another step forward, edging Lusse a bit closer to the ring boundary.

"Kara, trust me." Risk's words tore at her.

Unsure, Kara paused.

"Just a little more," Kelly choked out, her breasts heaving with the effort of holding both her half of the disk and the portion Kara had let slide.

"Kara..." Risk's plea was no more than a whisper, making it somehow all the harder to ignore.

Her eyes filling with tears, Kara dropped her arms. The sudden loss of power sent Kelly flying backward onto her seat. Kara stood there, panting, praying she had made the right choice.

Lusse weaved forward, a hand pressed to her chest, her

eyes filled with disbelief. Her gaze shot from Kelly to Kara to Risk.

"Good work, alpha." She grinned, her hands shooting upward.

Kelly's face fell, hurt and betrayal showing in how she turned her head, in her mumbled, "No, Kara."

With a laugh, Lusse stumbled forward, waving her arms, gathering power with each step.

The room fell silent, like the stillness of a mountain seconds before an avalanche strikes.

Something was wrong, Kara could feel it. Too much power, Lusse was pulling too much. Perhaps she could survive the delivery of her blow, Kara had no way of knowing. But Kara was sure of one thing, there was no way she or her sister could survive the strike.

Lusse stopped, her body bending, power flooding out of her arms, her legs, her torso.

"No," Risk roared. The ignorant witch had broken Jormun's one rule. She was delivering a death blow, and he had allowed it by letting her in the ring without Jormun's bracelet.

Without another thought, Risk leaped, flying toward the ring and Kara.

Behind him an even greater roar sounded. The skapt fell to their knees, their hissing combining with the hum of power flowing from Lusse, and the booming shriek behind him. Risk ignored it all, his only thought Kara and saving her from Lusse.

Kara staggered sideways toward her sister. Growling, Risk lunged in front of her. His teeth bared, he threw himself at Lusse just as she unleashed the first wave of power.

Dirt, power and the stench of obsession swirled around him. His gaze focused on Lusse, on the insanity flaring in her eyes, he struggled forward.

Another shriek split the air. The skapt threw themselves prone on the ground. Lusse's head shot upward, her eyes rounded in horror, she went shooting backward, over the ring and onto the bodies of the fallen skapt. She lay there quivering, her hair singed, her eyes rolled back in her head.

All sound stopped.

Dead. Was she dead? Afraid to look, Risk stood frozen, then he felt it. Something large, filled with power and slithering toward him.

On the ground a few feet away, Kara stirred. Her sister gasped, and Risk turned, his hackles raised and his feet braced, ready to fight.

A gigantic green serpent slid toward him, its tongue flickering out over Kara, her sister, and then Risk. "Calm, little forandre." Jormun's voice echoed inside Risk's head. "Your witch, she cheated." Jormun, the snake, rose; his head weaving above them, his tongue danced over Lusse. "She didn't wear the bracelet." He shook his head as if in disapproval. "Too bad. It would have saved her some hurt."

Risk stepped backward until he felt Kara's body next to his. Her sister scrambled forward, grabbing Kara's hand and attempting to pull her away from the snake and Risk.

"She won though, didn't she?" he asked.

The snake cocked his head. "And…" He flicked out his tongue again. "She lives." Jormun's rolling chuckle sounded in Risk's mind. "Well met, forandre. Take your witches and leave."

Witches? Risk blinked, unsure he had heard the larger shape-shifter correctly.

"Don't lose your advantage. Leave while the bargain still holds." With that, the serpent lowered his belly to the ground and slithered out of the hall.

The snake-men hurried them out of the hall toward the door where Kara had first entered what seemed a lifetime ago with Narr. Risk trotted along in the rear, his eyes alert, but avoiding Kara's gaze. When they reached the first doorway, the snake-men parted, allowing Risk to walk between them until he stood beside the sisters.

Kelly, her eyes narrowed, said, "What's happening? Why's this…beast with us?"

Her mind swirling, Kara ignored her. They were letting them leave; she didn't know what had happened, but Risk had been right. He hadn't betrayed her. *Jormun's letting us leave. Risk, too—just not…Lusse.* The image of Lusse lying immobile on the ground slammed into her.

"Is she dead?" she asked of no one in particular.

The closest snake-man blinked.

"Lusse, is she dead?" Kara repeated.

"Who cares?" Kelly muttered.

The snake-men glanced from Kara to Risk, as if he had said something. One hissed, then said, "She lives, just knocked out. She proved she was the stronger. Only the strongest can serve Jormun." His eyes gleamed.

"The strongest?" Kelly raised a brow.

Risk growled. To Kara's surprise, her sister snapped her lips shut.

"So, what happened to her?" Kara asked.

"Too much power. She couldn't filter it all," the snake-man replied. He reached into a small crevice near the doorway and pulled out the stick that Kara now knew opened the door.

"But…why didn't anything happen to us?" Kara motioned to herself, Kelly and Risk.

"Forandre?" The snake-man hissed, a disbelieving sound. "Nothing hurts forandre."

"And us?"

"Bracelets. They protect. The other witch was lucky. She wasn't wearing one. In the past, witches weren't strong enough. The power of Jormun's change overwhelmed them…killed them."

"But Lusse…?"

"Survived, strongest. She will serve Jormun well." The entire group nodded, their tongues darting in and out of their mouths.

So the other witch, Kelly's friend, Jormun had killed her, but perhaps not intentionally. Kara glanced at her sister, who was staring at the band around her ankle. Did it matter? Dead was dead. A shiver passed over Kara.

The snake-man swung his stick, striking the door. Even before the vibrations had slowed completely, the group had turned and began swaying away.

Something warm knocked against Kara, nudging her through the doorway. She dropped her hand, hitting fur—Risk still in his other form. Walking beside him, down the tube that lead to the portal, she let her fingers rest lightly on his back.

Strangely, she felt no fear—or even unease. Walking beside Risk felt normal, safe.

When they reached the portal, it was already open. One hand on Risk, the other clasped around Kelly's hand, Kara stepped out of Jormun's world and into the Guardian's Keep.

Risk herded Kara and her sister through the doorway and into the Guardian's Keep, then quickly circled around so he was between them and whoever or whatever might be waiting for them in the bar.

"Well, I didn't expect to see you again." The garm, in human form, leaned against the bar, his arms crossed over his chest. His gaze drifted from Risk to Kara's sister, where it settled and stayed.

The twin grabbed Kara's arm and shoved her way past Risk. "Let's go."

Kara balked. Using her body weight against her sister, she refused to move.

The garm raised an amused brow and turned his gaze back to Risk. "Were they worth it?"

Risk tilted his head.

With a low laugh, the garm pulled a pair of jeans from behind the bar and tossed them in a heap in front of Risk. "Heard you were coming. Thought you might want to change." He grinned.

Not in the mood for forandre humor, Risk grabbed the denim in his teeth and dragged it backward until he was a few feet away from Kara and her sister.

With a small amount of privacy, he turned his back to the others and began to shift.

"Damnation," he heard Kelly mutter. Ignoring her, he finished his change and began tugging on the jeans.

When he spun back around, both Kara and Kelly were staring at him. The garm bent down to rearrange some bottles with angry clanks.

Risk stood, dressed only in the garm's worn jeans, his gaze on Kara, feeling vulnerable and exposed—something he'd never experienced before meeting Kara, before loving Kara.

Unable to form words, he held out one hand.

"No way." Kelly placed a restraining hand on Kara's forearm. "We still don't know what happened back there. Maybe he's been sent through to watch us, use us somehow."

Kara shook off her sister's grip. "He saved us."

Kelly sputtered. "Not. How do you figure that? We had Lusse dead to rights. We were winning. Then he did…something. Broke your concentration. He caused us to lose the battle."

Her eyes focused on Risk, Kara replied, "But that's it. Don't you see? If we'd won, Jormun never would have let us go. Risk convinced me to lose. Jormun thought Lusse was stronger—that's how we escaped."

Kelly frowned. "He convinced you to lose? How? Just with that one note?"

"No." Kara smiled. "The note should have been enough, but it wasn't." She took a step toward Risk. "I'm sorry. I should have trusted you."

The band around Risk's heart loosened.

"Kara," Kelly objected.

Kara held her hand out to her sister, shushing her, then took the last few steps into Risk's arms. He pulled her to his chest. His nose buried in her hair, he inhaled her scent, her love, her.

"You can accept…" He let the words trail off.

She looked up, her eyes shining with tears. "Everything. I love everything about you."

When he started to speak again, she pressed her fingers to his lips. "What about you? Can you forgive me for throwing you out? For being so…" she glanced at her sister "…stubborn?"

He laughed, all the stress, worry and fear he'd been carrying evaporating like mist. "Anything, everything. If you can accept me, and all I've been, there's nothing I wouldn't forgive."

He lowered his mouth to hers. With a sigh, she met his kiss. His fingers tunneled through her hair, he held her there, forgetting where they were, who was around them, and all the unsolved problems that still lay ahead.

Then her fingers brushed the silver chain around his neck, and she pulled back, concern in her eyes. "What about this?" She gripped the chain as if willing it to melt in her palm.

He shrugged. "I don't know. I'm still bound to Lusse. Even with her in another world, the bond doesn't break."

Kara stared up at him, her brows lowered in determination. "Can we break it? You thought we could."

Risk glanced from Kara to her sister, who stood listening, her face lined with suspicion.

"It doesn't matter. Jormun won't let Lusse go. As long as she's trapped, I may be bound to her, but she can't touch me."

"That's not good enough." Kara pulled back, out of his arms. "We'll free you." She spun toward her sister.

Kelly shook her head. "No way. You haven't convinced me he's one of the good guys yet. We don't know what will happen if we unleash…that." She made a disdainful gesture toward Risk. "It's probably all part of his plan."

"Kelly…" Kara took a step toward her sister, her head lowered, her gaze fixed. "We are going to free him."

Kelly braced her feet and stared back. "No. We're not. Trust me. It's for your own good."

The garm chuckled. "Yes, be a good little witch and listen to your sister who got herself caught in the first place."

Kelly turned, her gaze slicing. "Stay out of this. I'll settle with you later."

The garm grinned. "I can hardly wait."

The sisters stood toe to toe, neither giving an inch.

Risk shook his head and stepped around them to talk with the garm. "Did Sigurd keep his word?"

The garm shrugged. "He hasn't been back here."

Risk nodded. Unsure what to say next, his gaze returned to the sisters. They still stood in the same confrontational stance.

"How long you think they'll last?" the garm asked.

Risk shrugged. "Who knows."

"My money's on the cranky one," the garm replied, pulling a bottle from under the bar and filling two glasses.

Risk picked up the glass and took a sip. Honey-tinged whiskey burned down his throat. They stood for a few moments watching the twins.

"Your son escaped," the garm murmured.

Risk turned. "Venge?"

The garm nodded. "Sigurd released him the day you left. Rest of the hounds, too. It's caused quite a stir in the nine worlds. Aren't used to hellhounds running around. Could cause trouble."

Risk nodded, his thoughts on his son. "Hear where he went?"

The garm shook his head. "No."

Risk nodded again. That was fine. As long as Venge got a chance, it was all Risk could ask for. More than he'd ever had—until now.

Kara stomped forward, her hand wrapped around Kelly's wrist. "We're doing it."

The garm raised a surprised brow and held his glass in mock salute to Risk. "Wonders never cease."

Risk wove his arm around Kara and pulled her to his side; with her sister glowering beside them, he pressed another kiss to her lips.

No wonders never did cease, and with Kara by his side, he had a feeling they never would.

Kara pulled back and motioned to her twin.

Her brow creased, Kelly stepped forward. "Remember, this wasn't my—"

"Just do it." Kara slipped her hand under the heavy chain around Risk's neck. With a frown, her sister mimicked her actions. Together they folded their hands around the heavy silver then grasped each other's free hand, forming a closed circle.

Rick stood frozen as the space around him swelled with power. The twins, their eyes shut, concentrated on their job.

The metal at Risk's neck warmed until he wondered how the sister's could bare to maintain their grip. Then suddenly the heat along with their hands were gone, but the chain still lay heavy against his throat.

Kara stared up at him. "So?"

"It's okay. I told you, it doesn't matter—" he began.

Kara's sister rolled her eyes. "It's done. We just left the final act…" She made a pulling motion at her throat with her hands "…to you."

He glanced back at Kara; her blue eyes smiled up at him. "So, show us."

His gaze locked on Kara, he wrapped both hands around the ancient metal links, then after expelling the long breath, he pulled. The chain fell from his neck.

He stood there, the symbol of his bondage stretched across his open palms. With a smile he let it coil to the floor.

Kara's hands wrapped around his forearm. "We did it," she whispered.

"You did it," he murmured back.

Her sister bent and plucked the length of chain from the floor. "You think this might be worth something?"

Still staring down at Kara, Risk replied, "You keep it. I have everything I need right here." Then he scooped Kara into his arms and shimmered out of the bar.

* * * * *

Mills & Boon® Intrigue brings you
a sneak preview of...

Dana Marton's Tall, Dark and Lethal

With dangerous men hot on his trail the last thing Cade Palmer needed was attractive Bailey Preston seeking his help to escape from attackers on her own. Could Cade tame the free-spirited Bailey as they fled both their enemies and the law?

Don't miss this thrilling new story available next month from Mills & Boon® Intrigue.

Tall, Dark and Lethal
by
Dana Marton

He would kill a man before the day was out. And—God help him—Cade Palmer hoped this would be the last time.

He'd done the job before and didn't like the strange heaviness that settled on him. Not guilt or second thoughts—he'd been a soldier too long for that. But still, something grim and somber that made little sense, especially today. He'd been waiting for this moment for months. Today he would put an old nightmare to rest and fulfill a promise.

In an hour, Abhi would hand him information on David Smith's whereabouts, and there was no place on earth he couldn't reach by the end of the day. He'd hire a private jet if he had to. Whatever it took. *Before the sun comes up tomorrow, David Smith will be gone.*

He headed up the stairs to his cell phone as it rang on his nightstand. Wiping the last of the gun oil on his worn jeans, he crossed into his bedroom. He was about to reach for the phone when he caught sight of the unmarked van parked across the road from his house.

The van hadn't been there thirty minutes ago. Nor had he seen it before. He made it his business to pay attention to things like that. At six in the morning on Saturday, his new suburban Pennsylvania neighborhood was still asleep, the small, uniform yards deserted. Nothing was out of place—except the van, which made the hair on the back of his neck stand up.

The only handgun he kept inside the house—a SIG P228—was downstairs on the kitchen table in pieces, half-cleaned. He swore. Trouble had found him once again—par for the course in his line of work. Just because he was willing to let go of his old enemies—except David Smith—didn't mean they were willing to let go of him.

"Happy blasted retirement," he said under his breath as he turned to get the rifle he kept in the hallway closet. From the corner of his eye, he caught movement. The rear door of the van inched open, and with a sick sense of dread, he knew what he was going to see a split second before the man in the back was revealed, lifting a grenade launcher to his shoulder.

Instinct and experience. Cade had plenty of both and put them to good use, shoving the still-ringing phone into his back pocket as he lunged for the hallway.

Had he been alone in the house, his plan would have been simple: get out and make those bastards rue the day they were born. But he wasn't alone, which meant he had to alter his battle plan to include grabbing the most obnoxious woman in the universe—aka his neighbor, who lived in the other half of his duplex—and dragging her from the kill zone.

He darted through his bare guest bedroom and busted open the door that led to the small balcony in the back, crashing out into the muggy August morning. Heat, humidity and birdsong.

At least the birds in the jungle knew when danger was afoot. These twittered on, clueless. Proximity to civilization dulled their instincts. And his. He should have known that trouble was coming before it got here. Should have removed himself to some cabin in the woods, someplace with a warning system set up and an arsenal at his fingertips, a battleground where civilians wouldn't have been endangered. But he was where he was, so he turned his thoughts to escape and evasion as he moved forward.

Bailey Preston's half of the house was the mirror image of his, except that she used the back room for her bedroom. Cade vaulted over her balcony, kicked her new French door open and zeroed in on the tufts of cinnamon hair sticking out from under a pink, flowered sheet on a bed that took up most of her hot-pink bedroom. Beneath the mess of hair, a pair of blue-violet eyes were struggling to come into focus. She blinked at him like a hungover turtle. Her mouth fell open but no sound came out. Definitely a first.

He strode forward without pause.

"What are you doing here? Get away from me!" She'd woken up in that split second it took him to reach her bed and was fairly shrieking. She was good at that—she'd been a thorn in his side since he'd moved in. She was pulling the sheet to her chin, scampering away from him, flailing in the tangled covers. "Don't you touch me. You, you—"

He unwrapped her with one smooth move and picked her up, ignoring the pale-purple silk shorts and tank top. So Miss Clang-and-Bang had a soft side. Who knew?

"Don't get your hopes up. I'm just getting you out."

She weighed next to nothing but still managed to be an armful. Smelled like sleep and sawdust, with a faint hint of varnish thrown in. Her odd scent appealed to him more than any coy, flowery perfume could have. Not that he was in any position to enjoy it. He tried in vain to duck the small fists pounding his shoulders and head, and gave thanks to God that her nephew, who'd been vacationing with her for the first part of summer, had gone back to wherever he'd come from. Dealing with her was all he could handle.

"Are you completely crazy?" She was actually trying to poke his eyes out. "I'm calling the police. I'm calling the police right now!"

She was possibly more than he could handle, although that macho sense of vanity that lived deep down in every man made it hard for him to admit that, even as her fingers jabbed dangerously close to his irises in some freakish self-defense move she must have seen on TV.

"You might want to hang on." He was already out of the room. Less than ten seconds had passed since he'd seen the guy in the van. "And try to be quiet." He stepped up to the creaking balcony railing and jumped before it could give way under their combined weight.

She screamed all the way down and then some, giving no consideration to his eardrums whatsoever. Once upon a time, he'd worked with explosives on a regular basis. He knew loud. She was it.

He swore at the pain that shot up his legs as they crashed to the ground, but he was already pushing away with her over his shoulder and running for cover in the maze of Willow Glen duplexes in Chadds Ford, Pennsylvania.

Unarmed. In the middle of freaking combat.

He didn't feel fear—just unease. He was better than this. He'd always had a sixth sense that let him know when his enemies were closing in. It wasn't like him to get lulled into complacency.

"Are you trying to kill us? Are you on drugs? Listen. To. Me. Try to focus." She grabbed his chin and turned his face to hers. "I am your neighbor."

He kept the house between him and the tangos in the van, checking for any indication of danger waiting for them ahead. No movement on the rooftops. If there was a sniper, he was lying low. Cade scanned the grass for wire trips first, then for anything he could use as a makeshift weapon. He came up with nada.

"Put me down!" She fought him as best she could, a hundred and twenty pounds of wriggling fury. "Don't do this! Whatever you think you are doing, I know you are going to regret it."

He did already.

"Are you crazy?"

He could get there in a hurry. He put his free hand

on her shapely behind to hold her in place. Smooth skin, lean limbs, dangerous curves. He tried not to grope more than was absolutely necessary. Yeah, she could probably make him do a couple of crazy things without half trying. But they had to get out of the kill zone first.

"Let me go! Listen, let me—"

They were only a dozen or so feet from the nearest duplex when his home—and hers—finally blew.

That shut her up.

He dove forward, into the cover of the neighbor's garden shed. They went down hard, and he rolled on top of her, protecting her from the blast, careful to keep most of his weight off. The second explosion came right on the heels of the first. It shook the whole neighborhood.

That would be the C4 he kept in the safe in his garage.

Damn.

"What—was—that?" Her blue-violet eyes stared up at him, her voice trembling, her face the color of lemon sherbet.

There were days when she looked like a garden fairy in her flyaway, flower-patterned clothes with a mess of cinnamon hair, petite but well-rounded body, big violet eyes and the cutest pixie nose he'd ever seen on a woman. She had no business being wrapped in silk in his arms, looking like a frightened sex kitten as he lay on top of her.